Dan Sherman is the author of *Riddle*, *The Mole*, *Swann*, *King Jaguar*, *Dynasty of Spies* and *The White Mandarin*. He lives in Los Angeles, California.

'Dan Sherman is that very rare thing, a natural writer with a fine ear for speech and with understanding and compassion. He is a someone we will hear from in the future, a man who bears watching and whose work is exciting and rewarding reading'
Howard Fast, bestselling author of *Spartacus* and *The Immigrants*.

By the same author

DAN SHERMAN

King Jaguar

GRANADA
London Toronto Sydney New York

Published by Granada Publishing Limited in 1983

ISBN 0 586 05809 5

A Granada Paperback UK Original
Copyright © Dan Sherman 1979

Granada Publishing Limited
Frogmore, St Albans, Herts AL2 2NF
and
36 Golden Square, London W1R 4AH
515 Madison Avenue, New York, NY 10022, USA
117 York Street, Sydney, NSW 2000, Australia
60 International Blvd, Rexdale, Ontario, R9W 6J2, Canada
61 Beach Road, Auckland, New Zealand

Printed and bound in Great Britain by
Cox and Wyman Ltd, Reading
Set in Times

For Phil Wimberly

Immediately the clock pinged, the cat opened his yellow eyes, the claws shot out from their sheath of cracked pad, to fight a duel of understanding.

– Patrick White

1

Simply put, Robin Turner met Julia Vegas and the two fell deeply in love. This had been in the fall and the cold wind had been stripping the leaves from the trees, slashing reflections out of the copper beeches. At that time Robin had been the resident martial arts instructor, a traditionalist, they said, with a legitimate Black Belt in Kenpo karate. He taught the juniors in the mornings, and gave his afternoon to agents in for refresher courses. These veteran fieldmen, said CIA legend, were a murderous lot to handle, but sooner or later everyone came to love that gentle Robin Turner.

As for Julia, she was the child of an embassy marriage. Her mother had been a consular aide from Texas. Her father was Brazilian. Victor Ross from the South American desk recruited her out of college, and she had been in for a bout of training before covert placement in Brazil.

There are those today who still recall how the lovers used to stroll along the red brick paths of the Langley grounds. You would often see them drifting through the blue hours of dusk, maybe mooning by the silted pond, or further down among the ghostlier pines. There was Turner, blond and thin, and there was Julia with her coal-black hair and blue-gray eyes. That year the fall had seemed suspended, neither budding nor fading.

They also said that Robin had a way about him, a halting diffident charm that knotted your heart, and that charm was what got him a place in Julia's run. Some even remember how he pleaded his case at a Georgetown party among the small talk, among the porcelain, tastefully dressed in a dove-gray suit. No one knew exactly what he had said to Victor Ross, but in the end he and Julia did leave for Brazil together, and everyone called it a milk run.

By all accounts Julia played it nicely at first. She stepped in smoothly to her case officer's role, and within a month she was running half a dozen stringers with a respectable take of low-grade political intelligence.

Then unexplicably Julia hit a nerve, and her house of spies collapsed. The bust was a classic. First came the boot through the door. Next came a little muscle in a concrete room. Finally there was the long prison breakdown.

When the first report of the arrest came in, Langley hit the roof. They wanted the two kids released or the head of the nearest Brazilian. The State Department, however, was afraid of a flap. It preferred the delicate route. Eventually the Company gave in, and John Poole from the Brasília Embassy was called in to negotiate. First he lodged a series of complaints with the local officials in Belém. On another track he met with friends in the capital. Yet nothing could be shaken loose. The Brazilians even denied any knowledge of the prisoners, which to knowing minds meant that the kids would be skinned alive.

Then came the incredible twist to the dismal story. Turner escaped. First accounts varied. Details were vague. Some said he bribed a guard. Others claimed that he actually killed one. Either way, however, Turner was out and the game was wide open again.

Six weeks passed, and Langley sweated through an intelligence blackout. Turner had completely vanished. In an effort to find him, every Company contact was tapped. Help lines were tossed out from one end of Brazil to the other. Poole was ordered to pull more strings, but all he got for his efforts was the final word on Julia Vegas. The

8

Brazilians claimed that she had been murdered by her fellow inmates. It was a pretty common excuse in the trade.

To all this, however, came a relatively mellow ending . . . it was well after midnight and an American consulate clerk was dozing at his desk. Then the telephone was ringing and it was Robin Turner calling from around the corner, wondering if there was someone still awake who would be so kind as to see him in. They got him out of Brazil the following night disguised as a diplomatic courier.

So Robin Turner came back to Langley, Virginia. He arrived at the end of a slow, mild winter. A long, black Dorchester limousine met him at the airport. His contact wore blue flannel pinstripes and a rich, maroon tie. He said his name was Andrew Aston, and he twirled his moustache ends to saber points. Turner had combed his hair before landing, but could only excuse the wrinkles in his corduroys. Aston called Turner's arrival 'The Coming Home,' and his eyes were crinkling as he smiled.

They drove with the windows down, and the air was wet and clean. They passed great homes of colonial white with gabled windows and marble steps. Swallows dipped and swooped to the dark branches of chestnut trees. There had been no snow, but the pavement was slick and shining from rain.

Debriefing began the following evening and Aston ran it like the old professional that he was. For intimacy and that cozy, rustic touch he requisitioned one of the north end cottages. These cold, stone hovels had supposedly been used to process the Bay of Pigs team, but only Aston still took incoming agents there. He liked these little bungalows. He liked the rough, boulder hearths and the knotty pine shutters. The cots may have been a little loosely jointed, but the quilts were warm. In the mornings you could make coffee on a potbellied stove. Then you could sweep the pinecones off the doorstep and have a smoke on the creaking porch. So it would be like father and son out for a week in the woods. That was the feel that Aston was after. While beyond the willow shadows, past these chilly elms, there was another fairy-tale cottage where the fellows from Security worked the mikes.

Aston sashayed in slowly at first. He was only prodding, talking around the issues. There was a roaring fire, and warm brandy. Turner balled himself up in the deep leather wing chair. Aston sat like an Arab, with his back to the crackling flame. 'You can start anywhere, Robin. Just begin where you feel most comfortable.'

But Turner only kept staring at the palms of his hands. 'I don't know what to say.'

'Then how about Brazil? Why don't we just start with you and Julia in Brazil?'. . .

Nothing, Robin confessed, had prepared him for Belém. The city lay to the north, along the hot belt of the Amazon delta. Each year the sun passed from Cancer to Capricorn, but midsummer was perpetual. Hard rain fell twice a day. In the afternoon the forest floor lay hushed and still. In the night the moon above the shaggy jungle hills was always blood-red and misshapen.

Belém may have once been some colonizer's decadent vision that had flourished in the rubber boom. There were wide boulevards with planked boardwalks and rococo streetlamps of black iron. The palms in green sawtooth hardly trembled against the pale pink stucco. Vines snaked around the foils of balconies, and the whitewashed lattice hung from low arcades.

Down along the docks boys tortured stray dogs for sport. Girls hustled tricks all morning. Slummers in mocha brown and Panama hats wandered in and out of the market stalls. Women slouched in windowsills. The day that Turner and Julia arrived a black man was killed in the Monkey Café, slashed to death with the broken neck of a whiskey bottle.

Their first days were fragmented. Both Turner and Julia soon became lost in the steamy disquietude. More and more they were rubbing their knuckles in their eyes. Possibly they were feverish. Certainly the tap water had afflicted their guts. At night the twisted mattress springs gouged at their ribs. There were lizards scurrying across the terra cotta floors, and mosquitoes breeding in the washbasin.

Afternoons were the worst. Then the rain came washing off the red clay tiles, cascading in sheets past their hotel window. Sometimes, Turner said, you got so blown out that all you could do was hang, half limp, gazing into the crumbling masonry, staring into the chipped mosaic.

In the evenings there was nothing else to do but go down to the purple-neon Mango Bar. There in the sultry plush you could slouch into cheap velvet and sip sloe gins while the air conditioners battered away uselessly at the sweltering heat.

Yet even through these warped and torpid days Julia had managed to lay the foundations of her networks. She met with stringers, established safe houses and dead drops. For runners she had a motley gang of street urchins, mostly little boys in ragged shorts. They all had switchblade eyes . . .

Now Aston began to slip in questions, but slowly, casually. The log in the hearth was split and smoldering, and the old man kept poking at the coals, chipping away at the blackened bark. Sparks were blowing up the flue. He wanted to know how much Robin had known, and his voice was as soft as flannel.

In the beginning, Robin said that he had known very little. 'I thought that Julia had been sent down just to keep a watch on a few low-grade operations. Her Langley control was still Victor Ross, and I heard that Mr Ross was famous for that sort of run.' As time passed, however, Robin admitted that he and Julia did talk a bit, and by the end of a month he had a pretty clear picture of the operational plan.

Foremost, Robin said, Julia had been concerned about a man named Kohl. Kurt Jurgen Kohl, he was her *raison d'être* in Belém.

Limping on down to the rock-bottom dregs of the Mango Bar, sipping pink gin fizzes, sometimes Julia would talk about Kohl. She was fascinated by the man, or at least with Kohl as a concept. She said that she most liked the contradictions. On one hand you had a German expatriate who was supposed to have once been in tight with Josef Mengele and the whole crew of the hard-core Nazi underground. On the other hand you had the cornerstone of the Brazilian industrial machine.

Robin Turner remembered one Mango Bar night in particular when Julia was especially open. While Robin watched a girl in lavender swaying to the samba on the tinsel stage, Julia rapped out the Kohl story. Apparently Vic Ross had been a Kohl-watcher from way back. She told him that Ross had always been concerned about Kohl's influence. Well, Julia could understand why. Here you had one of the prime movers and shakers in Brazil, and the guy was almost pathologically anti-American. Ross said that Kohl hated America because his wife had been killed when the B17's hit Hamburg. Julia, however, believed that he may have just resented American pressure in Brazil. But either way Kohl could be vicious. You had American exporters claiming that Kohl was squeezing them out of the Brazilian markets. and you had importers claiming that he was bleeding them dry. There was also trouble on the political side. For example, Kohl had been partially responsible for the Brazilian decision to tear up a twenty-five-year-old military contract with the United States. He told the Brazilian president that if he needed arms he could get them from the West Germans. Beyond all that Kohl was supposed to have snubbed the president of the United States.

As a footnote to her story, Julia said that Kohl looked like a balding Heinrich Himmler, except older and with features a bit more chiseled . . .

It was midnight and the Mango Bar was filling up with whores. One girl kept staring at Robin, palming a sweating glass of whiskey. Julia had reached a crucial point in her story. She kept gnawing on her knuckles, working away at the gin, wondering if she should go ahead and tell him everything. Obviously there was no real need for Robin to know. It was her run. Robin was only along for the ride. But on that dismal night, beneath a pointlessly spinning fan, surrounded by hookers, wedged in between the knife blade leaves of potted palms, Victor Ross's basic security manual seemed a long, long way away. So she told Robin. She told him everything.

The story began on an odd, silly, ugly note. It was about five months earlier, Julia had said, and a washed-out free-lancer popped into the local consulate and asked to see the Company resident. It seemed that this stringer had some information to sell, information regarding Kurt Kohl. Was the CIA interested? Well, at first there was an awful muddle because the resident had to contact Vic Ross, and Ross was fishing in Vermont. In the end, however, the word was go, and for three thousand dollars this walk-in laid it all out. He said that Kurt Kohl had recently bought a large tract of land along the Amazon tributary called the Xingú River. What was more, the stringer claimed that Kohl was barging some big equipment down that river and clearing out the forest.

Next came a bit of the anticlimactic. Ross ran the story down and found that Kohl's Amazon project was everyone's secret. The industrialist had picked up a large tract of land that had been under the control of a monastic order. Not unusual, Julia had said, because much of that jungle land had been picked up by the missionaries who had originally come to convert the Indians but ended up robbing them blind. By all accounts Kohl was going to use the land to start a tree farm for wood pulp. The idea was to clear the land of virgin timber and then plant fast-growing pine and Gemelina trees. Ross passed it on to the deputy director, who couldn't have cared less.

Had anyone else been calling the shots the game would have ended then and there. 'File and forget' had been the deputy director's word to Ross. Nobody wanted to know about Kurt Kohl and his Amazon tree farm. After all, this had been in the days of the terrorist craze. But Vic Ross would not forget. He had a feeling about this one, and Kohl was a fish he had been after for some time. Kohl belonged to him. So he went at it on his own with a scrap here and a thread there, pushing, shoving, all like the cadgy flimflam spy that he was.

The reward for Ross came a few months later. Julia had told Robin that she had actually been on the Ross team at that point, and so she remembered events pretty well. It seemed that one of Ross's consulate placements in Belém heard that a couple of kids from the Peace Corps had been kicked out of the Xingú River area. Well, Xingú River rang a bell, and he intercepted the kids before the regular consulate staff could process them back to the States. What came out was that the kids had been in the area helping out with the local tribes. All went well for a few months and then one day a crew of Kurt Kohl men walked

14

into the Indian village and rounded up the kids. The kids were told that they were trespassing on Kohl land and that they had to leave. The kids complained to the local officials, but what they got for their trouble was a swift kick up to Belém. The kids also had stories about how Kohl's men were shooting Indians for sport, but what most intrigued Ross was their description of the Kohl project. The kids claimed that Kohl wasn't really planting any trees. They said he was building a whole damn city down there. The deputy director was still not impressed. Ross, however, didn't care what the director felt at this point. He wanted to know what Kohl was really doing in the jungle. So he went full speed ahead. First he ordered an overflight. Then he had satellite photos brought in. Nothing turned up, because the jungle was too dense. Finally he set out trying to contact a Kohl worker. Only when all this had failed was Julia sent down . . .

As an afterthought Turner recalled that Julia had been pretty fired up in the beginning. Obviously Ross's excitement had been infectious. But by the time of that night in the Mango Bar the desolation of Belém had already begun to waste her.

Desolation may also have been wasting Turner now. Outside, the dawn was turning the sky the color of iron. Aston's log was barely glowing. The oak beams above them had begun to creak. A skin of cold air was knocking at the panes of glass.

Robin Turner had been shivering for an hour or more. His lips were nearly blue. His eyelids were swollen. He kept his hands jammed up under his arms. Earlier, Aston had vaguely thought he would push the boy to the breaking point, rub him raw and see what came out. But this Robin seemed like such a fragile fawn, with moist, naked fawn's eyes. So Aston packed it in. Transcripts of the debriefing tapes clearly showed that after this first night Aston played it very gently with Robin Turner.

By the afternoon they were up again, and Aston was jocular. He kept scratching his cropped head of gray hair while he banged around in the tiny kitchen. They drank mugs of honest coffee on the rough log porch. There were also eggs and coils of bacon spread on paper towels. Turner, however, only ate an orange, balancing the peels on the knees of his blue jeans.

A little wind had risen, shivering through the tops of the pines. Aston had to suck hard on his pipe to keep the tobacco going. Finally he chucked it aside and coughed out, 'Dirty, stinky Brazil. We left off last in Brazil.'

'Yes,' Turner said. He had made neat piles of those orange peelings. 'I was telling you about the Xingú River project. Is that right, sir?'

Aston began to tap the bowl of his pipe on his palm. His fingers were pink. He was talking out of the side of his mouth. 'What line did Victor give you?'

'I'm sorry?'

'What was the game plan. How was Julia supposed to have gone about it all. Was there someone she was supposed to have contacted. Someone in particular?'

Turner blinked. 'I think there was one,' he finally said. 'I remember that Julia seemed pretty concerned with contacting a certain doctor. But I'm afraid I don't recall his name off-hand, although I do remember that he was known as the Amazon Doctor, or Indian Doctor. I suppose he was a missionary of sorts, you know, the kind that goes down to help the Indians?'

'Jaques,' Aston grumbled. 'Michael Jaques.'

'Mmm,' Turner nodded. 'That's the one. And apparently he had some sort of loose arrangement with Mr Ross. I was never sure what it was. But I do remember that Julia told me that this doctor was at odds with Kurt

16

Kohl . . . on account of the fact that Kohl was killing the Indians to get the land away from them. She also told me that the doctor was a bit of a nut. Shot strangers on sight.'

Aston was picking at gray slivers, stripping them off the edge of the porch. 'But you never had much luck with Jaques, did you?'

'No, sir.'

'Too bad,' and the old man swallowed like the mangy horse that he sometimes resembled.

'We did, however, get close.' Turner smiled. 'It was Julia's first real lead, which actually was not much of a lead at all, but at the time she was pretty excited.'

It began with rumors, Turner said. One of Julia's stringers claimed that there had been a firefight in the jungle. No, said another, Kurt Kohl did the attacking. Either way, this much was eventually clear. Kohl had just driven several white missionaries out of the Xingú River area, and one or two were willing to talk.

Because the missionaries were frightened, living on the edge, the rendezvous was touch and go until the very end. Finally Turner and Julia skirted the quay and met them down in a corrugated iron shack at the hard end of the docks. They found two men, one old, the other young. They were father and son. The mother had already died. While they talked, Julia had a native boy keep watch at the end of the alley. The warped and faded ocher door was bolted from the inside. The missionary's son kept a loaded automatic in the waistband of his dirty cotton trousers. His father's hand had been swabbed in iodine and crudely bandaged.

The first hour was background. The old man cried a lot. He said that they were Jesuits and had been down in the jungle for seven years. They had lived and worked with the Widebelt tribe. He explained that disease had been taking a dozen natives a year. Half suffered from colds,

17

always coughing, some just wasting away. Then there had been measles and influenza. Once some government nurse killed over thirty of them when she inoculated the tribe with a dirty hypodermic.

With this as a preamble the old man launched off into Kohl. He claimed that Kohl had been bringing in big machinery from the north. He said that there were bulldozers and tractors, but everything else was crated so one could not tell exactly what had been barged down. A few days after the barges arrived Kohl's work crews began clearing out the primary growth. Again, the old man never actually saw a construction site so he had no idea what was being built . . . An hour into this monologue rain broke, and the light through the slatted blinds was fading into a bluer gloom. The old man had begun to cry again, and Julia was having trouble following the story. First there was something about roving bands of killers who shot at the straying natives. Next a boy from the village was killed. Then came the slaughter.

Kohl's men came in the night. First they set the huts on fire. Then they released the dogs. Apparently this was the way all the old Indian hunters attacked. When the villagers scattered, Kohl's men brought them down with automatics. The wounded were clubbed to death later.

This told, the old man dropped into a spell of sobbing. He rocked in his son's arms. The rafters were ticking with a gentler rain. A moth was beating against the tin. Finally Julia asked about Michael Jaques.

Oh sure, there's Jaques, the old man said. Everyone knew who the doctor was. He was the one who stood up for the Indians. Even against Kurt Kohl, Jaques would stand up for the Indians.

Julia went on to ask how she might get in touch with this Michael Jaques, but by that time the old man had grown suspicious. He told Julia to go to hell, he was saying no more . . .

By now the blue-green tones of dusk were falling through the forest's corridor. The wind had died, the pines were still, and the shadows were black between the trees. Turner's narrative had pretty much dissolved. He said that Jaques's . . . and Kohl's . . . trail ended in that steamy, nasty hut.

'It sometimes happens like that.' Aston sighed. He had been making a point of talking softly. Something about this boy made him feel like whispering.

'But I think that maybe we didn't want to find him,' Turner said, his eyes rimmed with red. 'Because then they would have let us come home.'

Aston found himself wincing at such honesty. 'Well, that's not uncommon. Lots of agents in the field . . .' He couldn't go on. He had not found a way to tell the boy that everything would be all right.

'I suppose it was just a lot harder than we thought it would be,' Turner added in a monotone. 'Kurt Kohl is an institution down there. The government, the police, everyone seems to be in his pocket. Julia and I felt pretty helpless.'

They were both pretty haggard by now, still squatting side by side on the woody cottage porch. The counterglow of fading light was on the forest floor. In a little while the twilight deer would probably come down to graze. When evening folded in on them Aston led the boy inside. Together they stitched a bed of kindling and laid down another log. Soon the pine limbs were crackling blue and watery. Coffee was brewing and the brandy was out. Turner shredded lettuce into long, thin ribbons. Aston salted and peppered the steaks, then began to slice away the fat. He wished he could have sliced the boy's despair away as easily.

Turner was describing those last days before the arrest. He said that Belém had been chipping away at their better sensibilities. Julia had begun to knock down half a bottle a day. He recalled one wretched morning in particular. Not even noon, and already the flies were cutting hypnotic circles in the muggy air of their room. Julia had spilled her papers all over the floor. An ashtray had broken. There were still brown shards of glass ground into the tiles. Turner remembered how she had been slouching at the window. An hour passed. She had hardly moved. When he knelt by her side he realized that she had been crying.

Paranoia, or something very much like it, had set in. Julia hadn't liked the way a boozing heavy had been staring at her in the bar. Next it was a van parked outside their window. Stenciled on the side panel was the name of a local cleaning company, but the windows had been blacked out and the antenna was too long. Then she claimed that she had been followed near the Ver-o-pesa market. Scared, half crazy, she ducked into a row of stalls, and before she could get out she'd been forced by some pushy vendor to buy a boa skin.

Operationally her only real fix on anything was a priest called Father Tomás Simeon. Julia had hopes for this priest. She said that he was the one who had sold Kohl the Xingú River land, that he was a force in that part of the country . . . he knew people, had connections. It was just a question of getting him to talk.

So a meeting between Julia and Simeon was arranged. Turner said that he had not known the details. All he knew was that Julia would not let him go along. She said that the priest was nervous, afraid of what he was getting into. She said that she had to make this one alone.

Turner recalled that she left for Simeon's villa around midnight. It was a bad night. Hot wind from the swamps was funneling in hard. The entire city felt capped beneath a thermal seal. The humidity sucked you out. Take a walk around the block, come home, tap your skull, and it felt like it would break apart in sections.

Turner finally took a couple of downers and fell into a patchy sleep. Two hours later he awoke and found Julia sitting by the window. She was staring at nothing. Her face was terribly white. He asked how it went with Simeon, but she wouldn't say. When he pressed her, she began to cry. So he gave it up and they lay in one another's arms, just lay there on the bed in their dirty little room until the police broke through the door not long before dawn . . .

The night was taking possession of their cottage. The windowpanes were blackening. The stone walls were turning cold. Once again the fire was only flickering out a weak yellow light. Aston could have chucked in another log, but Turner was speaking freely and the splatter of sparks and blue flame might have disturbed him. So the old man sat still in the armchair while Turner went on to the eventual horror of the prison . . .

Arrested. Even while it was happening Robin said that he could not believe it. They were secret police with their brains in their necks. They immediately slapped Turner across the mouth and began to work on Julia. After that Turner said that he didn't remember much. He and Julia were hustled into a waiting van and taken to a sort of compound where they took his wristwatch and kept him moving from room to room, also changing the guards so the night was pretty fragmented.

The first day was a green concrete room that smelled of disinfectant. They began with the hard sweats, but they didn't use any muscle. They didn't have to. Turner was completely raw. He had no fallback, no cover, and nothing to confess that they didn't already know. All he had to give them was the truth, which meant that his back was right up against the wall.

He didn't exactly break. He just didn't have anyplace to hide. They kept on asking him what he knew about Kohl. They wanted to know if Julia had found out anything about the Xingú River project. After a day of saying, 'Nothing, we know nothing,' things became a little crazy.

They did not, of course, believe that he was telling the truth. They wanted more. Also, they kept telling him that if he didn't cooperate they would tear his lady to pieces. After three days he had begun to believe them.

Four days in the hole, then the pace changed. He was moved from his private, drab-green room, into the main compound. The cell was packed with about forty men. The walls were blackened stone. The only light fell from a tiny, barred window. Once a large bat squeezed through those bars. The prisoners killed it and ate it.

It was a stratified society. The strongest had the bunks. Beneath the bunks lay their slaves, who served in exchange for protection. Sometimes they were buggered, sometimes they were beaten, but their masters kept them fed. Next there were the wall men. These at least had their backs against the stone and most had a bed of straw. In the center lay the aged and the dying.

Each day there were executions. The guards, always the same two, would pull a man from the cell. Then they would walk him into the courtyard and shoot him. You never knew who would be taken. You never knew why. Anything seemed possible so long as it was something very bad.

For the first couple of days all Turner could think of was Julia. He had no idea where they had taken her. He thought maybe they had a woman's cell on the other side of the prison. Somehow, thinking of her, he lived on through the fleas and the lice and rest of it . . . On the afternoon of the fifth day the guards came for him. Ratface and Bimbo were what he'd heard the prisoners call them, probably because one was short and wiry while the other was a bulbous hulk. They always came for someone, and this time they had come for him.

Pushed down the corridor, hands cuffed behind his back, his legs had been unsteady. At the end of the hall was a gray steel door. But the door hadn't been meant for Turner. Bimbo had just pressed his face up to the little square of a window so that Turner would be sure to see everything . . .

Inside the room, Julia had been tied to a chair. She had been flogged, her front teeth were broken. Hair had been torn out. Her eyelids had been stitched open. Their eyes met, and each was held in the other's gaze, until Turner began to crumple, sagging to the floor into oblivion. But when he raised his eyes again he was looking into another face. There were thick lips and an extension of creamy flesh for a nose. Then the face was speaking to him, yelling that it could see his lips move but couldn't hear him. Did he perhaps want some more?

After that things merely happened around him. The days ate one another. He was not sure how much time had passed. Every so often a man would die, but no one seemed to care except that after a death the breathing of the others would go shallow, softer than the buzzing flies . . .

Turner was half awake. Around noon the guards came for him a second time. Not that he really cared. He said that after a while you just stopped caring. They couldn't touch you beyond the pain. They took him to still another gray cement room. It was a visitor's cubicle, partitioned with a screen of rusty wire mesh. Beneath the screen ran a rutted wooden ledge. Steel chairs faced one another. There were also two fiberboard doors. One led to the prison side, the other must have led out. The guards jammed him into the chair. A minute passed, then another. Finally a priest came in and sat in the opposite chair.

Father Simeon. The moment the priest entered the room and spoke his name, Turner knew what the game would be. He was to play the contrite sinner. Except that at first he seemed mistaken . . . the priest said that Julia had come to see him. Indeed, he claimed that the reason he was with Turner now was that he felt involved, he had come to help. He said that he had liked Julia. Later he told Turner that he liked him too.

Nearly delirious, as he was at the time, Turner said that he could not remember much of his conversation with the priest. All he really had left were impressions. First among them was the priest's face. He said the man was bald, and he had big lips. He kept on touching them with his tongue. Also his cheeks were running with perspiration, and his eyes – Turner remembered that Simeon had heavy lids and that what should have been the whites of his eyes were muddy gray.

Simeon told him that the Brazilians would not release him until the Kohl matter was resolved. He said that Kurt Kohl was a very powerful man and the government would always stand behind him. That a secret representative of the United States had tried to spy on Kohl was a serious offense. Then he wanted to know if Julia had figured out what the Xingú River project was about. Turner said that she hadn't and everything went back to square one. The priest changed gears, became angry. He said that if Turner would not help himself then there was nothing he could do to help either. In the end he told Turner he could rot in hell, then banged on the door so that the guards would let him out.

Whether Turner had known it or not at the time, he now understood that the priest had been the last stop on a long way down. The guards took him back to the cell, and

24

for an hour or so he slept. When he was up again the nausea was rolling through him. He was moaning. Chills racked him. All options were gone. You get out, he had told himself, or you are going to die . . . the next day, the day after, one way or another he would get out or he would be dead.

As it happened, the escape was hardly more controlled by him than the death that would have come to him. He hadn't any plans. He hadn't thought it out. It just started . . . The guards came for him a little before dawn. They called him from the cell door, but he did not move. Bimbo had to kick his way through the heaps of prisoners and wrench Turner up to his feet. Next they were pushing him down the corridor again, through that concrete tunnel which was straight and dark for fifty yards, the only light coming from small blue bulbs fixed to the vaulted stone. And then Turner was falling, not pretending but really falling. Ratface kicked him and pulled on his hair. Keys slipped and clattered to the stone. Bimbo took another swing at his head and Turner parried it and began to move with the force, and now he was twisting with the ingrained combinations of a classic Kenpo attack . . . he went for soft targets – the eyes, the groin, the throat. He said that he would never be able to recall the details because the Kenpo attack was not contemplative. It was automatic. Flowing from a whipping arm to a crashing knee, the moves clicked in and you rode them out, possessed, detached.

Indeed, the rest was much like a dream . . . When the guards were dead he dragged the bodies into a crook in the wall, pulled off a pair of trousers, boots, and a gray-green tunic, put them on and walked on down the corridor. Perhaps he had had vague plans of somehow sneaking past the main gates. He could not remember, but in the end the sewer *felt* so much better, what with its

25

long, black tunnel beneath the compound. So he pried off a metal grate and climbed down the rusted steel ladder. The shallow water was tepid. The stench was terrible. But he recalled how he felt very good in that absolute darkness.

There was no light, none at all. Only the slow drift of water gave him direction. Now and then something solid brushed against him, and there were rats all around him.

Coming out of that tunnel, Robin said, was like coming out of a coma. There was only this flimsy wire screen, and it gave way at last. Then there was nothing except the open marsh. When he crawled through the tall reeds he saw that the prison walls lay a mile behind him. By nightfall he had walked well into the countryside, where the marsh gave way to wild grass. There were no homes, no lights, no roads . . .

Once again Robin's story did not run down until the numbing hours after midnight, when each man seemed empty and almost shy. Turner's face was pale. Aston's joints cracked whenever he shifted in that old leather chair. The light outside their cottage door was steely. Fog had drifted into the forest hollows.

But in the morning their spirits were high. Aston in particular felt bucked up. He even hummed a few bars of some old song while he banged around with the crockery and battered aluminum pans. Soon he had strips of fat sizzling away and a pot of fresh coffee perking. He even had to grin at Robin's thin silhouette outside on the porch as the young man tossed crumbs to the birds.

After breakfast they walked a bit, a little stroll down the pine needle path and out among the oaks and laurels. Overhead the cottony clouds were drifting in a clear, bland sky. Squirrels chittered from the tops of the trees. It might have been the first real day of spring.

Soon the forest was growing moist and warm. Moss was

26

squishing under their rubber soles. Earlier Aston had nearly clapped his arm on Robin's shoulder . . . he had wanted to, but the boy had looked too serious, too sad here in this milky light and ring of trees. So he had had to withdraw again into his more professional self, clearing his throat . . . 'There's still one thing that intrigues me, Robin.'

'What's that, sir?'

'It's about that last night of yours in prison. I was wondering what it was exactly that made you decide to escape.'

Turner shrugged. They had both sat down on a rotting log. 'I guess I just realized that I had to get out.'

'Of course,' Aston said. He hardly knew himself what he was driving at. 'But perhaps you remember more precisely how you came to decide. Do you see what I'm looking for? I'm wondering what would change a man from victim to aggressor?'

Robin's head had fallen back. He was biting his lip. He also may have been gazing at the light through the leaves. Finally he sighed. 'I suppose . . . that is, there was one thing, but I suspect it will sound rather silly if I try to actually pin it down – '

'No, go ahead,' Aston urged. 'I could use a revelation or two.' He said it with a straight face. 'Revelations usually sound a bit foolish, or mysterious, first off. They are supposed to.' He smiled.

Turner's eyes fell and he took a deep breath. 'There was this stain on the wall of the prison. It was about the size of my hand. Maybe it was a watermark . . . when the rain fell there was a good deal of seepage. At any rate, this stain looked sort of like a face. Then there were other times when it looked like a bird, or a . . . I don't know, except that on the last night it looked to me like a cat. A jaguar, as a matter of fact.'

27

'A jaguar?'

'Well, I told you it was silly,' Turner said, but his tone was less diffident than his words. 'I shouldn't have mentioned it.'

Aston had to recoup. 'Please, go on. I'm truly interested.'

But Turner had already started fencing him off. 'There's nothing much to say. I just kept looking at the stain and it looked more and more like a jaguar to me. And what with the fever and everything else, I suppose that jaguar became sort of . . . symbolic . . .'

But of course. Aston knew all about symbols. 'The animal's ferocity, that sort of thing?'

Robin nodded. He had been speaking very slowly and softly. 'It could have occurred to me because Julia and I had seen an Indian jaguar dance only a few weeks before. Each year the Waica Indians outside of Belém present their Jaguar Festival. Oh, it's only a tourist attraction now, but danced against the backdrop of a jungle at sundown . . . it is rather impressive . . .'

'So,' Aston said, 'this jaguar association became an inspiration for you?' It sounded condescending, and he was sorry the moment he said it. He didn't want to embarrass the boy.

But Turner was not embarrassed. On the contrary . . . 'It made me angry. It made me able to hate them.'

'Oh,' Aston mumbled, because what else could you say? He had never heard the boy use that word before. 'Hate . . . The jaguar made you hate the Brazilians?'

But Turner had abruptly turned his head away. 'It's silly, it doesn't mean anything at all. Forget it.'

Two days later Turner passed through the debriefing stage and was pronounced fit to return to his post. The Belém affair was over. Julia's arrest was clearly the result of her work, while Turner had been taken merely because he had been with her at the time. There was, however, one ironic twist to the story. Turner recognized the face of Kurt Kohl as the same he had seen outside of the cell in which they had tortured Miss Vegas.

As for Robin's own perspective, Aston noted that the boy seemed eager to let the past dissolve, the days collapse behind him. When he was informed of Julia's death, he remained still and apparently resigned.

To celebrate the end of debriefing, Aston took Turner to his club for dinner. They ate off gold-leaf plates. 'Somebody's legacy,' Aston joked. 'Although when I come they usually lock the good stuff up,' and he laughed at himself. Next came uniformed servants with steaming joints of lamb. There was mint sauce in a silver bowl, and another for the bubbling sprouts. Afterward they took brandy in the sky-blue room, and Aston smoked a Cuban cigar, one of a cache that he claimed to have pinched from some Moscow Center spy. And what with the brandy, the glow of burnished candlelight on Robin's blond hair, his rich but modest suit, his even voice, his thin hands, his clear eyes, who would have guessed that he was anything else but an elegant, charming young man?

2

Rain fell during March and April, but just as often the days were clear. Some nights were even velvet, the sky a vault of stars. Through these months the old guard of the CIA still met fairly regularly, either at their Georgetown clubs or their rambling brownstones. Years ago Andrew Aston used to play a lilting ragtime to liven up the spirits. Now gout had crimped his fingers, but on the whole these evenings were much the same as they had been. There was still the brier smoke wafting up to the coffered ceilings, still decanters of liquor rattling on the Hepplewhites, still the jibes in the cloakroom, still those shared gentlemen's innuendoes.

And as the last of these gentlemen spies, the flower of the Eastern Seaboard, there was that gentle Robin Turner. Or such was the sentiment that ushered the boy back into the intelligence community.

They had all known Robin's father. Aston, for example, had known John Turner from the war. They had served together under 'Wild Bill' Donovan's Office of Strategic Services. Later, when John had left the secret world for the diplomatic corps, their shoulders brushed again in such unlikely outposts as Tangier and Katmandu.

All particularly remembered Robin's mother, now also deceased, God rest her soul. They remembered her best as hostess for those embassy affairs. Like her son, she was a blond willowy figure with delicate features. Aston said that she had collected paperweights and painted dreamy landscapes with a child's set of watercolors.

They further recalled that Robin had been born in

Hong Kong, of all places. Pure chance, of course, but there you are. Leslie Deveron said that he was a frail child. 'I think they had to put him in an incubator.'

Hong Kong also explained Robin's love for all things Oriental. 'He actually speaks a few dialects,' Aston boasted one chilly night at Deveron's place. 'And he does lovely translations of the late T'ang.'

Deveron, who was something of an Oriental expert himself, agreed that the T'ang was best. However, he also pointed out that Turner's Eastern bent eventually led him to a controversial sphere – 'point of fact, that karate business.'

But over the last few weeks Aston had become a believer in the boy's martial arts. So he declared, 'It's not that "karate business" at all. It's Kenpo. That's the name of his style. They tell me it's a very versatile approach to weaponless combat. Good for the streets, if you see what I mean, but it's a soft style. That's how Robin describes it, soft. And I've seen him work out. All those little dances and circular movements, it's very beautiful. Besides, there's a rather esoteric spiritual aspect to Kenpo, which none of you know a damn thing about.'

But Deveron, more comfortable with his eggshell vase from K'ang Hsi family, or perhaps even his Chinese Chippendale, still believed that the boy might have taken that Kenpo karate business a bit too far. Oh, it was all right as a pastime, but no one actually made a career out of it. Wrestling on the mat with all those nasty special-op types. What would old John Turner have said?

Not a thing, Herold Pimm maintained, and Pimm should have known. After all, he and John Turner went back to before the war. They had even shared quarters in the Yard at Harvard, and later a desk in London. Which was why Pimm had become Robin's sponsor when the boy first stepped aboard three years ago.

'I see no reason to deny Mr Turner his wish,' read Pimm's original note to the director of placements. 'He's head and shoulders above any existing hand-to-hand instructors. They even have him ranked on the international circuit, and he does very nicely with the students. He is respected and obeyed.'

As for style, one had to admire Robin here too. No shoes were allowed on the mat, and the term was 'dojo,' not studio or gymnasium. Students were required to bow when entering, and the tardy ones were not admitted at all.

Only Turner wore the black Gi; all others wore a standard white. Their tunics were knotted with the belt of their rank, according to the tradition of the Shaolin monks.

Rice paper screens in lacquered frames partitioned the rooms of the dojo. The symbol of Kenpo, a dragon sparring with a crouching tiger, stalked along the bamboo shelving. Threads of burning incense wafted up from the mouth of a porcelain dragon. Petals of fresh roses floated in a tortoise-blue bowl of scented water. There was also a parchment map of the vital targets: the eyes, the groin, the kidneys and so forth.

So Turner had brought a new refinement to his section of the training program. Then one day Julia walked into the dojo. Then came Brazil. And then the rest of that horrible business. And now it seemed that Turner was asking for a transfer. His request arrived in the placement office some four weeks after his return. A copy was sent to Andrew Aston, which was noted by all as the polite thing to have done. The request took the form of a letter, written in Robin's own careful hand on a sheet of gray linen. The tone was reserved but candid, and in the coda came this tender edge:

I ask then for this transfer to the research department, not only because I wish to play a more pivotal role but also because I believe that the time has come to turn to something new. I do not think that I can pick up where I left off. If this is not best, then forgive me. For I always wish to remain yours,

Robin Michael Turner

They were all appropriately touched, so they sent him to Lyle Severson. To Severson's home, in fact, on a Sunday afternoon for coffee and sandwiches in the garden. Except that the wind blew, and the rain fell, and the branches of the sycamores were scraping on the window-panes.

Lyle Severson – Father Lyle as he was sometimes called – might have been the oldest knot in the school tie. He too had served with Wild Bill, but not from behind a desk. Severson was the real thing. During the war he had operated for three years behind German lines, and in the end he had fallen all the way into the espionage night-mare – his cover was blown. His agents strung up, and for eighteen months he squatted in the corner of a sooty French garret. They finally caught him a mile from the Swiss border. They pulled his teeth out one by one. He never broke, all he gave was the fallback story. Now he still trembled from time to time, and occasionally his gums ached. The nights were particularly bad. Once at a party for some West German colleagues, words were ex-changed. Lyle sloshed claret in the beet-red face of a hun, which wasn't very sporting, but hadn't he had the license of real pain?

Mutual pain may have been the basis for the initial bond between Severson and Turner. At any rate, the old man liked the boy. He liked the way he skirted between the wet lashing leaves on the walk to the oak door (Lyle was watching the boy's approach, unseen, from behind the rain-spattered panes of the drawing room window). He may have even liked Robin's clothes that afternoon, his forest-green corduroy suit, his belted London Fog with

33

the missing button and fraying cuffs. Not obviously intended to impress you, but neat all the same.

They walked in from the drafty entrance, under the coffered ceiling, past a long-case clock chiming behind the crystal. As always the paneled mahogany, the fluted drapery, not to mention the gloom, had begun to slow down time. Or so it seemed. While Lyle called back, 'I knew your father. But then I suppose they all say that. He got around, you know.'

'Yes,' Turner answered. His hands were clasped behind him. His oxfords were sinking into the faded Kulah rugs. All around him was the sagging Georgian furniture.

'That was in London.' Lyle was wheezing a bit. 'I believe it was at a shooting party at some lord's place in the Lake Country. Ducks or some such, and you were away at school. That was Eton, wasn't it?' Lyle was sloshing sherry into delicate goblets.

'Yes' Turner said again. 'I was there for a year,' and he had hated the sniggering masters, and the sneering lips of the older boys.

'I hope you like this.' Severson handed the boy a gilt-edged glass. 'It's Californian. Sometimes people like it, sometimes they don't – '

'Oh no, it's fine. Really, very good.'

Outside the rain was rattling on the shingles, the runoff splashing on the flagstones. For a moment Lyle appeared dazed by the melancholy of his own drawing room. 'Have you ever worked in Archives, Robin?'

'No, not really.' Turner was looking into the blue-gray light through the bay windows,

'Well, it's a funny world,' Lyle droned. 'Actually many find it frightening. They have a habit of drawing you too far in. The files, I mean. They'll rule your life if you let them. I've seen it happen. Something will catch your eye, a sweep job against a Polish radioman in West Germany,

34

for example. But then you say to yourself, "Didn't I know this fellow from another read?" And you're off. Yes, you find that he was with the underground until the forties. Then he joined the British commandos. "So why is he with the Communists now?" you ask yourself. You can end up chasing cross-references back thirty years. What's more, a lot of the files haven't been kept up. They're just stacked in the old archive room, and that's a spooky place. The light's bad. Everything is lying helter-skelter. You'd think they'd get it all in the computers.'

They had been sitting for some time now. Lyle had taken his burlap wing chair. Turner had the lumpy daybed. An Indian counterpane had been laid to hide the cracked and bulging leather. The light had grown pale. Again the stillness was lulling them.

But Lyle kept on. 'I bring this up only because I want you to know what you're getting into. It takes a particularly retiring mind to work the archives. Oh, naturally we have our moments. Someone in the field spots an unknown talent, and then you've got your mad rush to find out just who your mystery man is. But the long projects take patience.'

Robin brushed a spray of his hair. 'But I won't mind it. I think I'm going to enjoy it.' His knees were together. The glass of sherry was cupped in his fingers.

'Well, it's going to be a change anyway.' Lyle winked. 'I mean after what you were doing before,' and he cut the air with the side of his hand.

'Oh yes, well I still might take the Saturday class.' Turner smiled. 'If I have the time, that is.'

'Mmm. We don't normally work the weekends. Some go in, but I don't press them. Anyway there's the overtime pay to consider for the juniors. They always complain when I have to pay the overtime.' Then his milky eyes became fixed on the cockleshell molding. He was

35

growing as rigid as any of the empty vases on the mantle behind him. Finally he sighed, 'You should also know that we're a mangy, bumbling crew, half blind, half crippled. They tell me our time is about up. The old order, I mean. Andrew, Leslie, Herold, myself – we're all about to be put in the pasture. They say we're snobs, and we are, of course. So I want you to know just where we stand, Robin. Because I think a wind is beginning to blow.'

While outside the real wind was making tatters of the trees, leaves were dashing against the siding.

'Oh, they've been saying that for years,' Robin offered. All through the house clocks were ticking. Although time may have become irrelevant again. The minutes could not dent the torpor. Every object in the room was so frozen in the pallid light that it took on its own haunting presence. 'So that's why I think I love the archives,' Lyle said at last. 'They're dead, but they're also alive. Know what I mean? There's a real feeling of . . . oh, I don't know, continuity maybe. But remember, you can get lost in it.'

There were those, Andrew Aston foremost among them, who soon became concerned that Robin *had* become lost, not in the archives perhaps, but in his grief. There were no outward signs to point to, but as Aston put it, 'He seems almost too quiet, too sober. I'd love to see him out on the town with a girl. I mean, my God, he's only twenty-six.'

Others, however, saw nothing wrong with Robin at all. On the contrary, he was probably the perfect young man. Secretaries, particularly those elderly matrons without children of their own to mother, took to Robin immediately. They adored him. Oh that beautiful, innocent, charming boy.

Turner was living at this time on a shady suburban street. He had a small, one bedroom flat, serviceably furnished by the landlord. There was his dresser and his

36

bookshelves. There was his bed, narrow and firm, and the headboard of dark pine. The spread was white hobnail. The landlord's wife had given him a tartan comforter, and this he laid on the window box where he sometimes sat in the late afternoons and stared into the trance of trees.

The walls of these rooms were white plaster. The carpets were chocolate brown. The large bay window seemed to float in the basket of the sycamores, high above the courtyard. The garden below was encircled by a low stone wall. Within lay the beds of roses and snapdragons. There was also a lemon tree and a terra cotta bowl where the sparrows always bathed.

Not long after Turner had been living here, Andrew Aston came to dinner. Robin prepared the meal himself, fresh salmon on a bed of shredded lettuce. The table was modest, but neatly set. Some of the silver he owned, some he borrowed from the landlord's wife. The night before he ironed the white linen tablecloth on the window box.

Early the following morning Aston and Severson breakfasted at their club, and at this cold hour the dining room was nearly deserted. Yet a fire still burned in the grate, and the light glanced off the chandeliers. Around them lay the settings of crystal and beaten silver. 'Not that Robin's table smacked of poverty,' Aston was saying, 'but he did have these plates with windmills on them . . .'

'Well, you can go to hell, because I think it was a very nice effort on his part.' Lyle smiled. 'And now I'm sounding like my Jenny Rice.' A croissant was crumbling in his fingertips. His saucer was filled with coffee. 'She's positively in love with the boy.'

'Oh, don't tell me.' Aston laughed. 'They all love him. Do you know what Suzi Hall told me? She told me that Robin was a very clean young man. A *clean* young man!' Aston began to dab his mouth with the corner of his napkin. 'But it's true. That's what has always struck me

37

about Robin, even from the start. He *is* very clean. Everything in its place, his shirts, his desk. His room was immaculate.'

'Oh, I see, you made an inspection.'

'Oh come on, Severson, I'm serious. I wonder if it's compulsive.'

Severson was watching the falling flakes of browned dough. 'Don't be silly. If Robin is anything, he's not a nut, and believe me, I've known my share of them.'

Aston's eyes were straying away into the long rows of gleaming tumblers, each on a starched white cloth. 'Well, I'd like to see him get a girl,' he said at last. 'It would loosen him up.'

'Maybe,' Severson said.

'So we should give it some thought.'

Lyle began to nod. 'All right. If you must have it, Johnny Gaunt's daughter is giving a party next month. She's eighteen, or twenty-one, or something. Anyway, I'll see what I can do. Fair enough?'

Aston smiled and reached for another wedge of toast. He had carefully glazed them all with marmalade from a tiny cut-glass bowl.

On this first balmy evening of the spring, Robin wore a little something for everyone. His shirt was cream silk, his light beige suit had been precisely cut. How resplendent they all thought he looked, sweeping around the leafy corner in his midnight-blue MG. Nice, but not extravagant. And then how he gracefully stepped out under the porch light to take his hostess's hand, and give her a proper nod and smile.

Inside the gleaming parquetry had been cleared for the ball. The band was playing waltzes and sometimes diluted rock. There was caviar in frosted bowls, and iced legs of crabs. Young girls in fine gowns spied on Turner, not that he stood out particularly, not among all these beautiful young people. Still, there was one who trapped him beneath the balcony . . . 'I understand you work for my Uncle Lyle,' all the while toying with a string of glossy pearls.

'Yes.' Turner lowered his eyes to his own hands. 'I've only just started though.'

'Well, it must be exciting.' Spun into her hair was a diamond tiara, the lights were winking in its stones. 'And you're a karate expert. See? Lyle's already told me about you.'

Robin turned to see the old man smiling at him from far across the dance floor. 'Well, it's nice of you to speak to me' – and his head dipped shyly away – 'because I'm afraid I don't really know anyone here.' If he had shut his eyes just then, the image of the grinning Father Lyle through the needles of gold light might have still remained in his head.

'Well, *now* you know me, and I know everything about you, absolutely everything.' She gently slapped his lapel.

Now his fingers were knotted together.

'Oh, don't look so sad, sweetheart. Lyle only told me good things' – and again whispering – 'very good things.'

They danced. It was expected of him. So he took her by the arm, and they went whirling off. Compared to this spinning girl in pink, Turner felt stiff and black, but at least he thought his form was good. Perhaps too good? Later, while he ladled out the punch to her extended cup, he was horrified to learn that she had very nearly pierced him. 'You dance very well,' she panted. 'So smoothly. In fact . . .' and she paused to wet her lips, 'in fact, I think that if you're ever reincarnated you're going to be a cat . . .' She might have shrieked it out. 'Yes, a cat. And not just a tabby either. You'll be a leopard, or a panther, or some such . . . I can see it in you already. There, in your eyes. So what do you think of that, dear boy?'

He thought he had better get away from her.

The days, the months, passed gently. In the humid mist of summer the women gave garden parties in the evenings. Torches were lit to draw the moths away. Robin came whenever they wanted him, always looking dapper in white cotton or pinstripe.

For a time he dated Sally Bowls from the Finance division. On clear nights they were seen sweeping back from the countryside. The top of Robin's car would be down, and Sally's violet scarf would be whipping in the slipstream. Or else they rode horseback along the shady avenues of the park, and the white dust rose to whiten the leaves of the laurels.

As for his work, Robin proved himself here as well. He very nearly always came in early, made coffee for the others, then plowed into the archives. On Fridays they soon came to expect his fresh doughnuts from a wonderful little bakery he had found. Robin first brought them to help launch Jenny Rice's birthday. (She had been fifty-one years old, and proud of it.) Yet the doughnuts had made such a hit that the following week he brought them again. Then on the next Friday, then on the next, until they became a tradition of sorts.

Beyond the doughnuts they found that they could depend on Robin in other ways. He was always willing to run that odd errand, to stay late that extra hour. When Susan Meyers went in for tests, who else filled in as the night clerk for two weeks running but that lovely soul Robin? And wasn't Robin the dear to pick up the pieces of Danny Shore's work when the brakes gave way on Danny's Porsche and he went sliding into a wreck? Then there were those extra nights. Once they even found that he had stayed on through the morning, and not for the sake of anything really important either. He simply wanted to put the index tabs in order. Such a sweetheart, really.

They might have worried about him, working as he did, often ten hours a day, buried in a dusty alcove. But he was always so willing, so cheerful.

By the fall he had pretty much stopped seeing Sally, or joining the others on picnics, or even coming around for drinks. They knew he still worked out with karate . . . they saw him in the parks sometimes, there with his graceful shadows on the frosted lawns. But he had no other side to his life they could see . . .

It was Jenny Rice who first noticed that the spark was gone from Robin's gentle spirit. 'He's growing quieter,' she told Lyle. 'And last Sunday, Susan saw him in the graveyard. Just walking, mind you, but looking awfully dejected all the same.'

They did not take Jenny seriously, not at first. Oh, he's just going through a blue period, they reasoned. Certainly we all have those.

Except that some weeks later, Jenny found him softly crying in an alcove, deep in the gloom of the archive hall.

Robin's heart broke with a murmur. There was nothing of the usual hysteria, nor the fits of drinking. Merely, they said, the loss of his Julia had finally caught up with him. So first there were the extended weeks of depression, then the moments of gentle weeping, and finally he stopped coming around at all . . .

The doctor was a paternal, quiet man named Danby. He and Lyle had been friends for years. Rather than the more formal drying out, Danby said that Robin should just get away for a while. The boy took it all in stride. On

41

his last day he stopped by with doughnuts again, and a spray of roses for Jenny Rice. The women hugged him to their cheeks and wept. The men shook his hand or clapped him on the back. Then he was gone, and he left them with that trailing Cheshire smile.

Andrew Aston was perhaps the last of the crew to see him off. He and Robin said farewell on the broad lawns of the Langley complex. The previous night had been cold, and they crunched through the frost on the grass. More ice encrusted the leaves. A flock of sparrows watched from a length of radio wire that sagged above the trees. The bodies of the birds were black against the wafer of the sun. The two had little to say. Robin would drive north until he reached New England. Beyond this he did not know.

And later, much later, in the months that passed, Aston would review this moment. He would remember how their eyes had met, how Robin's had been shy and blinking slightly. Which was how the boy played it to the end. He had revealed nothing, absolutely nothing.

3

There were evenings when the possibility of an old age
restored left the old crew giddy. They could not control the
vertigo, not in their own club, not among their odd
memorabilia: Remington pistols, a fountain pen with
deteriorating cyanide capsules. The nostalgia was too
gummed up. Time had become too warped. Even when the
word was out that the new director would not be one of
their own, there were those who still had visions of a Wild
Bill Donovan lumbering back from the Bahamas. Only the
bravest could confront the truth – the old order was dead.
There was nothing else to it.

Historians of the clandestine world may mark the end of
the grand tradition with the advent of Stansfield Turner.
'Sturdy Stan,' he was called by those who loved him. While
to others he was merely the president's 'teetotaling Christ-
ian Scientist.' Either way, he was not Old School. He was a
Navy man, and as Lyle put it in a wry note to Andy Aston,
'He does not like us. He does not feel comfortable in our
milieu,' by which Severson meant the traditional marks of
their world – the school tie cosmos, the Georgetown club,
the elliptical wit. 'Turner does not like us,' Lyle wrote. 'He
does not like us one bit.'

Predictably, Turner's first move was to publish his state-
of-the-ship report. The findings, circulated to department
heads, were also predictable. The Company, read the
report, is a wrecked ship. Intelligence collection is shabby.
Dozens of ongoing operations have been blown. Interde-
partment fighting is rampant, and after three years of
unrelenting public whipping, the morale is out the bottom.

Next there were several ad hoc meetings wherein all the old skeletons were dragged from the closets. Monday went to the Phoenix program and all agreed that the project had been a terrible error. Not only had the project failed to curb any real Viet Cong threat, but many of the program's victims were not terrorists at all but peasants, and the whole incident became one disgusting mess with kids thrown out of choppers, electrodes to the balls, napalm and lengths of bloody piano wire.

Tuesday and Wednesday were lighter. The subject was assassination plots, and here all felt that the press had been unfair. Friday went to the MK-Ultra project and the rest of that mind-drug-death circus. Sentiment on this one was ambiguous. There were those who were truly upset, while others seemed only to lament that the Company had been caught.

Given the state of the ship, most agreed that the new director had only two alternatives. He could have the old beauty taken to dry dock and repaired, or he could scrap the wreck and build anew.

He chose the latter.

Less than eight weeks after Stan Turner took the helm the dismissals began. By the end of the first week over eight hundred regulars were given notice. Of the old hands remaining – Severson, Aston among them – the word was clear: The CIA will be a tight ship from here on out. There will be no room for the style of the Eastern elite, no room for the sly buccaneer, for the gentleman spy. Stansfield Turner wants only good sailors.

For a time the new ship floundered, buffeted by the bitter wind of fired agents, or else becalmed by indecision. Then they began to trim the sails. New talent was piped aboard from schools through the country. Old talent never used was ferried in from out-stations. Among these young hands came the counterintelligence contingency from Paris, and within this group came Kristian Badgery.

She missed her plane and arrived alone in the coldest hours before dawn. The first night she spent in a cheap hotel. There were warped country scenes in plastic frames on the wall. The television was clapped out. In the morning she telephoned the number they had given her in Paris, but there was no answer. Personnel had promised to find her an apartment, but when she checked, no one knew a thing about it. Finally there was a sleepy kid who gave her a list of available rooms. But the list was a month out of date. Everything had already been rented.

As for her office, there was a desk, but no chair. Again, no one knew anything. In the end she had to steal what she needed – the extra chairs, the filing cabinet, the stationery. And when you can't rob them, ran her unspoken, half-conscious code, then you charm them. Particularly the men, because she was a pretty girl, with very blond hair, platinum actually, but natural. If she was slim, there was still enough to call her fashionably slim. Especially since each breast fit nicely into the mouth of a champagne glass (she had tried that one in Paris, drunk out of her mind with some English actor). She had been told that her eyes were her greatest asset. They were green, definitely green, not blue, and with the merest hint of mascara to accent the innocence, who would have guessed that Kristian was the one who had filled her office by theft?

As a little girl they had called her cute, and she was. She was Colonel Badgery's darling princess whose mom had been queen of the base. Even among all those perfect children – officers always had beautiful kids because they married beautiful women for prestige – Kristian had a notion she was special. Now she had her mother's face, slightly rounded with a button nose, and her mouth in that perpetual slow, sly smile.

But with so much to entice with, Kristian often wondered how she came to be where she was. Oh, it wasn't merely being broke in Paris or Washington . . . why this spook business at all? There were no real answers, unless you said that you joined for the romance. Ah yes, the romance, and that wonderful Professor DeLisle who kissed you all over and then suggested that you talk to one or two people that he knew. So yes, she could say that she had joined for the romance – although they probably took her because she had a flair for numbers.

Originally they had tried to put her in their cryptography school. After all, they argued, everyone knew that ciphering was the backbone of the trade. Well, they could take their ciphering and shove it. Kristian didn't want the backbone, she wanted the action, and she soon got out of their cryptocrap school and away from all those acned boys with their slide rule sensibilities.

But now, here in what they told you was the heart of the Company, she wasn't sure that anything was much better. The heart of the Company somehow was more like the womb, hot and moist and dark. Paris had been great, really the choice assignment, but what did you do in Langley? Every day was overcast. The rain brought no relief from the heat. Summer had come, mosquitoes everywhere, and all the available men were jerks.

Then there was Father Lyle, Kristian's immediate senior. He was always dragging around, and you certainly couldn't charm him, not in the usual way. John Gaunt was the same. 'Gaunt' Gaunt, Kristian called him. There would be the two of them moping through the corridors while the dry trail of Severson's pipe curled behind.

Only Jenny Rice would talk about the death that they must have all been mourning, 'He's cut the poor dear's staff in half,' she whispered. 'He's locked him out of the upper-floor registry, and now he's about to close his operational account. So it's nothing in and nothing out unless the Committee approves.'

The 'he' was, of course, Director Stan. The 'Committee', was the National Security Council's Review Committee, which was supposed to be the president's latest check on the excesses of clandestine warfare. 'Oh, excesses my foot,' Jenny would complain. 'It's our effectiveness they're cutting. How can you run an intelligence service if you neglect counterintelligence?'

But Stan Turner and his Review Committee had no intention of neglecting Lyle and Jenny and even Kristian Badgery. Actually, they had plans for the counterintel groups. Their directive came down in the form of another intra-department memo, the Green Paper. 'This is a critical period of our development. Security is everyone's business.'

The Green Paper fell back on a reliable standard of the clandestine world – when you're down, look out. Not for some time, the paper reflected, has the Company been so vulnerable to foreign penetration. Unhappy staffers can be bought. Frustrated ones can be burned. So keep your eyes open, and your mouth shut . . . Any irregularities were to be reported to the Domestic Counterintelligence Group, which meant Lyle in general and Kristian in particular.

And how they ferreted out the undesirables then! From every closet, from under every bed were seen telltale signs of enemy infiltration. For a time Kristian was going at it some thirteen hours a day. Then came Jenny Rice to the rescue, explaining, 'Oh honey, no one expects you to follow everything down to the wire.' . . .

Tonight Jenny was powdered white and maternal. She had spread herself in Kristian's revolving, tiltable, chromium-plated chair. Papers littered the desk. Some had even drifted to the floor. There were cigarette butts in the corner. Jenny smoked Black Russians. Some said she drank gin from a silver flask, but on this Friday evening she only smelled of lilacs and her rich tobacco.

'But some of these must mean something,' Kristian insisted. An hour ago she had been crying there at her desk among the yellow pages and the empty coffee cups. But now she was composed again, perched on the edge of her desk with her knees locked together beneath her gray tweed skirt.

Jenny, sucking on a lozenge, began to mumble. 'No. No, no, no. They mean nothing. Here' – and she swiped a note at random as several others went fluttering away – 'some little twerp in the Service Bureau, eh? Well, what do you want, Mr Grimes?'

'It's just his work name,' Kristian said.

'Well, all right then, Mr Work-name Grimes. So what's your gripe?' She knotted her spun gray hair around one pink knuckle, 'Mr Gripy Grimes,' Jenny often muttered as she read. 'Look here, darling, this is just what I'm talking about. Your Mr Gripy Grimes has written to tell you that he found the drawer to the housing lists un-locked.'

'What are the housing lists?' Kristian's hands were clasped meekly in her lap.

'The home address and phone number of outgoing personnel. And it means nothing, not a bean of import-ance. If you want you can chit the lock-up men. Or file and forget. Or better yet – ' and she slowly began to shred the paper, smiling.

Next there was Miss Shelly Quinn from the Registry staff. 'I know her.' Jenny grimaced. 'She's that flam-boyant, tasteless one. Or maybe she's the prig . . . Somehow I always get her mixed up with that tart in Communications. Prig, tart, not so different really . . . opposite sides of the same coin . . . Anyway, here she

48

complains that the *gardener* has been giving her evil looks. My God! Evil looks!'

'Who's the gardener?' Kristian asked. Wreaths of Jenny's Russian smoke were floating past the gooseneck lamp.

'Who knows? Who cares?' Jenny puckered up her lips. 'My advice, hon, is to send a note to Shelly Quinn. Tell her to wear a bra.' And now the large woman began to laugh, her bosom heaving, her flowered print dress shaking. 'Oh, wouldn't that be a scream? Then you file it with Personnel.'

By midnight Jenny was still the flippant spy-catcher, not that they had found any spies. 'Not at all like the old days,' Jenny finally said. She was dreaming into the cigarette haze and settling flurry of paper. Yet tonight, here in this cubbyhole office, she probably felt closer to those old days than she had in years. Then there had been ornate gas jets on the blackened plaster walls. Smooth blue flames had cast halos above the brass pipes. All night you heard the spiked heels of the girls clacking on the floorboards. 'But the girls weren't that different from you, dear.'

Kristian was bleary by now. The flesh on her hands might have rubberized. Too much coffee. 'What about this one?' She held up still one more yellow sheet of paper.

'What's that, dear?' Jenny may still have been rocking to the lullaby of an old dream.

Kristian let the paper drift away. 'From Archives. Somebody can't find a file.'

Jenny began to stir. Her fingers began to crawl across the desk. 'Has he checked the master index?'

Kristian nodded. 'And the computer. It's a series of registers with a provisional classified rating.' She was so sleepy that she had to push out the words one by one. 'The material was withdrawn last January.'

'A name?' Jenny was again winding her thumb into a coil of silvery hair.

'I'm afraid not.'

'Then who was at the desk?'

'Doesn't say.'

'Day or night staff?'

'No, sorry. All we have is the lost-report.' Now Jenny was fingering the paper. As she read she became still. She was nibbling on the fleshy pad of her palm. 'This one,' she murmured. 'This could be something, dear. Ah yes, this really could be something.'

Later that night Kristian stood in front of the window of her tiny, muddled flat, and shivered as dry thunder cracked in a predawn sky. But thunder had never frightened her, so why shiver now? In the morning came the rain, flattening the dead leaves on the sidewalks. She might have stayed in bed all morning, snug in a patchwork quilt and unwashed sheets, except that she remembered the night before. And a dream, something about a paper chase and a handsome young man . . . all in a place not so unlike the hall of the Register Archives.

Archive scholars, said Langley legend, were like miners or bats. They hunted in a world of their own. Night vision saw them into the murk. They did not like intruders. To reach them, one walked to the lowest level of the Langley complex. There had been talk of incorporating the Registry into the Walnut computerized retrieval system . . . a few yards of microfiche would have done the job. But the talk had come to nothing, so the hall remained.

There were tall shelves here, the files stored from ceiling to floor. The linoleum was hopelessly scuffed. The air conditioner was on the blink, sputtering out drops of sooty water. The duty clerk at the turnstile was an arrogant one in blue jeans. He would have given Kristian a difficult time, perhaps even made a pass, but her counterintel stamp put him off and he checked her on through.

There were jokes about an archive ghost, a contrary spirit that teased you into the labyrinth, then left you to wander forever among the shelves. Kristian could have believed in the ghost now. Anything was possible here. She had been backtracking, on tiptoe, so as not to break the hush. An air vent was whistling. An elevator went clanking from behind the walls. Overhead were feeble cones of fluorescent light from drab green fixtures.

She stooped, ran her fingers along the cracked spines of files – orange for biographies, yellow for the industrial reports; all else was dark brown and forgotten, some going back to Jenny's time, some even earlier.

Then she had it, and tapped the wooden block that marked the missing section. The chalk-marked initials stood for the name of the one who had discovered the loss. Thirty feet of files from wall to grimy wall, and here was the tangible gap.

Jenny lived in an ancient brownstone behind an ivy wall, the path to which was lined with stone urns. The garden had run wild . . . tubers had cracked the flagstone, vines had twisted into the arabesque of black iron. Above the garden the trees were shuddering in the warm wind and cooling rain. Inside, the rubber plants had steamed the windowpanes.

'Sometimes I have to rap my head to let the world in here.' This wet and humid afternoon she looked unusually vast and snowy in her acetate bathrobe, submerged in the eiderdown love seat.

Kristian had taken the bentwood rocker, having had to puff away the tendrils of a mossy fern. The place was crammed with huge antiques: watery gilt mirrors, gargoyle statuettes in Dutch silver; four Irish candle lusters, stopped with the burnt-out stubs of wax.

'I get that feeling all the time,' Kristian said. They had

told her that Langley was the center. Well, yes, she supposed it was, but the center of what? Not the real world certainly.

'See,' Jenny laughed. 'It's already gotten to you.'

'What?' The orange tabby at Kristian's feet had begun to paw at her ankles.

'Why, the archives, child.' Jenny's eyes were wide. Just now she might have been a fairy-tale witch, but not the wicked one. 'You spent all morning in the archives, didn't you?'

Kristian, as the still-bedraggled Dorothy, shrugged. 'I didn't find much there, but at least we know there's definitely been a theft.'

'Ho, there!' Jenny giggled. She was pulling back on her imaginary reins. *Possibly* a theft. They might have just misplaced it. Or not returned it. Or who knows?'

But Kristian was rummaging in her battered leather purse. A rubber band snapped off, and flew across the wilted flowered rug, and the cat began to stalk it. 'I brought a photostat of the ledger,' Kristian said. 'For the night in and around – '

'And they let you take the copies out?' Strips of Jenny's eyebrows arched. 'Oh, there's excellent security for you.'

Kristian held out the glossy paper. 'I didn't understand how to read it, so I just brought the whole lot with me.' Now she was kneeling at Jenny's feet. Jenny's glasses kept slipping off her nose. 'Where are you, you little brat?' and she tossed a paper behind her, the sheet slowly zigzagging off into the musty room. 'Ah, ah yes. Look here, child.' The old woman was curling her fingers. 'Come closer, dear.'

Kristian's legs were tucked up beneath her. Her hands were clutching the arm of Jenny's seat. 'You've found it?'

Jenny shook her head. 'Not quite, dear, but look.' The pages were gently rattling together. 'You see, whenever a

52

file is removed, the time, the date, and the file's call number must be recorded in the ledger. That's what your poor wretch at the turnstile does. He records all in his little black ledger. He's responsible for making sure that everything is tidy-tidy. When the reader returns the file they simply check it in. There's the day duty and the night duty. That's the rough slot, night duty. No one wants night duty, all alone in that spooky hall. Oh God, not night duty.'

More papers fluttered away. Then Jenny's hand snatched a single sheet from the rest. She was humming, sucking on one blunt red fingernail. 'Oooh.' She started to drum on the japanned woodwork. 'Oooh.' The gold band on her finger was clacking. 'I think . . . we . . . have . . . it . . . now. Yes, come closer, child, and look here.' Their cheeks were nearly brushing together, and their hair, Kristian's gold was mingling with Jenny's gray fluff. 'Yes, this is it. Your lost flock, child, I've got it.' She clicked her tongue. 'There were actually three files in all. They were checked out by a . . . uh-oh. Here's our Mr X. The party is classified. All you have is the code, so you'll have to get clearance to get the name.'

'Is that difficult?'

'Depends, dear. I think they'll let you in. You check with Mr Severson come Monday . . . Because the code many times isn't legit.' Jenny's eyes seemed to bulge in the lenses of her glasses. 'Do you know what I'm saying? We can't rule out anything.' Her lips were puckering. 'Mmm, and here's a delicious name from the past.'

'What's that?'

'The night clerk at the turnstile when the files were taken,' Jenny answered, smiling. 'Night duty, child, and who do you think it was *that* night but our lovely beau, Robin Turner.'

'Who's he?' Kristian brushed a strand of hair from her eyes.

But the old woman was within herself again, humming softly to herself.

'Tell me, Jen.' Kristian laughed. She could play this girl's game too. 'Who is he? Come on, give.'

'Oh, wouldn't you like to know . . . pretty girl like you, and not a decent boy in sight,' and as she said it running her fingers through the fine strands of Kristian's hair.

Kristian submitted her petition for a provisional four-digit security rating to Severson on Monday. This had been the bolder approach. She could have simply requested that the identity code found in the ledger be declassified to her existing level, but Jenny Rice, who was more or less running the show from the grandstands, was very keen to see Kristian kick up her heels. 'Let them know you're a serious mind,' she had instructed. 'Let them know they got a bloodhound when they took on Badgery.'

But Kristian felt far less the hound-dog spy-chaser, more the frightened new girl in town, particularly when the trumpet began to sound from above.

They called for her at noon, and not on the telephone – a seventh floor runner came down to fetch her. An elevator swept her up and left her at the end of a long narrow corridor. There were no windows and no doors. She might have been inside some sanitized machine, her heels clicking away on the clean linoleum.

Severson met her at the laminate door, and she walked behind him until they came to a circular room. Through the smoked glass lay a broad stretch of the Fairfax County countryside. The shag was dark brown. A portable bar had been set in the corner. A round, squat man was brooding before the window. They called him Humphrey. 'Mr Humphrey Knolls.' Severson beamed. 'Humphrey, meet Kristian Badgery.'

The small man whirled forward, scratched his head. His

pudgy hand was dangling out for her. 'Oh, how do you do.' There were food stains on his drip-dry shirt. His glasses were taped at the bridge.

'Humphrey is our money man,' Severson explained. 'Aren't you, Humphrey?'

'Oh, well . . .' He began to blush. Money man or no, he couldn't keep his eyes off Kristian's creamy legs. He began to pull at the tufts of his carrot hair.

'Humphrey and you have apparently crossed paths,' Lyle went on. 'That's to say you've both stumbled onto the same problem.'

'Yes,' Humphrey said, his voice striking Kristian as a chirping sound. 'Go-between.' He may have been trying to impress the girl with his own shabby style. 'Go-between is the word, all right.'

'Uh, Humphrey . . .' Lyle laid his hands on Knolls's rounded shoulders. 'Kristian hasn't actually been briefed yet.'

'Oh, I'm sorry.' Humphrey swallowed.

'So why don't I just fill you in now, dear.' Severson was pulling out a chair for her. Now they all sat at the round varnished table. 'From the beginning, then.' Severson smiled.

'Yes, please,' Kristian returned primly. My God, it was like some tea party and she was Alice.

'Ah now, dear, you've just sent up a petition regarding a certain identity code found in the archive ledger, right?'

Kristian nodded. Her lips were tight. 'Because of the missing files, sir.'

'Very true.' Severson's fingers were lacing together for a long and serious chat. 'You see, the situation is something like this. The identity code you found in that ledger, the same used to check out the now lost files, is not the code of a single individual. It's an operational code. That's to say, whoever took those files did so on behalf of an operational group. In other words, the files were removed at the request of a special operations member or members. Rather than using his own name, or work name, he merely used the code of the operational group. In this case, Operation Go-between.'

Humphrey had been pulling at his earlobe, digging his fingers into his scalp. Now he perked up. 'Yes, Go-between. There's the problem. I don't mean that the operation is a problem in itself. I mean that it's a problem because it doesn't exist.' He began to rock back and forth. Nervously.

'Doesn't exist?' Kristian glanced at Severson.

'No,' Lyle said. 'Not as a bona fide operational group. It exists on paper, yes, but not as a functional entity with the power to extract classified material from the archives.'

Suddenly Knolls was vehement. '*Or* to receive funding.' Whereupon he sagged back into his chair.

'Uh, that's right.' Lyle nodded. 'Go-between has, it seems, received money for expenses. Which is, of course, odd, because how can they have expenses when they don't exist. Which is also how Humphrey here became involved. He was tracing missing money and Go-between turned up.'

Kristian could have sighed and rolled her eyes at this mad tea party with Father Lyle and his Humpty-Dumpty Knolls. 'But who is Go-between?' Which seemed like the logical question to ask.

'Exactly,' Humphrey put in. 'Who indeed?'

'We don't know, dear.' Lyle told her. 'Go-between is merely a shadow now. We have found the tracks, but we haven't yet found the beast.'

'Odd, isn't it?' Humphrey was staring at Kristian.

'Very.'

Through it all Lyle kept pulling at his tattersall cuff, saying, 'Naturally there are others, uh, a bit higher up the ladder who are also dealing with the Go-between problem. So there may be some areas which we don't know about. However, I've been given full rights to the problem as such. So the two of you might as well work together.'

'Humphrey and I?' Kristian was looking at her hands. She couldn't bear to glance at Humphrey Dumpty, or even at Lyle.

'Yes,' Severson said. 'I think that would be the best way to go,' and he crimped his forehead while his accomplice kept on scratching his throat and glowering at Kristian's breasts.

Humphrey's office was an awful mess, not that Kristian had expected less. But the place might have been alive, organic, like mold. Piles of papers had long since spilled over from the cabinets, across the desk, and onto the floor. The walls were lined with memos. Crude block graphs in red and blue ink had been thumbtacked to the door. There was a scatter of paper clips, rubber bands, stray matches, and the stubs of colored pencils. Growing in the bottom drawers were millions of curled eraser shavings, not to mention the more infectious crumbs of sandwiches, including shreds of dried lettuce. There was more that Kristian could not identify, some sort of decomposing library paste, or something.

On the chase, however, Humphrey Knolls was said to have been as gallant a man as any. He had been a hunter under Allen Dulles. Under Richard Helms he had headed the team that traced the checks of Soviet paymasters in the Eastern bloc. But internal tracking was his specialty . . . certainly he knew all the alleys.

By the early evening he and Kristian had a fairly complete picture of the Go-between history. The line began clearly in the Plans division where the operation had been discussed formally some eighteen months before.

'Go-between,' read the summary brief, which was an

eyes-only report circulated up from the deputy director to the president, 'is a three-prong support grouping.' Target names, agent names, dates and locals were omitted. They were only to have been supplied if and when the president gave a 'go.' In this case there was no such word, and it took Humphrey and Kristian the better part of a day to secure a security pass to the deputy director's files.

The eventual release of these early Go-between minutes was a substantial victory for the hunters on two counts. It validated the importance of their work. If the deputy director was willing to open his closet to this quirky team, then he obviously cared a good deal about their success. Humphrey, however, who had played and won at the status game before, was less impressed with the seventh floor support than Kristian. What excited the myopic little man was the data itself – contained in the minutes of the meeting.

Go-between was to have been a fairly straightforward purchase, with all strings neatly attached. The merchandise was one General Aldo Castillo Roso. The playground was Bolivia. The asking price was small. The general wanted a few cases of automatic weapons, some light artillery and a handful of mortars. In exchange he was willing to play the generalissimo puppet game. All he wanted was to be the star.

Project sponsor had been Raymond John Getty, then covert operations man of the South American desk, now retired in Alabama. Pulling up Raymond John's rear was none other than the Company's famous 'Dancing Allen' Cassidy, who had missed a step in a soybean scandal and was undone by a legendary killer from 'Operations' named Josey Swann.

Opposition to the Go-between plan came primarily from Steve Grinder, who was representing the Review Committee's voice. Grinder's objection was simply that the rewards did not justify the risk. Arms into a South American country was just the sort of stunt that the White House would scream about. Debate followed, and the upper hand clearly went to the opposition. When the meeting was over, Go-between was not dead, but it was pretty well beaten.

There were one or two later references to the operation, halfhearted attempts to revive it. Then the trail died.

Through the following days Kristian and Humphrey became friends of sorts. Such was the bond between those who walked the tortuous path of the archives. They often lunched together on the broad lawns beneath the trees. Humphrey always brought bread crumbs for the birds. Other days they met for breakfast on the red brick patio of a small café where they could watch the cold mist rising and curling off the black slate roofs. And if Humphrey was still that grubby, scratchy egg-man, then at least he was a very good egg. Kristian had come to like him best when his glasses were off . . . he looked particularly naked and mortal, with the red rings around his droopy eyes and the groove on the blob of his nose. Once he even brought her flowers, a dozen crisp daisies. 'Why, Humphrey, you're a true gallant, after all.' But she didn't kiss him, lest he get the wrong idea.

In time their search took on a profound unreality. The path became dark and twisting. They might have been on some desolate dream street that rose and dipped into perpetual twilight. The had even come to fear the Go-between beast. While in the shadowless hours of an early evening they often became so listless, so frustrated, they would have to leave Humphrey's wretched room to wander through brambles at the edge of the Langley forest.

By the third week Humphrey had established without a

59

doubt that Go-between was the sole recipient of the missing funds. He calculated the sum to be somewhere between one-hundred and three-hundred thousand dollars. 'The big table,' he told Kristian. 'Anyway you look at it, Go-between was playing for keeps.'

But Go-between was also much more than a common thief. Humphrey was quite sure on this point. 'The ends,' he would tell her, 'have nothing to do with money. Money was only the means.'

But the means for what? So many hours were spent hunched over desks in the night that the journey might have taken place during the space of one long night. Then too there were moments when the files seemed as if they would turn on the hunters and devour them. Certainly Go-between could seem alive enough at times.

Toward the end of the first junction they had seen that Go-between had been a functioning organ unto itself. The operation had actually conducted a lengthy research project, utilizing all four branches of the Langley library system. Field intelligence had been siphoned off regular channels and fed into the mouth of the beast. There were even one or two cases in which agents unwittingly worked exclusively for Go-between.

To all this there was proof. They had seen the research requests to Archives. Kristian had found the mysterious Go-between code on classified subscription lists. Humphrey had traced an order to a French stringer through his case officer, back to Langley and finally to the European desk. Yet for all this they had not yet glimpsed the beast. They were able to see where it had stalked, but they were no closer to the kill. Which was to say, they had no names. The actual Go-between members still remained hidden.

It was as if there were no members, Humphrey complained one particularly bad night at the headachy, sour-stomach hour. 'It's as if the thing just sprang to life out of red tape.' All evening he had been moaning, tearing at his empty coffee cups, gnawing on the Styrofoam. 'A red tape monster, that's that we've got.' He was surrounded by a pyramid of notes. The lights seemed to be throbbing at him. His eyes were bruised with purple rings.

Kristian lay sprawled on a bed of files. She had lost her shoes, literally buried beneath debris. Around them lay the remains of glum prodding. There were half-eaten sandwiches congealing in the wastebasket. Wads of candy wrappers had been tossed on the floor. One of them had broken a bottle and kicked the glass into the corner.

Now Kristian stirred. 'I don't know. Damn it, I just don't *know*.' There had been moments when she even thought she had heard the beast breathing. For sure the thing had taunted them, led them down one awful blind alley after another. 'Maybe we should go back over the master code lists? Maybe we missed something?'

Humphrey spat out the flakes of his coffee cup. 'We didn't miss anything.' Tonight he was grim and nervous. Possibly he had seen the glimmer of something that scared him. 'You can look again,' he finally told her, not that you'll find anything there. I've checked.'

But Kristian hadn't heard. She was idly nudging a pile of papers with her toes. 'No members,' she said. 'No members. Well, maybe that's the key? You said it yourself. Humph. Go-between doesn't exist. Well, maybe *that's* the point? I mean, what if we've been looking in the wrong place? We've been hunting for a mastermind on the inside, but what if Go-between has been run from the outside?' Then the teetering stack of papers rocked forward and fell, and the notes went skidding across the floor.

So it was that on this night Kristian and Humphrey found a name in the maze. Neither would admit that they had uncovered the moving force behind the whole thing, but they had definitely found something. For whenever files had been removed under the auspices of Go-between research they had always been checked out through the same clerk. Further, this clerk had also doubled as a runner, picking up all sorts of material with a pass bearing the Go-between code.

And so it was that on this night Kristian had her first substantial brush with Robin Turner.

4

More and more through the humid summer Kristian had been feeling that she was close to something that would soon engulf her. This morning in particular she had begun to notice her good old flippant self receding in the dead calm. Leaves hung limply all along the avenues. You could almost hear the rats of suburban anxiety gnawing behind the brownstone walls. There were hardly any people about. She had only seen a few dogs squatting on the lawns. She might have been caught in a vacuum of sorts. The day had not yet properly begun.

Better to put these nervous palpitations down to the weather, she had told herself. Kristian may have had a schoolgirl's figure, but she frowned at the schoolgirl's taste for dramatics. Besides, what with the mauve light soaking through the puffs of clouds, there really was an unreality to the morning.

She was driving Humphrey's battered Rambler. 'Runs like a top,' he had told her. Except that the tires were bald, and the suspension was shot, and whenever she braked the glove box clattered open and all kinds of junk came flying out. This tallowy wreck might have been an extension of poor Humph's office. Or his mind? No. Beneath those perma-press shirts, those flapping Hush Puppy loafers, there was a pretty levelheaded guy. Not a hero, but Humphrey had his moments all the same.

Closer now, Kristian eased the pedal down and rattled to a stop. Here there were once firm and quiet family dwellings. Most of the homes had since been subdivided.

Students lived in those rooms, she thought. Also lonely working people.

Then she was out on the sidewalk, stepping up to the iron gate. The hinges squeaked. A dog was barking. There were birds splashing in a bath. Her footsteps sent them fluttering to the bridge of leaves above the street. When she pressed the doorbell she could hear the chimes faintly tinkling from within.

'No, I wouldn't say that he left in any rush,' said Mrs Williamson. 'Robin wasn't the sort that wouldn't give you notice.'

Kristian sat on the edge of a velveteen sofa. Her handbag lay in her lap. This morning she was Deedee Lamont from Hartford Insurance. She had three plastic cards to prove it.

'He told us he was leaving about a week before he left. And he paid up for six months beyond that,' Mrs. Williamson continued. She was a shriveled woman with dollops of wispy gray hair. She wore saggy stretch pants and a green dressing robe. Her leather slippers might have been her husband's.

'A week?' Kristian was fiddling with the brass clasp on her bag. 'You're sure it was a week?' The heads of birds had been painted on china plates now fixed to the wall. One had been broken. There were also somber landscapes, one a craggy shoreline with thrashing breakers.

'Oh' – the woman nodded – 'I'd say he gave us about a week. My husband would know for sure, but he's at the Builder's Emporium.' Her fingers picked at a ball of fluff on the sleeve of her robe. 'My husband's name is George. He liked the boy too. Robin, I think everyone must have liked Robin.'

A portable fan was mixing the lingering fumes of roasted meat and cleaning polish. 'Always quiet,' the old woman droned on. 'Never heard a peep. Always a kindly word. "Hello, Mrs Williamson," he'd say in the morning. "Good evening, Mrs Williamson." And wasn't he always around to help with the trash when George's back was acting up?'

Kristian smoothed the lace antimacassar on the arm of the sofa. 'I wonder if I might see his room?'

The old woman frowned. Her cheeks ballooned out. 'I don't know if that would be right. He's still paid up and all.'

'Yes, but I wouldn't have asked unless it was absolutely vital.' Then with her sweetest smile, 'You can understand, can't you?'

They moved through the groves of waxed and dusted furniture. They passed a low harmonium. Behind a crystal case sat seven porcelain ducks. The ring of keys was clanking in the woman's fist.

Outside, the birds had returned to their bath. A narrow flight of wooden steps climbed sharply to the overhanging eucalyptus. Once they had to stop so that the old woman could wheeze and suck in air. Then they stood before the door.

'This is where he lived,' the landlady said. She had begun to pant. Her hands were trembling. She couldn't get the key in the lock. Then she was turning the knob. The bolt clicked back, and Kristian eased on through.

Strange. Kristian couldn't quite get herself going. She had to hang there, poised just inside the door. Ahead, each object lay taut in the stillness. Well, what else had she expected? There was his table, there his chair, there his fiberboard dresser. *This is where he lived*. They could have roped it off.

She was treading cautiously now. She might have been afraid of the reverberations if she so much as disturbed the dust. Her handbag strap lay smartly against her shoulder.

Her hair feathered on her back when she turned her head. Behind, the old woman had begun to mumble, but Kristian ignored her and moved to the desk. Inside she found a stack of paper. Next to the paper there was a pen; all in order, all perfect.

Except in the bedroom there was the painting. Here at eye level, here was this incongruous face of a cat. 'That's his tiger,' the old woman was saying. She had folded her arms and leaned in the doorway. 'He likes tigers.'

But Kristian was already shaking her head at the too exact oil in its simple black frame. 'Not a tiger,' she muttered. Then louder, 'It's not a tiger. It's a jaguar,' and she stepped in closer to the dabs of paint. 'Why?' She was actually touching the canvas. She even wanted to pick at the swirls of encrusted paint. 'Why?'

'Because he like tigers.' The old woman was squinting, rocking a little from side to side.

'Will you leave me alone, please?'

'Why? Has Robin done something wrong? Is that it? Did he steal that picture?' The landlady's fingers were twitching. 'He was a good boy. He was very good. I'll tell that to anyone. He didn't steal anything.'

Then Kristian turned quickly around. 'Leave me alone, will you? Just wait outside, okay?' Because the eyes of the cat were sucking her in.

Alone now, Kristian was able to cope with the animal's glare, or at least wrench herself away. She moved to the dresser, and slid back a drawer. Here too there was that total order. There were his socks, his underwear. Everything was neatly folded and stacked, one to one. But then she was peeling back the elastic seam of his cotton briefs, and her nails clicked against a plastic finish. She fished the thing out, now holding a spool of magnetic tape. There was no label, only this reel of recording tape. She dropped it into her purse, and snapped the clasp shut . . .

Outside, the first tepid drops of a blown summer rain had begun to shake the garden leaves. As if the vegetation wasn't vicious enough already. Every shrub was trembling in the hothouse wind.

The old woman stood by her birdbath pelting bread crumbs onto the grass. 'He hasn't done anything wrong, he's a good boy, he didn't steal that picture, I was there when he bought it . . . I just remembered.' The light was almost incandescent now under the cap of purple-gray clouds. 'I just remembered, he paid for that painting. He bought it at the outdoor sale.'

But Kristian had already flung back the gate. She was almost running. Around her the rain kept splattering while above the clouds unraveled.

Humphrey propped against the doorjamb. Kristian sagged into the Naugahyde. They had shared a pizza from a greasy bag, although Humphrey's cynicism may have been more nourishing. Nothing could rattle him today. He was lumpy and jocular, blowing out, 'So what.' Then again, shrugging, 'Soooo what!' He had an elbow on the cabinet. His hair stuck out in wired curls. 'Maybe the guy just likes to live clean, you know? Clean,' and he kicked at the wastebasket, knocking the balled-up papers from the heap.

'You had to have been there. It was weird, that's all. I think he's a weird person. You can tell that from the way he lives.'

Humphrey languidly reached for another half-eaten slice of pizza. 'Well, so what. I'm weird. I know it, but I'm proud of it.'

She had to smile weakly now. 'You're weird in a nice way. This Turner's weird in a . . . oh, to hell with it. Let's just play the tape.'

They called down for a proper recorder, but there were

no available runners with security clearance above the fourth floor. So Humphrey had to lug up the machine himself, his round thighs pumping away on the stairs while Kristian trotted behind with the cords, laughing. 'You're going to break it, Humph. You're going to break it,' every time he banged the wall. And when the dangling wire snapped in the elevator, she couldn't help calling out, 'It's closing, Humph, look *out*, the door's closing.' She could have shoved him through, but the hilarity doubled her over.

When Humphrey finally stretched the tape tight through the spools, he might have been stretching their nerves as well. They had both become taut. Then the speaker was crackling with static, and then came the chanting . . . or was it singing? 'Like Indians,' Humphrey murmured. 'There must be hundreds of them.' While over and over the same droning syllables were echoing on.

Kristian could only shake her head. The plastic lid was buzzing with the rolling grunt of deeper voices. Until she couldn't take any more. 'Shut it off, Humph. Shut if off. I don't like it.'

In the aftermath and silence, she began to bite her lips. 'So?'

Humphrey's forehead was studded with sweat. 'Hell if I know. Maybe it's nothing, you know? Maybe it's just some tape he had.'

But Kristian was frowning. Her eyes had narrowed. 'No, Humph. I think he wanted us to find that tape. I really do. He was so *neat* . . . nothing left to chance.'

That evening they met with Roger Jasper from the language lab. Jasper was a ragged little fox of a man with a silver beard and horn-rimmed glasses. Humphrey said he was crazy, but then they were all crazy to Humphrey Knolls. Still, Kristian found a few quirks here and there scattered about in Jasper's office. Like the linguist kept hamsters in a glass cage, and on the wall hung a stiff portrait of a dog. It was a rather glum terrier with a dead bird in his mouth. Beyond this, they found Jasper rocking slowly in his chair. He was chewing pistachio nuts. The fragments of shells had been ground into the Mexican rug.

'You gave us a real workout on this,' he said. His glasses hung on the end of his nose, all the better to see Kristian's knees. 'We ran the sample through the main library and came up with nothing. I had my kids going, let me tell you.'

Humphrey's fingers had been inching toward the bag of nuts. Now he froze. 'But you found it, right?'

'Oh sure, we found it.' Jasper grinned. 'Want some?' He shoved the bag to Knolls. 'What you've got there is definitely a chant. My guess was that the syllabic configuration was South American Indian. Which was right on the money. Not to blow my own horn, but I guessed it from the start.'

'So?' Kristian prodded.

'So, it's South American Indian, all right. Brazil, the Amazon Basin precisely. Even more precisely it's from the Xingú River area.'

'But what are they saying?' Humphrey had even forgotten about the nuts now.

Jasper finally pushed his glasses up. 'Three word grouping,' he said. 'Same thing over and over.' Then he held out the bag to Kristian, but she shook her head. 'The modulation changes, but the grouping is always the same. He crushed another shell between his molars. 'They say,' and he spat out the shreds of a nut, 'they say, "We sing it is bad. We sing it is bad." There you go, Knolls. Over and over, it's the same thing. "We sing it is bad." And that's all I can tell you.'

Humphrey had picked up the phrase. '. . . it is bad . . . bad . . . bad. . . What the hell do you think, Kris?'

But the girl was watching a rampant hamster pawing the glass of its cage. Then, too, she may have seen that jaguar again.

That night Robin Turner became the quarry, but not without some reservation. Humphrey Knolls, in particular, had trouble seeing the boy as the man behind the deception.

But to counter Humphrey, Kristian presented a rather neat set of figures. By correlating the known dates and times of Go-between activity with Turner's duty schedule she was able to strengthen her case. In every instance that material had been routed to Go-between, Turner had either been directly on the line or else near enough to have been of consequence. Granted there were several times when Go-between functioned without probable Turner involvement. Further, the operation often moved in circles denied to the likes of the boy. But you had to expect that Turner would cover himself, Kristian argued. And besides, she said that she had a feeling.

So Turner remained. Humphrey still wouldn't cast him as the star of the drama . . . there was no way that Turner could have gotten the money. But as a member of the supporting cast, Turner did indeed show definite promise.

They began with his records. First there were Andrew Aston's debriefing reports. Next there were the sixty-odd pages of tape transcription. (Even during those walks in the Langley forest, a mike on Aston's belt had recorded their conversations.)

The primary sources contained the main of Turner's story. There was a fair amount on his affair with Julia Vegas. Aston had made several probes into the scope of the relationship. Had the Brazilians been correct in assuming that Turner had been involved with Julia's clandestine work? No, Aston concluded. The boy had known nothing. Why, then, had Turner been arrested? Because, Aston said, he was with the girl, and that was all. Except that as an ironic footnote, Aston spelled out the reason for Turner's stay in Brazil as 'love.' He then added a vicious comment on the Brazilians' crude intelligence system, and Kurt Kohl in particular.

As for the details of Turner's prison experience, these were at once explicit and vague. There were moments when he seemed able to speak freely. Other times, however, his descriptions were sketchy, terse. The tone was charcoal gray. The dominant theme seemed the despair of loss. To Humphrey, the boy's reticence was understandable. It had been a nightmare. No wonder he was unwilling to dredge up the memory. And so Humphrey was prepared to gloss over those sections of the report.

But there was one area that Kristian could not get enough of. She was drawn back to Robin's words again and again.

ASTON: *There's still the matter of your escape, Robin. I wonder if we couldn't go over that a bit closer.*

TURNER: *I killed a guard.*

ASTON: *Was that one guard, or two?*

TURNER: *Yes, I killed two guards.*

ASTON: *How?*

TURNER: *I just killed them.*

ASTON: *Won't you tell me exactly how, Robin?*

TURNER: *Why does it matter? I don't remember.*

ASTON: *Well, did you use a knife, or . . .?*

TURNER: *I used my hands.*

ASTON: *I see. Thank you.*

TURNER: *I killed them with hands. I also kicked them. I killed them with my hands and feet. Then one was blind.*

ASTON: *The guard was blind?*
TURNER: *I did it. I did it with the claw . . . my fingers.*
         [Faster breathing.] *I tore out his eyes. I tore out
         his eyes, and then I hit his head against the wall.
         And my form was perfect . . .*

There were one or two other places where Turner's
narrative dropped to this kind of detached violence.
Kristian noted that when he spoke of the guards' brutality,
for instance, there was a feel of what she called a sort of
'wry existentialism.' She smiled her apology for the pre-
tentiousness of it. He spoke of the torture. He spoke of
the deaths. He said that the Company's training program
designed to prepare agents to overcome such systems was
very good. Naturally the actual situation could not be
duplicated, but the Company instructors managed a very
accurate facsimile of the Third World prison.

Overall, however, there was a lilting, aerial scope to the
Turner files. Long passages of the Aston debriefing were
filled with jaunty polemics. They discussed art, the classi-
cal in general. Specifically Turner favored the T'ang for
their shimmering porcelain, though he also admitted to a
fondness for the German Expressionists – Emil Nolde
and Max Beckmann; he said that he liked the way they
dealt with unhappiness. In another mood Robin said he
also liked the French: Matisse, Gauguin, especially
Georges Seurat. There was something about the way they
handled light in the afternoon, he said.

As a touching coda to his sessions with the boy, Aston
submitted three of Robin's 'Translations from the
Chinese.' Joy, sorrow, death: the sort of poems that could
have meant anything.

A less equivocal vision of Robin Turner's soul appeared
in his honors essay at Harvard College. The yellowed
manuscript was contained in his entrance file, along with

72

chummy letters from professors and the rest of that school-day memory. The paper was a look at the Sun Tzu classic, *The Art of War*. Although the effort ranked well in the class, there were some who felt that Turner stressed too much the art, and not enough the war. Yet, as Turner himself noted, 'The supreme art of war is to subdue the enemy without a fight.' Was this still Robin's touchstone? Kristian somehow doubted it.

Throughout, the Turner files were filled with praise. From the first entry to the last, everybody seemed to like this golden youth. There was Robin as the scholar, walking with his tutor along the college avenues, a quiet boy popular among his mates. Professors especially seemed to have enjoyed his company. Next there was Robin the gentle instructor with all his admiring students. He left notices for his Saturday class on the bulletin board in the lounge, all most carefully worded. And finally there was the shattered but still polite Robin, and how they had all sympathized for the pain and the loss in his life.

The phases of Robin Turner. Each a succinct picture of a wonderful, wonderful boy. Or else, dear Robin, Kristian thought, or else you've been conning us all along . . . and your form *is* perfect.

Along the flagstones, past the formal grounds, the wild evergreens began. Here too Turner and Aston had sat . . . perhaps on that long fallen tree, talking, flinging an occasional pebble into the coils of brush. 'Did he ever take you into the forest? I understand that he liked the wood.' Kristian walked with her hands in the pockets of her green corduroy trousers. The ends of her red flannel collar lay over her sweater. She might have been a child on this late afternoon, kicking at the carpet of pine needles, feeling the trunks of trees.

'Yeah, I think he took me out here,' said Sally. But she

was hardly dressed for the woods now. Her skirt kept catching on thorns. She was a tall, angular girl. Pretty, yes, but Kristian couldn't help thinking that this horsey Sally Bowls had been an odd match for the slender Robin Turner.

'And on the weekends, you went walking into the country. Is that right?' Kristian was watching the girl as she talked.

'Yes.' Sally nodded. She was stepping high to save her nylons from a cluster of thistles.

Kristian had a sort of bumbling kid's walk. If alone here, she might have dug at a rabbit's hole, or simply mooned about. Now, however, she was digging at this finance clerk. 'Did he know a lot about the outdoors? Did he know all the birds, that sort of thing?'

Sally scowled. 'We didn't talk about nature.'

They had come to the edge of a gully. Kristian had hoped for a view, they always spoke better to a view. But all they saw now was the wall of pines and below the greenery of soft broad ferns and poison ivy. 'So then what did you talk about?' Kristian eased down to a damp stump.

Sally smoothed her skirt and joined her. 'I don't know what we talked about. I suppose just the usual things.' She was sitting very straight while Kristian was hunched with her toes turned in.

'Did you ever talk about the future?'

'How do you mean?' Sally whipped her hair from her face.

Kristian shrugged. 'You know, life, love, marriage.'

Sally smiled. 'Look, I'm not a fool. Robin is a very kind person. He never led me on. But let's face it, I never had a chance with him.'

'Why not, he liked you.'

'Oh, I know he *liked* me. But he didn't *love* me.'

Kristian began to pick at the bark on the stump. 'Why do you say that?'

'I could tell, that's all. I could just tell.'

A long strip of bark had peeled away in Kristian's hands. Her nails were clotted with brown dust. 'How do you feel about him now?'

'I don't know. Maybe I still love him. I mean, you can't help but love Robin. Everyone loves him. I don't care what you think he's done. They're going to all still love him. He's got a way about him.'

Kristian sensed the girl was on the edge of crying. Her face was hidden behind a curtain of brown hair. 'Why don't you tell me about him, Sal. You can, you know. I'm just going to sit here with you and listen. So why don't you just talk about him.' Kristian's voice was a lullaby, although she was grinding the bark in her fingers to dust . . .

Sally and Robin had met at the garden party of Irene Van Houten. Late May, it was, and the last chill had been mingling with the first warmth. How clear that night had been. The sky was studded with stars. The patio was glowing with blurring lights in orange paper lanterns. But it wasn't silly, Sally insisted. There was really something special about that evening. You had the feeling that time had rolled back to some half-remembered elegance. 'Oh, it was very twenties.'

She first saw Robin by the buffet table. He was serving melon balls and rum to a grinning Andy Aston. 'And I thought, isn't he the pretty one, there in his white jacket and button-down collar.' She did not remember exactly how they came to talking. Only that there they finally stood under the branching wisteria. Robin was shy at first. He brought her punch in a paper cup. They talked about travel. Robin said that he had always been intrigued by those chance surreal moments that one encounters in distant cities – London, Athens, Paris . . . like a dream, he said.

They had eased into the relationship. Robin seemed to take his time. 'He was beautiful,' she said. Beautiful, even if he was kind of subdued and rather formal. One somehow had the impression that he was from another era. Maybe he had been born too late.

He took her for drives on Sunday afternoons. They lunched on patios of open cafés. They walked in the park along the paths of red leaves. Once they saw a small production of *Hamlet* and afterwards wandered through the streets that still glistened from an early rain. Finally they came to rest in a stark cone of lamplight and he told her that he had never understood why Hamlet had waited so long to murder his uncle, but now he knew . . . Hamlet was not the sort to consciously choose revenge. He'd fallen into it, into the persona of the avenger, into the scheme. And that persona, and scheme, were greater, larger than Hamlet the mere man was. And so he became lost in it . . .

Now Sally hardly knew why she recalled that moment under the lamplight. Unless it was because she had never seen Robin so intense. At any rate that had been the first time Robin had actually frightened her.

'But there was another time he frightened you, wasn't there, Sally?' In the time that had passed, Kristian had smoothed the lump of bark into a point. Now she was casually grinding the wood on the edge of the stump. 'That's why you stopped seeing him,' she continued calmly. 'He did something that wasn't very nice.'

Sally was stiff. There were tears on her cheeks. 'No, you've got it wrong.'

Kristian ran her fingers along the crude blade. 'Have I?' She was pressing the point into the stump. 'I don't think so. Why don't I tell you what I think, and then we'll see,

76

okay?' She began, still playing with bark, speaking almost carelessly. 'Oh, it must have been about three months after you met. Things were nice and simple. Maybe you'd meet for lunch. Then he began coming to your office. He had clearance by then, although you didn't know from where. Maybe you asked, and he said he was working on something that gave him the run of the place. So you forgot about it. Time went by, and after a bit you thought nothing when he came into the finance office. In fact no one gave him much thought. . . "Oh, that's just Sally's boyfriend . . ."'

Through all this Sally remained rigid, but shivering, maybe from the growing breeze, maybe from the grief. The sun was also falling. Behind the line of trees, shadows were spreading. Kristian was speaking softer now. Her fingers had whitened around the bark. 'Then one day Robin asks for a favor. Oh, it really wasn't much, but it sort of broke the rules a little. "Out security," you told him. "Oh, come on," he said. He said that he had to have this favor done to save his job. He had botched up something, you were the only one that could cover for him, and he looked so sad, didn't he, Sal? He looked so very very sad, and, of course, beautiful. Well, you just couldn't refuse him, could you? You just had to do it.'

Suddenly the girl heaved. 'Oh God, please!' She was crying and running her hands across her eyes.

But Kristian still twirled the point of her bark-knife into the stump. 'What was it, Sal? What was it that he wanted? Come on now, come on . . .'

'He wanted . . .' She wiped her nose on the back of her hand, then finally got it out. 'He wanted an operational funding order, and he wanted it blank.'

Kristian bit her lip. 'The funding order. That's what you'd need to get money out of Treasury, isn't it?'

77

'Yes.' Sally's arms were laced across her breasts. 'But it's no good without a valid operation code.'

'Oh, he had that,' Kristian said.

Sally hadn't heard. She was rocking gently in the breeze. 'And it wasn't like you said. He didn't beg me for it. He just asked me. He told me that he needed it for something he was checking up on. Something to do with security arrangements. Anyway, we had tickets to the ballet that night and he had to have the packet or we would have missed – oh my God,' and she began another long cry.

The tones of dusk were spreading across the forest floor. Sally's breath was jagged. Her body trembled some. Then she sniffed. 'I knew, I knew he was going to steal the money. He never told me, but I knew.'

But still, Kristian couldn't leave her there in the dark, alone. So she took that horsey girl in her arms, and rocked her, and when Sally whimpered, 'I'm cold. I'm cold,' Kristian held her even tighter.

So. Robin Turner had forged a funding request. Then he had authorized the form with his Go-between code, and slipped the papers into the Treasury's list. The money followed routinely. The cash had probably been left for him in a local bank. This then was the thread that untied the knot. 'And what a clever knot it was,' Humphrey had to admit. Even now there were small details that still eluded him. How, for example, had Turner gotten around the various security checks?

Charm? Kristian offered. Yes, that graceful Turner charm could be heard tinkling all through this. However, Humphrey had also seen a different Robin. Witness one February night when Turner had needed an open-end pass through the Registry. Danny Shore had been slotted at the archive turnstile that night. Yet Danny hadn't reported in. There had been an accident. The brakes on his Porsche went out and he went sailing into a traffic light. All very fortunate for Turner, since he was then able to take the night shift. As a favor for Danny, one was to understand. What a good sport that Robin was. Except that Humphrey was now fairly sure that Turner had drained the car's brake fluid that afternoon, which would have accounted for the two-hour gap in his day.

On the evening before filing the first stage of the findings, Kristian went to Jenny Rice. You owed the poor love that much, Kristian had told herself. You just can't let Jenny learn the truth by way of grapevine.

She rode the bus as far as St Mark, then made the shambling walk from there. The sky was mottled with clouds. There had been no rain, but the wind in the leaves made them look liquid black.

Jenny became a rag of a woman. She couldn't help sobbing into her sloshing goblet of sherry. She sucked her sticky knuckles. 'But you don't know for sure,' she said. 'I mean, you can't know positively.'

Kristian could only chew her lip. Her hands were linked beneath her knees. 'No, Jen, we know for sure. Really I wouldn't have come otherwise. Humphrey's made out a timetable. He's broken it down to minutes in some places.'

Jenny flung away a soggy tissue. 'Oh that Humphrey Knolls, what does he know? Grubby little creep. You know he's got a skin disease. Ugly flakes all around wherever he sits.' She lumped up her cheek. Her eyes were puffed, but suddenly dreamy. 'Oh Robin, oh, Robbie.' She was singing out the name. 'You mean all those months? He was at it from the start.'

Kristian nodded. 'Yes, all those months.'

Jenny shuddered and slurped at her sherry. 'Well, I'm

not going to hate him. I can't hate him. I just can't. We take him to our breasts and he bites us in the throat, but I won't . . . I can't hate the boy. I'm sorry. I can't hate him.'

No, you couldn't hate Robin Turner. Even Humphrey, Kristian suspected, had come to admire the beautiful traitor. Robin, the skulk of foxes was also the prince of thieves.

Not that the others would dub him so gloriously, she knew. Soon they would call him a mangy cat burglar, with torn ears and a cocky eye. He killed the canary, and then padded off to the tin-can, rawboned rat's alley whence he came. But alone, in the yellow half-light of her bedroom, gazing at his photographs held to the lonely shine from the china lamp, Kristian settled on a new title for Turner. He is not the hungry tom, she whispered. Robin is the king of cats.

The photographs offered no insignificant perspective on her cat-boy. Humph had pulled them from the entrance file. 'Here's a couple of good shots of our beast,' he had said, and tossed them into her lap.

There were two pictures. Each was an eight-by-ten-inch glossy. The first was a rather conventional portrait, but with a white sun falling at his shoulder there was a trace of sorrow in those eyes. The second was Turner as the Black Belt Karatica, poised in midair. He had obviously leapt for the camera, but he just as well might have been leaping to kill. There was no pretense, none. They said that the Kenpo attack was both physical and mental, that Turner had a way of overwhelming his victims before he even struck. Well, you could believe it from this shot. His speed had apparently shredded the time when the shutter clicked, creating an eerie blur.

But what most intrigued her was the face. She had seen

that sort of face before, and never had been able to explain its attraction for her . . . unless there was some psychic link that tickled her romantic self. Over the years she had come to suspect that everyone had an image of a face that belonged to them, that haunted them, and in turn . . . in Turner . . . She was drowsy enough to let herself be taken over by it . . . him tonight. Later at least his face would give the hunt a special edge . . .

At midnight she lay down and twisted the screw on the china lamp. Now she saw only the dimmest outlines of furniture. A pale blouse hung from the doorknob. Her stockings were coiled on the floor. If she shut her eyes the fatigue absorbed her. Or was that Robin's face absorbing her? Certainly she felt close to him tonight, close enough even to whisper, *Robin Turner, why did you do it?*

In the cocoon of his high-intensity lamp, Humphrey was also tackling motive that night. His feel for Turner as a king of cats may have been sketchy, but he knew Robin the spy rather well. So watch for the subtleties, he had told himself. You've got a clever one here with a graceful style.

On this line he began with a look at the photostats of the archive index. This would have been the list of all Go-between research requests. From the index he moved to the call tags, asking just what had Turner sought? Now he felt the breath of Go-between. The animal was definitely within range.

Outside was the ebb and flow of night-time traffic. Pigeons rustled on the rainspout. Now and again came the rush of water through the ancient plumbing. For Humphrey none of these predawn sounds was as real as the growling of the Go-between beast.

Then, checking and cross-checking again, he had it. Checkmate; there were two names that had been of manifest interest to Go-between. The first, and as far as he could tell the most important, was the Brazilian industrialist, Kurt Kohl. The second was more ambiguous. Go-between had only seemed to dally with the figure. Yet, here too there were links. Like Kohl, the name had appeared in the Aston transcripts. Then too, Go-between had also demonstrated interest in any information contained in the archives. So in the end Humphrey added Michael Jaques to his list, and then there were two.

Only minutes before the dawn broke, Humphrey had been muttering to himself. He had been dithering across the floor, crumpling sheets of crosshatched foolscap. Now, however, he stood transfixed at the window. He may have been even stunned a little by the vision of a dead street in first light, except that since the hunt had begun Humphrey had often stood before this window and looked out to a deserted city. So what's it now, he might have asked, but didn't. There was no need. He knew very well that he was just one more tubby little bureaucrat. Whereas, you, Turner, you are a very dangerous boy. They put you in prison. They starved you. They killed your lady. And now what?

Humphrey knew, of course. He thought quite calmly, now I know. Go-between had never been intended as merely cover. Nor was the operation dead. No, Go-between was alive. There had been a plan, a timetable, and a target. In short, there were all the trappings of a bona fide search and destroy operation.

The day had taken on the misty pinks and yellows of sultry weather. Kristian had her air conditioner blasting away. Humphrey sat at the Formica breakfast nook. He had brought along the entire mess of his garbled night-notes. Earlier he had also stopped at Severson's and left with still one more hefty file. Now the heap of it lay on the kitchen linoleum. A wrinkled map lay spread on the table. 'I want to try something on you.'

Kristian was banging about with pots and pans. She had broken a cup. Coffee grounds were scattered on the draining board. 'I'm half asleep, Humph. Give me a break.' This morning she felt a drowsy wreck, not that Humphrey looked much better in his sloppy pullover and untied sneakers.

'You won't be when I'm through,' he said. His glasses were misting in the rising steam from his coffee. 'I've just come from Lyle's.'

She gave him a bleary laugh. 'Like that? You went to Lyle's dressed like that?'

Humphrey was too tense to smile back. His hands were sweating around his cup, he was staring into the curling white steam.

'All right, Humph.' She yawned. 'At eight in the god-damn morning.'

Then Humphrey laid his hand flat out on the table. 'It's eighteen months ago,' he said. 'Turner is in prison. John Poole, a Company regular who's attached to the embassy, has been trying to get him out, but it's no go. The Brazilians are holding Turner on an espionage charge, and that's a pretty stiff rap down there. Familiar? Sure, it's in the Aston tapes.'

Kristian was sniffing and nodding. She felt lukewarm and groggy, and just now this job they had given her seemed like the dumbest thing in the world.

'Okay,' Humphrey went on. 'What is this espionage charge all about? Well, again the answer is in the Aston tapes. Julia Vegas was sent down to keep an eye on Kurt Kohl. You know Kohl. He's the big money in Brazil, He's agriculture. He's shipping. He's steel, He's everything. He's worth something like three billion, right? Now this Kohl has recently gone down to the Amazon to plant trees for wood pulp. Only Victor Ross, who was Julia's case officer, doesn't believe in this tree planting business. Or maybe he does believe it, but he also thinks there's something else that Kohl is doing down there in the jungle. He's gotten a few reports that indicate that Kohl is building something along the Xingú River. Kohl's clearing the area of missionaries. He's got in big equipment. He's tearing out the forest. Ross has a few satellite photos and a Big Bird overflight, but Kohl has covered everything up with the brush. So down goes Julia Vegas, and Turner goes along for the ride.'

Kristian had pulled herself up to the draining board. Her bare feet were dangling down. She was frowning, slowly drawing finger circles in the coffee grounds.

'Now I give you one Doctor Michael Jaques. Jaques. He's French, but the name's been Anglicized so you pronounce it with two syllables. This guy's been down in the Amazon since the end of the war. He's the missionary type, sort of an Albert Schweitzer but a lot more militant. Now Jaques and Kohl are naturally at odds. Kohl is killing the doctor's Indians, and Jaques is out to stop him. Well, somehow Victor Ross hears of this Jaques and decides that he would be the perfect contact for Julia Vegas. The old doctor would be a willing stringer because he hates Kohl, and if anyone knows what's going on along the Xingú River it's Jaques, because the Xingú River is his territory. So that's the background. Vegas is down in Belém trying to contact Michael Jaques.'

By now Kristian had grown still, although she kept on tapping her heels on the cupboards. 'How much of all this had Turner known?'

'Good question. And the answer is everything. You can hear it in the Aston tapes. Julia poured her heart out to him on a fairly regular basis.'

'So' – and Kristian began to pull at her hair – 'so when

84

Vegas and Turner were finally busted he knew the whole story.'

'Right, which now takes us to the bust. It went like this. Julia had no luck in contacting Jaques. After all, the guy lives in some native village way down in the jungle. If you don't know where to look you'll never find him. However, Julia managed to get another lead into the Xingú River project. A priest. Father Tomás Simeon. He was the one who originally sold Kohl the land. Apparently Julia met with him on the night before the bust. My guess was that Simeon was probably the one who blew her to the police. The sequence fits very nicely. Vegas meets with the priest. Three hours later the cops come through the door. We might also add that the priest visited Turner in prison. He came in as the good guy, which I'd say takes the cake.'

Humphrey had gotten up. He was pacing now, sipping at the dregs of his coffee. 'From here on out I'm only guessing, but all the facts still point in this direction. Okay, Turner is in the can. Then he makes his break. Now we're into his six lost weeks. According to Aston's tapes, Turner claims that he hid out along the Belém docks. Says he lived from hand to mouth. Eventually he got it together and crawled back to the consulate. Okay, that's Turner's story. That's the way he tells it. He's on the run and living by his wits. It's an acceptable image for Aston too. Aston sees Turner as a nice young man, horribly mistreated. That's not exactly how I see Turner. Not at all.'

Humphrey was slowing, wedging himself back into his chair. His fingers balled up to a tight, moist fist. Coffee always made him sweat. 'Turner. Here's a guy who killed two guards, even clawed out the eyes of one of them. Here's a guy who has just seen his girlfriend wiped out. He also knows that it was Kurt Kohl who pressured the police into putting her through the wringer. Right? Kohl was even there outside of Julia's cell when Turner was taken to see her body. So let's say that this beautiful Turner is riding full steam on hate. I mean this boy really gets wired on a revenge trip. So okay, Turner is out for revenge. He wants Kurt Kohl. Well, he knows that Michael Jaques is the number-one Kohl enemy. He also knows that Jaques has a reputation for being a pretty rough character. So?'

Kristian shut her eyes. 'So Robin breaks out of prison, gets himself down to the Jaques camp, and the two of them work out a plan to destroy Kohl.'

'That's it.' He was gazing up from the top of his foggy glasses. 'Our beautiful boy Turner is out to stick it to Kurt Kohl. Jaques has a bunch of savages. Turner comes back here and gets the Go-between scam running. Pretty soon he has enough money to buy them weapons. The target is probably the Kohl outpost.'

Kristian had grown very still, looking into the yellow space of her wallpapered kitchen. Robin, she thought . . . one day, I'll meet him.

'Lyle's the only other one who knows all this,' Humphrey was saying. 'I just got it last night.'

'Last night,' Kristian mumbled back. She had slipped off the counter and moved to the slatted window. Outside on the telephone wire a string of small birds was lined against the white sky. 'You got all this last night?'

'It was all there to begin with. We just never put it together properly. But it's always like that. You get the parts first, then you get the whole.'

'And Lyle?' Kristian was still peering through the venetian blinds. 'What did he say to all this?'

'He just listened, that's all. I don't think he can quite conceive of Turner as this man yet. Know what I mean? I think he's having trouble seeing this boy Turner as the ingenious avenger.'

'Well, I don't,' Kristian said abruptly, shaking her head.

86

Outside the birds were stirring, several had wheeled off the telephone wire, scattering above the black-shingled homes, spinning out of the trees. 'The boy . . . why do we always call him that?'

She shook her head again. The birds were now circling and then reeling off toward the sun. Because, by God, he's *not* a boy. She couldn't say it to Humph. It was too personal, too close. Turner was very much a man, and more . . . ?

5

Summer died, and the autumn wind swept across the green heaths of the Schleswig-Holstein. Hamburg was cold. The rain fell often, clattering on the rusted sheeting of the factory roofs. Turner could not sleep, not that he was sleeping much these nights anyway. Since he had entered Hamburg, he had begun to live nocturnally.

He had come to this place for the weapons. The Paris connection had disconnected. Three thousand rounds of 9mm ammunition had been lost in Madrid, and then the Czech deal fell through as well. So Turner had come to Hamburg. He lived down a gray street, up four flights in a small, drab green-plaster room behind three dirty windows, that some suicide had nailed shut. Frau Aiekman, the landlady, had told him about the windows. She was a glum woman with sleepless bruises beneath her eyes. The suicide had fascinated her. Here had been this young student from Bad Zwischenahn, she said. A nice sort, if you liked students. Anyway, he didn't speak to anyone, then one day he nailed shut the windows and a week later he crashed through the glass. She had a photograph of the body sprawled on the concrete stoop.

The apartment lay near the Reeperbahn on the wrong side of the St Pauli district. In the evenings there was often light rain and gray mist, diffusing the cabaret neon across the slick pavement. Sometimes Turner walked these streets. He passed sulking teenage hookers and even younger dogs cadging pfennigs and dope. To hell with the vibrant new Germany – this was a neighborhood where glass still broke every night.

Turner usually ate in a small vaulted tavern near the U-bahn station. He drank beer, ein Kleines, and the glass was always smudged with fingerprints. Sometimes he ate the Leberwurst. On other days there was firm blood sausage. The waitress was a dour girl, not over-bright, who thought that Germany had won the war; her father had told her so. She always served Robin thick slices of rye, but he wouldn't touch bread. He liked meat, beer and red meat.

He also liked the symmetry of the Gothic stone. He liked to stand in the cold groin of St Katherinen on sunless afternoons. Through the flying buttress ran a long view of the wet slate roofs of the east wing. He also liked the clean line of the Grindelberg apartment blocks and the grassy stretches of the promenade. Only the *Germans*, he hated. Turner, after all, was the jaguar now, with a cat's distaste for humankind.

Sometimes there were whole days when the jaguar was nothing more than a conscious symbol, a discreet and aesthetic beast. During these periods he had been known to move for weeks in perfect goose step with this place. But when he was scheming, or spying, or preparing to murder, then you could believe . . . he could believe . . . in the integration of man and beast.

In a sense, the jaguar had been responsible for everything. First there had been the cat in the cell. *And this jaguar became an inspiration for you?* Andrew Aston had asked . . . Well, Andrew, one could say that. Although maybe obsession would have been a better word. There he had been, crimped against the prison wall, and there had been the cat with its best Cheshire grin. And Turner had met that grin. He had gazed back easily, knowingly, until his vision had constricted and the fleas jumped away. And when their common sweat had fallen, each flinched and they lapped it up together.

It had been the jaguar-man again keeping him alive . . . or he it? . . . while he hid among the wharf-and-shanty-town of Belém's filthy quarter. And it was the cat that manipulated his way onto a native boat and down the river until he found the doctor . . .

Jaques and Turner. Sometimes Robin couldn't help wincing at the memory of how they finally came together in that jungle hollow. The first night they talked until dawn, two walking wounded plotting farfetched revenge against Kurt Kohl. Oh, it was happening, all right, even though there were moments when Turner felt entirely lost. There was still going to be his revenge.

Jaques had seemed comfortable with the plan from the start. 'These people will follow me,' he had told Turner. 'You get me arms and my people will follow me right to Kohl's doorstep.' Initially Turner had been skeptical of the doctor's ragged platoon of half-caste jungle survivors. Most had been only a step away from the Stone Age. There had also been those dispossessed tribesmen, back from the cities, sullen and angry. There were even a few killers with at best self-styled political links to the Indian cause. These would have fought for anyone – all they wanted was a fight. Finally there had been the actual tribal warriors, many of them ill, each of them fingering a machete.

But there in the jungle, which was also the home of the jaguar, anything had seemed possible. And later in Langley, all through those months of conniving and stealing, Robin had barely stopped to consider the practical details . . . how you trained the soldiers, how you launched the attack on Kohl's land . . . These aspects he had left to Jaques. Langley had been a dream fed by a nightmare.

Hamburg was also a dream of sorts. And definitely a nightmare, what with the waiting in this throbbing, illusionless city. There was nothing else to do but wait. Each evening he rode the underground to the Steintorwall, then walked three blocks to the post office to check his iron box. Occasionally there were notes from Gabrial. The traveling man, Gabrial called himself, and one could believe it. The wiry little fighter was ubiquitous. Turner had already met him in London, Madrid and, of course, in the Amazon Bush. Soon they were to come together here, and perhaps stroll through these streets, and have a beer in that tavern. Then they might chat, not business, but just chat, because each was all the other had. For the soul of Gabrial was the soul of the Waica tribesmen, and he had recognized Turner from the start. He had actually *recognized* him, which was to say he had seen those telltale traces of the jaguar.

Other than the letters from Gabriál there were progress reports from the arms deal. Baden, the dealer called himself, although from the Langley files Turner knew his name was Kurt Essen, a one-time wet nurse to the terrorist Baader-Meinhof gang. He was also a vicious little fag, and Turner hated him. You took, however, what you could get.

Strangely, there were days when Germany actually suited him. You could never love this stolid, morbid Fatherland, he had told himself, but he rather liked the dark undercurrents. After all, this was werewolf country . . . he smiled to himself at the thought . . . and not all that far from the Black Forest . . .

Nine weeks had now passed, and the lakes of the Das Alte had grown cold. The white-timbered skiff lay moored in gray water. The leaves of the Tiergarten were brittle and littered the walkways. Finally Baden wrote that the arms were coming, and Gabrial flew in from Brazil.

They met on the Lombard Bridge at sundown. Turner walked east across Stephansplatz. Gabrial came plodding from the opposite bank. Spread across Lake Binnen was a dark and fluttering chop. Small flags on the iron bunting snapped in the wind. The crowds were treading beneath light fog. Each man's eyes were fixed to the stone before his feet. Most were grim clerks in woolen coats. But there were also factory women with scarves knotted beneath their chins. Among this flow, Turner and Gabrial appeared to be nothing more than two of Hamburg's dispossessed.

Their first move was a silent passing so that each could check the other's trail. Then they rendezvoused on the steps of St Michael's. Turner entered the square from the shadow of the cathedral tower. Gabrial was waiting on the damp ledge. He held a ball of white bread, and the pigeons had gathered at his feet.

Turner covered half the square when Gabrial rose, shouted and then swung his arm into the air. The pigeons scattered. Some even flapped up around him so that when the two men finally met they stood amidst this white flurry. While Gabrial laughed and said, 'Hello, Robbie. Hello, hello . . .' Which was how it had been in every city. Hello, hello, until one day you could be caught and killed . . .

'The doctor sends his love, ' Gabrial said. 'And he asks that God be with you,' Now, as always in Europe, Gabrial was dressed as the immigrant laborer. He was too swarthy to play German. Today he wore cheap polyester, dark green to clash with brown loafers. He might have been some Latin boxer. He had the shoulders.

But Turner was always the slender intellectual type. This afternoon he wore a knee-length leather coat . . . he might have been a recluse painter. He would have been the abstract sort. His work would have been simple and clean in water-color.

They were tramping slowly now among the lingering crowds, beneath the circling pigeons. Turner walked with

92

his hands in his pockets; and his voice was even and soft, almost whispering, 'I'm sorry, I'm afraid I couldn't get the grenade launchers. We'll have to use mortar instead.'

Gabrial shrugged. 'Mortar. That's good too, isn't it?'

Turner hardly knew himself, but he nodded anyway. 'They tell me so.'

'What kills you with the mortar?' Gabrial was gazing up to the spires of the cathedral. The swirling stone and buttress converged some sixty feet above them. 'Concussion?'

Turner nodded. 'And the shrapnel,' he said. 'The mortar fires an exploding shell.'

Now Gabrial turned to watch the pigeons reeling through the foils and arches of Gothic stone. 'What about just the hand bombs. Did you get them?'

'Hand bombs?' Turner visualized some smoking black ball.

'You know.' The Brazilian pulled an imaginary pin.

'Grenades. Yes, I managed to get them.'

Gabrial hefted his imaginary hunk of steel. 'Because those are pretty powerful, aren't they?'

'Mmm.' Turner was sagging a little from the seeming unreality. 'I suppose they are.'

They had come full circle. Now they sat on the ledge again. A blue-gray mist was curling out from behind the cathedral walls. 'Everything has been crated,' Turner was saying. 'You'll ride out on the barge, then they'll load it all on the freighter. I've got you a berth.'

Gabrial had begun to look agitated. 'Bunk bed? Do I sleep on a bunk bed?'

He's like a child, Turner thought. I guess we all are. He racked his fingers through his hair. 'You have a private cabin. You're traveling as a government engineer, but everyone will assume that you're CIA, which should keep them away.'

93

Gabrial began to roll another ball of bread for the birds. 'That's good? They think I'm a CIA person, and that's good?'

'Yes, it's good. Our cover is cover. Do you understand?'

'Oh sure, I get it. Sure, it's a house of mirrors. They see us everywhere, but they really don't see us.'

Turner had liked it once too. In fact there had been moments when the simple beauty of the trick had left him spellbound. But perhaps this house of mirrors had one reflection too many. He was often afraid he had also tricked himself.

'Those cannon,' Gabrial was saying.

'Mortar.'

'Yes, mortar. Are they special?' The birds had returned, bobbing at Gabrial's feet.

'In what sense?'

'Oh, you know. Are we going to have any trouble aiming them?'

'They're standard. Your man should be familiar with them.'

'Hector?'

'Yes,' Turner answered. 'Hector.'

Gabrial flicked another lump of bread to the birds. 'Oh yes, he's really good. Hector was a commando in the army. Is that how you say it? Commando? Yes, well, we're very lucky to have Hector.'

A large bird began to scrape and peck at the stone. The others reared back. Their throats were undulating. Turner was speaking languidly into the flock. 'I should think the training will take about nine weeks. I've looked into it – nine weeks.'

Gabrial was peppering the birds with bread. 'Hey, Robbie, you're a real fanatic, aren't you? Just like the doctor. Yup, I've got a couple of real heavies on my hands

94

. . . Hector, he's already begun training our guys. Sure, we could be ready, maybe three weeks after the guns. But, I know, you want to wait. You and the doctor want to wait until Kohl comes home to his plantation. That's all I hear. Kohl, Kohl, Kohl. Okay. You want to wait until Kohl is there to personally catch it. Okay!'

Two birds had begun to tussle over a piece of bread. Their feathers were bristling. Small bits of down were flying off. Gabrial was smiling, watching but not seeing them. 'You know the doctor's got this big secret. That's his secret plan. He says that Kohl has some big deal in the jungle. Okay, so we're going to blow it up. Big secret. Big deal. He won't tell me. He won't tell anyone. Big secret – '

'You know something here?' Robin's voice was abruptly hard.

Gabrial flicked another crumb in a high arc over the bobbing pigeons. Some began to scamper back. 'Hey, why ask me? What do you think this story is all about, uh? You, your lady, God rest her, me, the doctor? Hey, it's Kurt Kohl, and he's got his secret jungle business. But *I* don't know anything, so don't ask, okay? . . . Some crazies, I'm working with. Not that I care. I'm, as they say, doing all this for the future generations. I'm not an angry guy . . .'

They had begun to walk again. One was harder to catch on the run. This was early in the game. But he had become a good academic spy. He always made a point of following the classic moves of the Lyle Seversons, the Andrew Astons, and all the others he had used.

Here there were narrow, twisting streets. Each morning, immigrant labor swept the cobbles clean. They passed shops with gabled windows, saw the blank gazes of porcelain dolls from Dresden. The pine eaves of the shops had been grooved into quaint Bavarian swirls. Gabrial had even stopped to smooth his fingers on the filigree of a window splay, entranced as well by a spread of knives behind the frosted panes.

Turner was speaking to his back, while the glass threw out both of their reflections. 'I want you to understand,' he was using his gentlest voice, 'these people, the Central Intelligence . . . They're not that quick.'

One long dagger in particular seemed to be needling Gabrial. 'Sure, Robbie, I know.' He was fishing for his wallet.

'One day they'll catch me,' Turner went on, 'but right now we have them chasing about.' He was toeing at the cobblestones. 'Do you know what I mean? They're like any bureaucracy. There's imperfect coordination. It could take them a year to put it together. I want to disabuse you of the mystique.'

Gabrial only nodded, shrugged. Now the cobblestones had grown smoother. The winding street was plunging into narrow alleys. Overhead were the rustic suggestions of wooden balconies and sloping country shingles. 'Simeon,' Gabrial had begun to chant. 'Simeon, Simeon, *he's* the bastard priest for you . . .'

'He saw me in prison,' Turner said.

Gabrial sidestepped a soapy pool of water. 'Hey, I told you, I'm not an angry guy. I'm not a butcher, okay? But Simeon, he knows you. He knows the doctor. Maybe someone puts two and two together and then they go and talk to him. You know Simeon will talk if someone asks.'

Turner was swaying a little, rocking with his hands in his pockets. 'He's at the Convent of Sainte-Odile. I heard that he goes there every year at this time. It's outside of Strasbourg. He stays at the guesthouse there, keeps to himself, wanders in the forest.'

Gabrial's image was smearing in shop windows. 'Convent with nuns? He's a priest . . .'

'Sainte-Odile is a shrine,' Turner said. 'I guess Simeon prays, I don't know.'

'Sure, you don't know, I don't know. But I know Simeon's a dangerous character, priest or not. First he steals Indian land. Then he sells the land to Kohl. Now they both kill the Indians. Simeon is a bastard. I'm not an angry guy, but I hate the ones like him who – '

Turner in the same dead voice broke in, 'Well, I will be going to the convent.'

'Yeah, Robbie, you do that.' They had come to a cul-de-sac. Gabrial was whistling, shuffling on the stones and whistling. While there on the face of a crumbling wall someone had spray-painted a dripping black swastika.

There were the inevitable delays. Baden complained about the shipping manifest, said he needed more money. Then there was some supposed trouble at the docks. Meanwhile the air had turned cold and Gabrial became disheartened. He did not like the endlessness of this German November. Paris he had been able to deal with, had even liked Madrid. But Hamburg, he said, this was a city that seemed to have been founded on some kind of death.

On the seventh day Turner and Gabrial drove out into the darkening countryside to meet with Baden. They passed valley meadows, and thick patches of pines. They stopped at an inn with a thatched roof and a nest for the stork on the chimney. Inside there were cuckoo clocks. But Gabrial didn't like the stares he got, so they left. His nerves were all over the place. He had even brought a knife.

Baden, it turned out, wasn't looking for a fight. They found him stoned and dazed, rocking back on the porch of his farmhouse. A sullen blond boy sat at his feet. They were passing beer, and a tiny gold box of cocaine.

Turner eased onto the railing. Gabrial edged up behind him. To the east lay the forest of Sachsenwald, the last light of day glowing in the tops of the pines. 'We were wondering . . .' Turner began. He had suddenly become a coy and cheery fellow.

'Exactly.' Baden grinned. 'Of course, I realize that you wonder. But I am sitting here to assure you now. Nothing indiscreet has taken place. I have been as straight as an arrow.'

Turner smiled. 'Only, we really could use the delivery now.'

Baden's nose was running. He kept on sniffing back and twisting up his lips. 'Oh, you want delivery now. Well, how can I succeed in doing this? I ask myself, how? Even for the Central Intelligence Agency I don't make the impossible. But naturally I also don't cheat the CIA.'

Which Turner thought was probably true. The little pig would play with expenses, but was too afraid of the Company to run a solid burn. Still, Turner always made a point of pushing home his cover, which he now did . . . 'Langley wonders' – he nudged the word forward – 'you understand how they can be.'

Baden threw up his hands. 'I know, I know.' He began to pull at the flesh beneath his chin. 'I tell you what, I'll get everything loaded by Friday. Two days more, and you'll be out to sea.'

Now Gabrial was tapping Turner's arm. 'Ask him about the incendiary.'

Baden started to fan himself. 'Who is this guy?' He was puffing. His ears were red. The buttons of his flannel shirt were straining at his chest. 'What? Incendiaries? I got them, so what? You're going to set fires. Well, then go ahead. I don't care.'

Turner was also nodding. 'I've seen them,' he said to Gabrial. 'They're French.'

98

Baden looped his thumbs through his large brass buckle. 'Sure, you've seen them.'

The trees behind were burning with the falling light. Overhead dusk was blacking out the sky. 'Friday then,' Turner said quietly.

'Exactly.' Baden laughed. 'Friday,' and his arm snapped up, flat-handed for the Nazi salute. 'You have the word of a Prussian gentleman and an ex-Hitler youth.' Then his head went lolling back and he was shaking, spitting up hard laughter, reaching for the thigh of the boy at his feet.

On the evening before departure Turner and Gabrial wandered along the Steinhoft wall beside the old canal. The rising tide was sweeping through Hamburg. They sat on the bricks above the black water.

For a long time they were silent. The water was gurgling in a rush against the wall. Then Gabrial said that he was afraid, that tomorrow he would be on the high seas with nineteen crates of weapons and ammunition and he was afraid of the sea. Behind them burned the lights of the Rathaus tower. Ahead on the cobblestones two lovers were sauntering arm in arm. Turner heard their murmuring Slavic. Gabrial was also watching this drifting couple, and a bottle of wine was swinging from his fist. Finally he said, 'You had a sweetheart, didn't you? Sure, the doctor told me you had a lover. Kurt Kohl killed her. So that's why.'

Turner's boot heels were knocking on the chiseled edge. No one had ever pinned him down so easily, but he supposed it was true, in a way. 'Yes.' He smiled. 'That's why.'

'The doctor,' Gabrial said. 'He's the same way. Me, I'm not doing it for vengeance. I'm doing it because Kurt Kohl will eventually kill us all. So, like they say, it's kill or be killed. And my way is better, my way is for the future. You're too young for vengeance, Robbie. Vengeance is what you do just before you grow old . . . you must forgive the pomposity of that.'

Turner had taken the bottle now, was toying with it, holding it up to see the lights of Hamburg wink in the rim. 'Those incendiary bombs, why does Jaques want them?'

'Who cares? Who knows? It's part of his big secret. He's got a plan. Okay? You listen to me, Robbie. I tell you, a guy grows up and people crap on him. Like Doctor Jaques. They killed his Indians, they killed his family, and now he's about to be old. He's maybe sixty. So before he gets old he gets revenge, spends his last days in peace. That's the Indian way too. When I'm about to grow old, that's when I get them all back too.' A rush of small waves had come rolling up the canal, the water was sloshing at the stone. 'But you've got some time, you don't have to be so mad after it. The doctor, he's got to even the score. But you Robbie, you've got time.' And he let the bottle fly off his fingers, craned his neck to see it inching under the Heiligengeist Bridge. 'To hell with it. When I leave you're going to find Kurt Kohl, aren't you? You're going to spy on him, make sure he doesn't give us a hard time. You're going to watch him for us, correct?'

Turner's arms were crossed at his chest. He might have been cold. 'He's supposed to have left Brazil about six months ago. He could be anywhere now. He has homes all over the world. Still, I'll give it a try. So yes, I'm going to try and find him.' He dropped his eyes to the water below. 'There are standard ways you enter a household. You can go for the servants, or the delivery boys. I hope to be able to use the bugs.'

'Okay.' Gabrial laughed. 'That sounds good to me. You'll be just like any old spy with your little microphones.' He slapped his hand on the bricks. 'You must

100

have really loved that girl, right?' He began to shake his head. 'Yeah, that's love all right. That's really a famous love, you know? Hey, you got a good story to your life. Here you loved this girl so much that now you're going to kill for her. That's quite a story. Except if it was me, being just an *ordinary* person, I think I'd say to hell with it and throw the goddamn fish back.'

Turner said nothing, but his look shut Gabrial up. Finally.

The next morning Gabrial boarded ship. Turner saw him to the launch, and as the sun rose he stood on the wharf to see the gray hull heaving in the glassy slick of the harbor, then stalked back into the crowd.

Alone, his less civilized self always seemed to take control. He could almost feel the advent of the cat now. Although perhaps one had to define civilized, because the cat could be a very cosmopolitan creature. After all, it was a very clean animal, and this jaguar in particular had a thing about order . . . walking through an outdoor market, for example, he had often found himself in love with the smooth fruit, oranges and lemons, he liked these especially. Then there were eggs. The eggs he liked best of all. Eggs were perfect, white and smooth . . . Oh yes, there were moments when Robin worried about himself . . .

Just now, during his last hours in Hamburg, he had never been more the cat-man. He ate a simple meal of lean meat and beer, then moved through the mechanized crowds until he came to his room. Packing was another ritual, everything folded and laid in its place. At the sink he shredded still one more passport, then burned the scraps little by little, washed the black ash down the drain.

When he was done, his suitcase by the door, the room far neater than he had found it, he began the most arcane ritual of them all. Fully contained within himself, succinct, flowing, he moved through the formalized steps of the kata, the dance of the karatica. His feet swept round in arcs. His hands snapped to form the weapons, or swung for blocks. All circular and absolute, until there was no wavering identity any more . . . because in this moment he knew the jaguar was only a name he had given to his most essential self.

There was a low mist on the Rhine, but the sky above Strasbourg was clear. Banking into the Alsace Valley the jets began to shudder and whine. Turner saw snow on the distant peaks while beyond lay the brown-and-green checkerboard of the French vineyards.

They passed him through customs, through the double doors, and an hour later he was entrenched again, milling about in this French city that had been fleshed out with German fat (he had changed his name so often each new town was like an illusion).

He took a room for the night at the Maison Rouge, and in the early evening went down to move about in the streets. Here too there were gabled shops, the timbered beams fluted and tooled with filigree. He drank beer in the galleria of an old café. A young boy sold him a paper. The chimes rang, struck by the wooden doll that stood for death. And they had a bridge where they told you that heads of traitors had been hung on spikes. But what did they do with the spies today? Or those who murdered Catholic priests?

Later that night he walked along the glittering finger of the Rhine that eased through the canals of this city. He had come to the edge of a village square. Four towers rose up to the purple sky, and the darkness was soon absorbed in medieval stone. Now, moving closer to the water, he saw a girl, there under the eaves of a carpenter's shop. She too was mooning at her reflection, and what with the deepening shadows, her pose, her hair flung back, Robin could have wept for Julia, who looked so much like this girl. Except that he never cried any more, which, of course, was what revenge was all about.

He rented a car in the morning, a white Volkswagen convertible, and drove with the top folded down. The air was crisp. Light winds sailed down from the icy cliffs of Zorn. Most of the cars on the highway had probably come from Ribeauville, or further south from Mulhouse. There were ruined castles in the Vosges mountains where storks were said to have nested in the battlements. But all Turner saw on the Wine Road today was the carcass of a dog.

By the early afternoon he began to climb through the shivering pines. Some pagan wall ran along the road. There were campers in red and blue tents, pitched in the meadows. The convent lay at the summit.

Nuns received him in their guesthouse as they would have received any tourist or pilgrim. He followed one bent sister up the flagstones to the low half-timbered chalet. Dark wood had been laid on white plaster. His room was furnished with simple jointed oak. Above the narrow bed hung the portrait of the patron saint, and a cross had been nailed to the door.

Alone again, bolting the door, then drifting to the window, Turner slid the brass latch down and threw back the leaded panes. Now the curtains were billowing around him and he could see the cold stone towers of the monastery peeking through the evergreens. And later, still lingering by the window, he actually saw the halting figure of Simeon weaving through the early evening.

A logical killer, a conventional Langley man, would have waited now, would have given the target plenty of time, would have mingled with the other guests, established his cover. And when the body was found he would have stayed on to wring his hands, provided he had been able to make it look like an accident.

But waiting was the worst, and night the lowest ebb for him. So by evening he had decided. Go. Nothing else mattered. Go, and then it's done.

By midnight he was pacing about the room, first by the window, then by the door. He had tried to sleep but he was too tight. So in the end he was merely hanging there by the window again, gazing through the trembling curtains . . .

Half past the hour, and the sun was climbing. Simeon came into the garden alone, moving slowly out to the forest. For a minute Turner nearly froze, then it was on and he was actually stepping to the door, climbing down the stairway. A nun on the patio smiled and nodded. A young couple were drinking coffee in the garden. A boy was dropping pebbles in the pond.

Turner followed the flagstones out through the rows of hedges, crossed the narrow bridge, and now among the pines walked softly over the needles, past one last veil of leaves . . . there, the priest was walking, strolling still further into the woods.

They met in a clearing, face to face. 'Do you remember me, Father?' Then Turner looked away and began to nudge a pile of brown twigs.

'Should I?' The priest cocked his head. His hands were fumbling in the pockets of his trousers.

'Oh, I don't know,' Turner replied. His voice was subdued. 'I suppose it's been a long, long time now. My name is Robin Turner.' It had less of a ring than he had hoped.

The priest glanced up to the sun through the boughs.

'Belém.' He smiled and hunched the shoulders of his shaggy knit sweater. 'They said you are a murderer and a spy.'

Turner, still toeing the clump of twigs, 'Oh no, Father, not me. They must have been speaking of someone else. I've only come to ask your forgiveness.'

Simeon shook his head. 'This is not what I see in your eyes.'

Turner stepped closer. Ahead lay the granite boulders of a deep ravine, and when the breeze stopped whipping through the trees, they could even hear the water cracking in the gully below. 'Well, then what do you see, Father?' Turner glanced back over his shoulder.

Now the priest was watching his profile. 'I'm not a political man.' He coughed. 'You think perhaps I know something . . . you've come to question me. About what? The Americans? Is that it?'

Turner twisted back around. 'You would have let them kill me, Father. You would have let me die in that prison. Why?'

Simeon had suddenly grown very still. 'Oh, I see. This is your day of reckoning, is that it?'

Turner dipped his head, frowned and reached for Simeon's sleeve. 'Won't you come with me, Father?'

They walked to the edge of the gully. Below, the stones tumbled down some twenty feet or more. The priest was stiff, staring across into the thicker trees. 'Why?' The word came gushing out. 'Why . . .?'

Turner put his finger to his lips. 'Shhh, Father. We must be quiet here. This is hallowed ground.'

Simeon tried to twist free, but his sweater only stretched. 'Then ask me some questions, for God's sake . . . ask me anything, I'll tell you – '

Turner had become liquid, gliding in the crosshatched light. His elbow hooked up into Simeon's throat. The priest crumpled backward. Turner caught him and wrapped an arm around his throat. Then jerking, the body stiffened, air broke from his mouth, and he sagged back down to earth. To hell, Robin thought.

Turner stayed on the mountain for three days following the death. He even hung from his window to watch them stumble with the stretcher up the path to the convent. He drank coffee with the other guests all through the dream-play of police and inspectors. In the end they called the death an accident. The unfortunate man had fallen into the gully and broken his neck. Yes, an accident, and just as well, because they could hardly have convicted a cat of murder . . .

From the mountain of Sainte-Odile he moved southwest and lost himself in the shadows of the Alps. There were lodges along the route. One night he lay awake until dawn, with the curtains back, the window ajar, and stared at the faraway blue cliffs of Mont Blanc, its peaks fogged with night clouds.

From the mountains it was down through the wooded crags to Grenoble. Here too he was able to lose himself, this time in the gray stone and black, slate streets. Except one evening he happened to catch a reflection in the window of an inn where he sat and munched cold meat. Was that solitary figure really himself?

He reached Nice the following week, and moved right onto the prowl, talking with bellhops, mingling with delivery boys, whose guidance brought him to the gates of Kurt Kohl's estate. From a sullen youth who cleaned the pool he learned that Kohl was out of France. 'Where?' Turner asked. The boy didn't know.

In the nights he hung around the Bay of Angels, where he might have been just one more hungry young shark on

106

the make. But Turner had specific targets now. By the end of the fourth day he was firmly resolved to use the beautiful Mrs Kohl as his way in.

To this end, came Jack.

Turner met him, or tracked him down really, in a bar off the marina. 'Sure, I'm Jack.' He was a lean, dark hustler, a pretty boy with a shambler's grin.

He and Turner slouched at the counter with whiskey sours. The strains of disco were snaking all around them. 'They told me you took care of the boats,' Turner said. The sweat from his glass was oozing on the bar.

'Sure.' Jack grinned. 'You looking for a gig?'

Turner nodded slowly. 'But I was also wondering if you could help me with some introductions.'

Jack spit out a little whiskey laugh. 'Oh, well I understand you now, man. But if you're really after the good stuff you got to be native, right? I do all right, but the native boys are the only ones that really score. That is, unless you're after native chicks. If that's what you want, then I can get you more ass than a toilet seat.'

Turner was watching Jack's ringed fingers drumming on the wood. 'What about a one named Kohl?' Then again so that there would be no mistake – 'Kohl?'

Jack had been scanning for action through the cigarette haze and expensive sleaze. 'Yeah, she goes. But she's a bitch. You got to be clean, *and* cool. Know what I mean? You've got to be quiet about that one. Anyway, she's a Nazi.'

But Turner was resolved. He needed an in to the Kohl estate. 'Still, they tell me she can be rewarding.'

Jack tipped back his glass to crunch on the ice. 'Yeah, she can be all right. Horny little slut. But then you'd be looking too if you were married to her old man . . . I mean, Kohl's got to be thirty years older than her.'

Once again for final confirmation . . . 'So she does go?' Turner said quietly.

Jack shrugged, and the ice tumbled back. 'Yeah, I told you. She goes.' . . .

That night Turner and Jack became friends of sorts – at any rate they were fellow tomcats on the hunt in this exclusive alley. Jack was really John Sweaten, but his street name was Sweet so it was Jack Sweet from New York. But New York also turned out to be a lie. When he was drunk enough, and the two had gone reeling through the back streets, Jack confessed that he had come from the Midwest. 'Goddamn wheat. That's all, for miles and miles and miles, just your goddamn wheat.'

He had been a good boy then, with a mother and girlfriend and a job at the Texaco station. But then came Vietnam, which he didn't want to talk about, and now he was here. 'Because I went back to the old soda shop, and the can-you-believe-it high school dance, and I walked my old lady's sad-assed poodle around the block, and I couldn't hack it, so I'm here. Cadging off rich women, staying out of trouble with the law.' Whereupon he sank to the bricks and became sloppy. 'And this is just bloody heaven. I'd kill myself, except I know heaven couldn't be any better than this.' While he spoke he had been grinding a shard from a broken bottle, and now his fingers were covered with blood.

They sat along the waterfront above the unlit strand of docks. Beneath heaved the oily water. The fronds of palm trees were jostling and rustling together. A black Rolls-Royce came up behind them. They were watching the lights of luxurious yachts twinkling from far out at sea. 'Money,' Jack was chanting. 'Money, money. All those beautiful spoiled brats with money. See this?' He held up a finger encrusted with gold and winking diamonds. 'Some chick. I screw her only one night and she gives me this.' He shook his head, spewed out laughter.

'What about Kohl?' Turner asked. Enough had happened to safely make another stab at it.

'Kohl . . . Ingeborg Kohl. Why you care about her?' Their feet were dangling over the seawall. Jack was rocking with the falling tide, the whiskey.

'Why?' Turner shrugged. 'Let's say that I have a perverse heart.' He even smiled.

Jack bounced his heel off the salty concrete. 'Oh, not you too,' Jack shook his head again. He was fishing for a smoke in the flap of his short leather jacket. 'You're too nice a boy.' He laughed.

Which was what they all thought, Turner could have told him. But he was more intent on planting his question right into Jack Sweet's head. 'So tell me about her husband. Where is he?'

'Germany maybe. They've got a house in the German Alps. Or then maybe he's in Rio. Or maybe he's in Berlin having his way with monkeys in the freak show. Know what I mean? He could be anywhere.'

'When does he come back?'

'A week.' Jack burped. 'A month at the outside. He's always back for the season.' Now he held an elegant lighter, smoothing his fingers on the thin sheath of gold.

'And what's she really like?' As the nonchalant hustler, Turner had stretched himself out.

'Frau Kohl.' Jack grimaced. The flame from his lighter was shining on both their faces. 'She's a cunt, I told you. I know one stud who made it with her. For a few weeks things were good. He was scoring . . . she took him to the Alps as her houseboy. What a life, right? Here's this guy with Ingeborg Kohl. Ingie, he calls her ass. Yeah, and they're up in some posh chateau watching the snowflakes through the picture window, toasting their buns by the big fireplace. And every night he's banging her trolley. Typical scene, right? But then one day he gets a visit from one of Kurt's guys. Konrad, and this Konrad is one big bad Nazi. Anyway, he tells my friend to lay off Herr Kohl's wife. Then just to make sure he gets the point, Konrad beats the crap out of him. So that's the scene. But if you still want it, then you can have it, friend.'

By now the night had grown thick around them. The white moon had risen above the palms. A strand of light lay from the bay to the horizon. A drunk in top hat and tails came wobbling out of the blackness. He was whistling. They heard the faint strain of an old waltz and the rap-rap of a cane on the stone. Jack had begun to mumble again . . . 'This town, Nice, like I said, this is bloody paradise. Since I've been here I must have made it with at least a hundred chicks. But let me tell you something, sport, what's really important is true love . . . yeah, surprise, surprise, Crazy Jack is a romantic at heart. Damn right. I think everybody in the whole crap-assed world has got one special out there, right? Can you dig that? You got a girl out there right now, sport. You don't even know her, and she doesn't even know you. Me, I'm just killing time until I find mine. Just killing the time. Or maybe the time's killing me.'

Turner remembered an old favorite word . . . 'bathos' . . . Jack was awash in it.

Overhead the stars had retreated some from this touching scene. The moon had become warped, sailing through a bank of clouds. Out at sea the white yacht was rocking slowly. They could make out the rise and dip of her running lights. Now and then the onshore breeze brought them wisps of music from across the bay. 'But if you want to go the flesh route, sport, well then you're welcome. Yeah, I'll be more than happy to introduce you to the trade. And who knows, maybe we'll even have a good time, while true love waits. Here we are, two happy-jack playboys in the fucking jewel of France. And yeah, yeah, I can really feel those good times coming deep down in my wasted little soul.' He laughed, and slammed his palm against the stone. Just to see his blood again?

And Turner whispered confidentially, 'Yes, Jack. I believe we'll have a wonderful time.' And he meant it too, for the moment.

6

Winter had come to Virginia. Occasionally there was snow to mottle the sidewalk and hang in the branches of the black oaks. More often there was only rain in wavering sheets. As for the hunt, Kristian and Humphrey now stood on the edge of Robin Turner's world, and here they saw a landscape far greater than they had imagined. In the booming silence they saw new figures along the horizons. Each had his own passion. Time seemed to be unraveling faster than either could catch it.

Although completed on a Friday, the first published findings on the Go-between case were not submitted until the following Monday. This was Humphrey's touch. He knew that the material was so explosive that a late-in-the-week submission would have surely dragged them into a Saturday conference. Normally Humphrey wouldn't have minded giving up his weekend, but this Saturday his mother had come to town. Kristian, who had been straining at the chocks all week, became angry. She said that she would never let him live it down. 'Yeah?' Humphrey had countered. 'Well, you tell that to my mother.'

True to Humphrey's word, however, the findings created no small uproar. The report, all had to admit, was nothing less than a devastating comment on Company security. 'Go-between,' read the summary brief, 'existed within the seams of departmental cooperation. The subject's [Turner's] success was his ability to exploit security negligence.'

Throughout Humphrey made no attempt to minimize

the boy's deft running of the Go-between scam. On the contrary, there were those who even suspected that Humphrey and Kristian were proud of their fox. See how they smugly applaud him, said some, that wretched traitor Robin Turner.

Perhaps the most dramatic result of the submission was that suddenly Turner and his Go-between ruse were top priority. The alarm had sounded. Lyle Severson as chief huntsman was given a new expense rating. There was money at last. Then too, Victor Ross made his entrance, he and his guard dog, Toby Pitt.

From the outset there was the Ross group and the Severson group. Ross had once been a nondescript Naval Intelligence person, but the president was supposed to have liked him. Which, of course, also meant that Sturdy Stan liked him. And so it was not long before Ross was running the South American desk. Not that Victor had had any real feel for the job, but he was a spit-and-polish regulation boy, and this was the new CIA. Beyond all else, Stan Turner may have liked Ross's style . . . he was a pusher and a shover, and every morning he jogged. It was said that Vic Ross even got on well with the Justice Department. At any rate, his right arm, Toby Pitt, was ex-FBI. There were also rumors that the Justice people owed Ross favors for services undisclosed.

Ross's claim to the Go-between case was quite naturally Kurt Kohl. Kohl has been my baby from way back, said Ross. Well, Severson had another story, and so the jousting began. Finally the deputy director ended the squabble with a compromise. Let us bury our hatchets and work together. So the two factions made an uneasy peace, sufficient to meet the next Friday.

In one corner were Severson, Humphrey, Kristian, and their fairy godmother, Jenny Rice. In the other were Ross and Pitt. Ross, however, had also brought along his industrial expert, Lewis Dixon, who was a lanky birdlike fellow with a greasy nose and bad complexion. Some said Dixon had been cut from the same mold as Humphrey; they were both quirky introverts, but to Kristian's mind Dixon lacked the Humphrey charm. Rather, Kristian saw Dixon as just one more pencil-neck. Every math class had one, you always saw them sucking up to the teachers.

As referee, there was Harlon Watson from the Plans division. Watson had always been a fence-sitter, but push come to shove, Severson thought he would probably touch down in the old school camp. After all, he had been with the British for many years.

Security had also sent their watchdogs – two dark internal warriors armed with lethal briefcases. Word was that Security was blaming Severson if only because he had been the one to bring bad tidings. Officially, however, Security was there to protect its own. They had even supplied the conference room, a circular laminate chamber with a long refectory table. Now and again the electronic mufflers whined faintly from the walls.

Watson began tentatively, wrestling with the words that he may have been afraid of. Words such as 'compromised intelligence,' and 'undisclosed damage.'

'But that's assuming that Turner was acting at odds with us,' Humphrey said. He was misting a tumbler with his breath, staring into the cut glass. 'Because Turner was, or should I say is, not working against us. He's working within us. Ah, and that's really an important point, I believe.'

Except that Humphrey had been too cryptic for the likes of Victor Ross, whose pen went rapping on the ash veneer. 'Does it matter? I mean really.'

Humphrey spun the glass. 'Yes, it really matters. If you want to understand the situation, I think it matters a great deal.'

114

Severson snapped forward to make peace. 'I think what Humphrey means is that there is a certain, well, attitude to the case.'

'Oh, hell,' Pitt muttered. He had little affinity for anything as nebulous as attitudes. He liked things he could feel with his hands.

Humphrey, however, was only now moving into the mystery space that was Robin Turner. He was still twisting the tumbler in his fingers, still eyeing the light in the stem of glass. Finally he said, 'Turner. Robin Michael Turner . . .' His voice had fallen to the most elaborate hush. '. . . Here you have a classic situation. Turner has, quite frankly, pulled off one of the most dramatic intelligence coups in recent history. Go-between was a fully active operation running right into the heart of Langley. And none of us knew a thing about it. So let's not minimize anything, shall we?'

For an instant they might have all been dazed. Then Watson picked up the standard of the opposition, saying, 'I don't think any of us here is actually trying to minimize the problem.' He glanced at Ross. 'In fact, I think it's just the opposite. Uh, so do you want to go ahead now, Vic?'

Kristian held her breath, the others tensed. Only Humphrey played casual, now twirling a pencil, now pulling his eyebrows, but he was waiting to see if Ross would show his cards just the same.

As it was, Ross not only opened his hand, he let them see the whole deck. Once launched, there was no stopping him. He seemed to take nourishment from the limelight, not to mention the odds. 'And it is very big,' he said across the tabletop. 'It's potentially very big indeed.' While Pitt, the guard dog, bared his teeth for his first real grin of the day.

Kurt Kohl: The man had been on the Company Watch List for a long time. To be sure, Ross explained, here was a German who had been battered around even in the days of the OSS. For the bare facts, Ross had a clothbound notebook. Now and again he rushed through the pages. Sometimes he even licked his fingers to get a grip on elusive dates.

All began neatly enough on the day of Kohl's birth in 1918. The Great War had just ended, and Germany stood on the brink of an even more explosive peace. Kohl's father, Martin, however, had done well enough in the coal trade to see them through even the worst of times. So the boy was born in a comfortable villa on the outskirts of Stuttgart. He lived in a kind of austere luxury . . . winters in the Alps, summers on the Baltic spent lolling in the grassy dunes beneath a striped cabana.

By the time Kohl had entered the gymnasium he was a bony, awkward, miserable boy. Ross even had a photograph that he had planned to show around but no one was particularly interested, so he went on with his lecture, explaining that from the gymnasium Kohl proceeded to the University of Stuttgart, where his record was not good. He was, in fact, a lazy student, and worse there were incidents with young women from the village, one of whom even tried to bring suit against him, claiming that Kohl had raped and then beaten her with a riding crop.

British Intelligence first took notice of Kohl and his family in about 1936. By then father Martin was no insignificant figure in the German industrial machine. Coal remained the backbone, but he was also well connected with oil and potash. Kurt, by now, had taken control of three lesser but promising concerns; to get his feet wet. Beyond all this the British were concerned about the Kohl political stance. They were Fascist, and as Hitler prospered, Kurt in particular became more and more active within the Third Reich's financial circles.

There were a couple of dark years now. Ross said that

the British may have let Kurt fall a little. The thread picked up again shortly after the German conquest of France. Kurt opened a potash processing plant in Mulhouse, which with two sister plants later became the focal point of war-crime investigations. Foremost among the charges was that Kohl employed slave labor – Jews, Poles, political criminals. Six Kohl executives were indicted, but Kohl himself slipped through on technicalities. There were, however, some ugly rumors concerning Kurt's sexual mistreatment of women.

By the war's end Kohl's father was dead of heart failure, his mother had been killed in an American bombing raid, and Kurt was living alone in a run-down villa on the edge of the Black Forest. No one quite knew how he passed the time. Obviously he had not been welcomed into the ranks of the new Federal Republic.

Then came Brazil, and with it the second coming of Kurt Kohl. Records first placed him in São Paulo around 1950. He had money, though it wasn't clear from where. In any case, by 1950 he was entrenched with the elite of the surviving German Right, swimming in the luxuriant aquarium of those exotic South American Nazis. Here was society based upon grotesque unreality. But there was money in Brazil, lots of money, and Kohl began to rebuild what he had lost.

This time his key was diversification. There were holdings in land for mining and agriculture. Then came the shipping lines and steel mills. Net worth estimates varied, but Lewis Dixon's figure was about two billion dollars.

As an epilogue to his story Ross provided a quick character sketch of Kurt Kohl, drawing a rapacious, steely little man with gross lips and beefy jowls. So their Kohl appeared a very nasty man indeed, and his pig's-snout face might have been cut in the hard lines of some satiric German Expressionist . . .

An interlude of questions followed, some speaking only to insure their place in the minutes. Humphrey tapped his fingers on the marquetry border. Kristian had begun to scowl . . . she didn't like Toby Pitt, who she knew had been undressing her in his mind. Finally Watson took control, and the floor was returned to Ross, who had grown truculent, and cocky.

'The Amazon . . .' he announced. 'I think we can safely begin three years ago in the Amazon Basin.'

Humphrey rolled his eyes and sighed.

Ross was flicking through the pages of his notebook again. 'Kurt Kohl buys a tract of land in the Amazon,' he said loudly. 'Everything remains above board. The land is government. Kohl says he wants to plant trees for wood pulp. There are some wisecracks in Brasilia, a few laughs within the industry, but Kohl can afford to blow a deal or two. So . . . everyone get the drift here? Kurt Kohl is growing trees in the Amazon – ha, ha.'

Lanky Dixon has a word to add. 'There's nothing to say that he couldn't create a pulp industry in the Basin climate. There's the time factor, of course. There would be, oh, maybe ten years before you got out of the red. But certainly it could be done – '

Humphrey could not resist. 'Well, that's nice, Lewis.'

Ross must have known he had just lost a point. His ears were flushed. He was speaking quickly to recover. 'Yes, well, ah, we're not actually interested directly in the wood operation. I think we're rather interested in what's happening a little south of the plantation. That's the Xingú River area.'

'Impenetrable,' Dixon proclaimed, then smacked his lips like a wise man.

'He means the jungle,' Ross explained. 'And, yes, the area is pretty remote. Which is part of the problem. It's easy to hide anything down there. We can't get a thing out

118

of the overflights. So you can all imagine . . . jungle, miles of it. But anyway, these are the facts as we have them.'

Ross could not decide if he should tick off his points on bent fingers, or slowly draw them out. He chose the latter, and began to pull at his earlobes. 'We have,' he began, 'that is, there are reliable reports that Kohl has recently purchased a large piece of land along the Xingú River. Okay, we all know that. The land was formerly owned by the Catholic church, under the control – '

'That should be management,' Dixon corrected, pimply furrows on his forehead.

'Yes, all right,' Ross swallowed. 'It's under the management of a Father Tomás Simeon. Familiar?'

'Oh, we've seen the name.' Humphrey smiled.

Ross returned it. 'Good enough. So Kohl buys the land from Simeon. I might add that Simeon retains some mineral rights. They're nominal, but there you are.'

Now Kristian had begun to stir, tapping her finger against her lips. Humphrey caught it and they exchanged looks.

'So now we have Kohl entrenched secretly some thirteen miles south of his officially sanctioned plantation,' Ross continued. He was still pulling at his fleshy lobe. 'Next we learn that Kohl has attacked some Indian village in that area.'

Watson couldn't help shaking his head. 'I've read the reports.' He sighed. 'Messy stuff. It breaks your heart.'

'In themselves the attacks are not unusual,' Ross went on. 'It's a way of life down there. The Indians get in the way. The whites kill them. Terrible, but that's the way it is.' Ross could not have sounded more reasonable.

Watson was still the compassionate man today. 'And no one is doing anything about it. The agency set up to protect the Indians is as corrupt as they come.'

Ross might have been embarrassed again. He laced his fingers together, his eyes lowered. 'Well, that's all true, Harlon, but there're a few other points here. Uh, what's inportant is that the missionaries were deported.' His hand was gently lowering to press on the desk. 'Yes, Kurt Kohl had the missionaries deported. Our feeling is that the missionaries were removed so that they could not bear witness to Kohl's activity. In fact, not only were the missionaries forced to leave, but the entire area was cleared out.'

'These missionaries, they're in there for the Indians, right?' Watson asked.

Ross nodded. 'But the small ranchers, the settlers, these people would not have objected to an Indian's slaughter, and yet many of them were also removed.'

'So you're saying,' Watson continued, 'that Kohl did not remove the missionaries because he was afraid that they would write about his Indian slaughter in . . . oh, I don't know – *National Geographic*?'

'How about the *New Republic*,' Humphrey suggested, but only Kristian smiled.

Ross let his eyelids flutter. 'Yes, that's exactly what I'm saying. Kurt Kohl has sanitized the area of *any* potential witness.'

Watson's face went red with the word. 'Witness. Witness of what?'

Humphrey could not resist pricking this ridiculous balloon of tension. 'Kohl has a secret project. Yeah, a *secret project*. Haven't you heard, Harlon?'

Ross waited. The pages of his notebook were cutting his thumb. Finally he managed, 'Point is, we don't know what Kurt Kohl has going. Obviously he's moved in some equipment. We know that much. He's cleared the land, but he's also camouflaged the land. He's even got an antiaircraft unit down there. So where do we stand?'

Watson nearly raised his hand. 'But you must have some idea, surely there's some notion – '

Dixon caught the question and snapped it back. 'Not a word. Maybe he's found gold. Maybe he's training an army to take over the world. We don't know, can't even guess.'

Humphrey cracked his knuckles. 'Well, we certainly know that he's up to no good, don't we, Lewis?'

This might have been too much for Pitt. The man was straining at the leash. 'Do we need that? I mean, Christ!'

Ross, however, took the safest route and ignored them both. 'The Brazilians.' He frowned. 'They have definitely been acting cagey.'

'Cagey?' Watson tolerated his own ambiguities, but no one else's. They said that all the Plans people were like that.

'Politically,' Ross added, and then tossed out another indefinite – 'financially too . . . Oh, they've been balking at trade agreements, balking at our aid projects – '

Here Watson could help him out. 'Balking at our sphere of influence?'

Ross hated the old-style honesty. 'All right, yes. Yes, if you like. They've been talking it up with the French, talking it up with the Germans. Which all may mean nothing, but – '

'But the president is concerned,' offered Watson, using the old-style diplomatic cliché.

'Among others,' Ross said. 'Then of course there's Kurt Kohl himself to consider. The man has never been a friend of ours.'

'He hates us.' Pitt scowled, at home with the feeling.

To this Ross could also add, 'Kohl will never act in the American interest if he can help it. So assuming he's – how shall we say? – increased his power base, we can only wait for the other shoe to fall.'

Severson stepped in to the heart of the matter. 'Why? Why all this over the Amazon? I mean, the Amazon for God's sake.'

Dixon became so eager he nearly began to tremble. His spider hands were flicking at the knot of his polyester tie. 'All right, the Amazon. Here you have potentially the wealthiest area in the world. You've got uranium, you've got diamonds, you've got bauxite, you've got . . . well, you've got a lot of potential.' He might have been trying to sell off parcels. 'Look, I could go on, but it's all right there, okay? So now you've got a possible trouble spot in the person of Kohl, and who knows what he's doing down there. We simply can't afford to remain in the dark.'

'Yes, dark,' Kristian murmured, which brought them around again to that cad Turner.

The ball was back in Humphrey's court. 'We know some,' he said, 'but not all by any means.'

'Well, we do know that there's a tie-in.' As the seventh-floor representative, Watson felt he had to prod for hard intelligence.

'With Kurt Kohl?' Humphrey was going forward as slowly as possible.

'Yes, with Kohl.'

'Well, I'd say we could go that far.'

Ross was close to a pout. 'Well, I'm naked, I don't see why Severson shouldn't be naked, Harlon?' He was almost whining. 'It's only fair.'

Then came Dixon. 'Yes, it's only fair.'

Now they even had Harlon Watson on their side. 'Because we all know that you must have more.'

'All right.' Humphrey sighed. 'In a nutshell then, we do have reason to believe that Turner had some sort of contact with Michael Jaques. Jaques?'

'We know,' said Ross.

'Okay then. Turner meets Jaques shortly after his

122

escape from the Brazilian prison. They very possibly have something going, and that's as far as we can take it.'

The moans began. From Ross especially. 'Oh Jesus Christ! Come on now. What does that mean? "They have something going." What? They have just opened a string of taco stands? What?'

Even Watson was becoming angry. 'Yes, Humphrey, spell it out. We want you to spell it out.'

Humphrey rolled his shoulders. 'Okay, we believe that Turner and Jaques may be planning to launch a . . . I don't know how you want to say it . . . a paramilitary operation, or at least some sort of attack?'

Ross was still hanging, waiting. Then, 'You mean against Kurt Kohl? You mean they're going to hit Kurt Kohl?'

Humphrey shrugged, 'Well, yes. Yes, we think that the two of them may have thought about that, but no one had better start screaming bloody murder yet.'

Pitt snapped again. 'I think you're holding out.'

Humphrey returned to his innocent pose. 'No, really. It's just too early to say anything. That's all we have, and it's mostly conjecture.'

Severson scooped up the ball. 'Of course we can't know anything for sure, why we've only just begun. First and foremost this Michael Jaques still remains a very shady fellow. I mean, what kind of man is he? Is he a tiger, or kitten? What's his profile? How does he spend his Sundays? Follow? We simply must find out this sort of missing factor. Anything else is just too dangerous.'

Watson nudged him. 'But you *will* begin right away. That is, you will keep the time factor in mind.' He wanted to be remembered in the minutes as the man who got things done.

'Of course,' Humphrey said, not so much to placate as to take the floor again. 'The main thing is that we want more time. We don't want Turner bugged, beaten or buried until we find out just what it is that he *wants*. Okay?'

'Sure,' Pitt said, 'and while we're at it, Knolls, we mustn't forget to send him a birthday card.'

'Now Toby,' Watson soothed . . . 'these people have their own methods, and they do get results.'

Ross came in with his own smoothing effort. 'What Toby means . . . in fact, what we all mean is really that we're a little afraid of this Turner fellow. I mean, my God! For all we know the boy is right this moment loading himself down with arms. And for what? You tell us that he may be planning to *kill* Kurt Kohl. Well, the White House would just love that. Oh boy, they would love it so much we might even get off lightly. Like only having to go out and get another job.'

Humphrey was rapping his hand on the table. 'Which is exactly why we *shouldn't* do a blessed thing right now. Who knows what we might walk into. Let's say that Turner is out to get Kohl. Well, then what? If we stick our noses in it, even in an open investigatory manner, we just might very well end up holding the dirty laundry. Or so it would seem to the Brazilians. And the White House, if you like. So just think about it, gentlemen. A man with a bona fide link to the Company goes out and kills their foremost industrialist. Of course we'll do everything in our power to stop Turner. But don't you think we'd better know exactly what the hell we're doing before we start to muck around. We're talking about Kurt Kohl here.'

With such a buildup Lyle couldn't resist his own dry snipe. 'Could be a bit of a strain in our relations with Brazil. No?'

When no one smiled Humphrey continued, 'So let's face the facts. Turner is playing a dangerous game, and I'd say we better get the rule book before we try to join in.'

Then Watson to Ross: 'They want more time to get a definite fix on Turner. They want to find out exactly what Turner has cooking before we create a very embarrassing situation for ourselves. That seems pretty reasonable to me, Vic.'

But Pitt bounced his pencil down. 'Well, I'm frankly sick and tired of all this worry about Robin Turner . . . I mean who the hell is this guy? You've got some punk. You say he's turned us inside out. Well, I say he's just a pencil-pushing punk who doesn't have the guts to upset a tea party.'

Humphrey leaned out far across the table. He was even aiming his little finger now. 'May I? A few moments ago we spoke of the priest, Father Simeon. Certainly he would have been a wonderful man to talk to. He knows Kurt Kohl. He knows of Jaques. He even knows Robin Turner. Beyond that, he's fundamentally implicated in the plot. So it would be a wonderful thing to chat with him. Now, we can't find Turner. We can't find Jaques. We obviously can't speak to Kohl. But the priest, yes, he would be available. Except that we can't speak to Simeon either. In fact we'll never be able to speak to Simeon. And why can't we do this? We can't do this because your punk Robin Turner killed him three days ago.'

For a moment, silence. Then Severson began to speak. 'Supposition,' he said. 'Still, there are some rather convincing bits of evidence.'

Humphrey laid it out. 'He was found at the bottom of a stream. His neck was neatly snapped in two. Simeon was staying at the Convent of Sainte-Odile, he stays there for a few weeks every year. They found his body not far from the convent walls. Accident, the report reads. He's fallen off the silly cliff, poor ass. Except that we had a man check it. And who should have arrived at the convent the day before Simeon's spill? A nice young American boy with lovely blond hair.'

Watson rubbed his eyes. 'Well I think that's fairly clear now. I think we all know just where we stand.'

Except that Pitt was straining at the leash. 'So that's it, huh? We wait?'

'No.' Humphrey was tugging at a thread from the sleeve of his shabby blazer. In the heat of battle his tie had come undone. A button was loose on his belly. But now, well in the lead, he was easy, almost slouching at the table. 'We don't merely wait. We certainly don't just wait. We hunt – ' and the word came popping out. 'We hunt and see what turns up. Who knows, we may even decide to let Turner run all the way around the bases. Who knows?'

If Severson was cringing, trying to shrivel under the table, Humphrey didn't seem to notice. He heard old Lyle seething his name, but he just couldn't stop. He was a roly-poly spy on a power trip, saying, 'I mean really. We've always wanted to get rid of Kurt Kohl. Well maybe Turner is just the ticket. Let's just say that Turner does go out and take care of Kohl. And let's just say that he does get away with it. I mean really gets away with it so that there's absolutely no way anyone can even remotely connect us with the man's death. Well, that would change the picture entirely wouldn't it? You've got Kurt Kohl gone and the Amazon wide open. Not too bad.'

Kristian kept her head down, not daring to look at him.

Pitt nearly wrenched the arm off his chair. 'Jesus Christ Almighty! Who is this guy anyway?'

No one could defend Humphrey now, and for a moment they all just sat there and fumed. Finally Severson attempted to drench the flames with a weak try at humor. Hardly his long suit. 'Did you hear something?' His head was swinging back and forth. 'I didn't hear anything. Did you, Harlon? Did you just hear something, I mean something about a wild scheme that no one would ever take for anything but a joke?'

And finally the forced smiles and laughter began.

So once again the hunters submerged into the twilight world of the archives. And time became warped, because now they had to contend with over half a century. There were moments when the years seemed to stretch until they snapped, and they both felt the reverberation of history.

They began with the Register biographies, but Michael Jaques only had the smallest mention. From the Registry they plunged into the heart of the high security field reports. Here Jaques appeared as an occasional stringer of questionable loyalty and dubious reliability. Still, there was a link. Jaques had been used to spy on Kurt Kohl as early as the sixties.

His case officer of the era described him as a feisty visionary, 'a South American Albert Schweitzer. The Indians love him. The government outwardly respects him, but inwardly fears him.' When Jaques was finally passed on to another control his former resident admonished, 'Don't talk politics. Don't talk money. Jaques may ask for a case of penicillin now and again. Also, if you rub him the wrong way his Indian warriors are likely to cut you up and serve you for dinner.' So much for the owner's manual on one mad Amazonian doctor . . .

On the evening of the seventh day Kristian found a key to the lock on the Jaques door. To wit: the doctor's relationship with the secret world of clandestine warfare had begun years before any Brazilian bits-and-pieces effort.

Now alone, crammed into the cubbyhole of an archive reading room, Kristian felt as if she could have leapt off the edge of her chair. The temptation frightened her. Then too there was no ceiling on the dingy scuffed-cream fiberboard cubical to keep her from floating into the forty-odd years. She was only partitioned from the other lonely archive scholars scattered throughout the great basement hall. So before she actually began the journey she chiseled her name into the desk with the tip of her ballpoint pen so they'd know it was she that the files had swallowed up.

Then, honestly trembling a bit, she was off. The first concrete mention of Jaques spun her immediately back to Paris. The year was 1937. The young Doctor Jaques lived near the rue Moufetard. There were hardly any more details. The reference appeared as a British in-house MI6 request for agent potential in the French environs. Not surprisingly the files were a mess. The order was broken with irrelevant material. Series numbers were missing. Whole pages had been torn out. There were even prewar tea stains.

Ushering Kristian into the tangled intrigue of fallen France were a host of clubbable secret warriors from the British office. There were dry memos with wisecracks passing for sympathy whenever some flamboyant partisan was shot against a wall. There were even grimmer jokes from the 'Brighton Girls,' those damp woolen typists who kept the files for a Leslie Beaver of the Resistance Coordination Group. Then from one tattered carbon came the first hint of the essential story, all with the code name 'Bitch.'

At first the name confused her. Bitch, it appeared so suddenly. There was no explanation. As if you were supposed to have known. Well, of course, one didn't know. Kristian even thought the files had soured on her again. Or worse, the index clerk had bungled it, thrown it in with another series. But no, there was indeed a reason here. By 1943 Michael Jaques was a shadowy French Resistance hero known to all parties as the Bitch.

For a while this Bitch eluded her, just as it had no doubt

eluded the collaborationist Vichy government and even more organized elements of the partisan underground. So, Jaques had been a loner from the start. And ruthless, the files were quite firm on that point. 'Bitch,' wrote some nameless British observer, 'remains fairly useless from a traditional viewpoint. However, there are profound psychological implications here. He's got the Germans hopping mad.' Another report, this one written by the now ubiquitous Neil Abbey, explained that the Bitch had very likely been the one who shot and killed the wife of Frederick Milch, Hauptsturmführer of the 33rd Waffen SS.

Next came the impressions of the Germans, eighty pages of clumsy translation, mostly dry Gestapo stuff. One bit, however, held Kristian for a full twenty-five minutes. The passage dealt with the killer's operational habits. The Germans were concerned because Bitch was clearly no amateur. On the contrary, he was thoroughly professional . . . his weapon, the Germans deduced, was a long-range hunting-sniper's rifle, probably a Mauser K98K with a ZF 41/1 scope. Furthermore, the weapon had been modified with some sort of silencer.

The murders too were marked with professionalism. Usually the Bitch struck from a distance. Sometimes he fired from windows, sometimes from beneath a garden hedge. He often liked to wedge himself into the crooks of walls. Once they found his shells in the vestry of a bombed-out church. Most especially, however, he came to favor the rooftops.

For the pure romance of it all, there was nothing in the file to beat those cartoon panels in *Stars and Stripes*. Obviously Public Relations loved him. He was their 'Phantom Avenger of Fallen France.' The story's title page read, 'Heroes of the Underground.' It must have been a series. Below was a pen-and-ink of the Bitch hanging from a blackened rainspout high above a glittering Paris. The next frame had him leaping across the glistening shingles into the velvet night.

What seemed most to disturb Gestapo Center, however, was that Bitch played it dirty all the way to the bone. He not only hunted officers, he also killed their women. There was Frau Hilda Stauffer, the wife of Hauptsturmführer Sepp Blomberg. There was the mistress of a Stabwache commander, shot while boarding a train. He even killed the daughter of a Vichy official while she was entertaining friends in a Paris apartment. In all there were some thirty known Bitch killings. *Stars and Stripes* claimed double that, but even the Germans admitted to at least thirty.

Finally there was the paragraph she suspected would come back to haunt her, so she let the pages fall together and then slouched out between the shelves, all the while wondering, just as the Germans must have wondered, had Jaques killed those women because their men had once killed his? As, say, they had killed Julia, the woman of Robin Turner?

Ross began to complain. There was altogether too much time spent on this background stuff. What was the point? Well, the point was that they were stalling.

To these charges the hunters appealed to Lyle, who in turn appealed to Harlon Watson. 'My people are very close to something,' Lyle argued. 'You've got to give them more time.'

The two had come together at their club on a Friday. It was the blue hour. The sky was washed with dusk. The evening was nudging at the oval panes of glass.

'Have you been there?' Watson was rocking back on the heels of his brogues. He was studying the print on the wall that had been papered so many years ago with quaint hunting scenes.

'I'm sorry?'

Watson tapped the glass of the print. 'Dublin. I remember this very street.'

Lyle scratched his head. 'Yes, I was there,' but his stomach had been curdling for an hour. Then he mumbled it all out. 'There is something rather touchy in the works.'

'Come again?' Watson was still dreaming himself into the print of a misted Dublin street.

'I said that we are to witness something very important. My people, Humphrey and the girl, they're close.'

Watson suddenly came back. 'Of course, Lyle. I know there are numerous possibilities here.'

'So I'd like to press for more time,' Severson added. 'I want you to keep Vic Ross off our backs.'

'I'll give you time, Lyle, but I'm also going to give you this. You've got to prepare yourself for the inevitable. There's going to be a few more players in this game. There's got to be.'

'Well, I'm aware of that, aren't I? There's Ross for starters.'

Watson's attention went swimming across the room. His lips were tightening. 'I just don't want you to be upset in case things don't work out as you planned.'

'Yes,' Lyle said very slowly. 'I do believe that I understand.'

But for the moment the hunters were given the field. Even when the track meant London for the weekend there were still funds. Granted they had to book their own flight, because the service officer said that Counterintel staff were not entitled to use their travel arrangements. Nor would the European desk help with contacts. But Finance had already gotten the word from the top floor, so there was plenty of money, except that Kristian had to bluff her way past some unwitting bank manager because a security twit would not release the funds directly. Then, and about par for the course, the check bounced off another red tape snarl, and two days were lost while everyone passed the blame. But in the end they made London, worn out from a flight that had gone bumping and humping through a storm.

And London charmed them, even possessed them. On the first crisp morning, they took coffee in a marble room of creamy browns. Nine fluted pillars held the ceiling, lit with crystal shades to shroud the electric candles. In Kensington Gardens Humphrey cupped his hands to hoot at a bird while a blue jay caught a butterfly and the gold shreds of the wings were lofted above a pond.

In the afternoon they took a clacking train into the countryside. They stamped about on the railway platform, and when no one met them they took a cab past the village and deeper into provincial England. Along the potholed road they saw lambs nosing at the gnarled fences of their pastures. Here and there were sagging farmhouses and the billowing smoke from brick chimneys. When they finally stood before the green shuttered cottage at the edge of the garden path, they were hardly conscious of having crossed the sea at all . . . a hunt was a single tunnel, and all around were the hedgerows to hem them into this universe of clotted history.

History may indeed have been all that Neil Abbey had now, now that he was an old man, and the war was over, and all of his friends were dead. 'Hang my hat on a pension.' He laughed and swept his arm about this room. He was a frail man swaddled with flannel, wrapped in the cocoon of his rocker. A sleeping dog lay on the hearth. Beneath a rusted cutlass hung still more assorted junk. There was even the prop of a biplane on the wall, and of course those photographs of the lads, not a trace of fear in their eyes.

They eventually came round to tea. Kristian brewed the stuff on a hot plate. There was milk from the can. Then they settled. Abbey took his favorite chair. Kristian and Humphrey sat on the flowered sofa with its sagging springs.

In between the awkward introductions, everyone's china was rattling. The old man dropped a spoon. He said that he was no longer visited much these days although sometimes there was a daughter on the holidays. Last year the neighbor died of a fever, but you really just put it down to old age.

But Abbey still lived well enough in the files, Kristian said. 'Over and over we saw your name.' She smiled . . . she seemed to have a way with the elderly, not that she had ever stopped to think about it.

'Oh yes.' Abbey beamed. 'But that was then.'

'And Lyle Severson remembers you,' Kristian added.

Abbey wheezed for a bit of a laugh. 'So how is that Lyle? What a little grubber he was. And what did he tell you about me? Did he say I was doing a book? No, it's the memoirs they want. Well, they can have the bloody stuff. The dumb sods.' . . .

Before he would speak in earnest he required the letter from London. 'As if I give a tinker's dam. Official Secret, my aunty fanny. Lord, the whole story ended thirty years ago. But still, they dragged poor John Millstone back for blabbing it all to the Sundays.'

By now Humphrey had lost all hope in this crusty spy with walnut eyes. He was gulping down tea, anything to change his perspective.

But once the story began, Abbey proved to be the treasure chest that Kristian had promised. No one knew the Jaques case like old dog Neil Abbey. 'The Bitch was, so to speak, my hobbyhorse,' he said. 'I couldn't get enough of him. Entirely unique chap. So I pitched it to them. No names, no departments. I won't give you those. But just the same, let me tell you that I pitched it to them. I said to those that be, "See here, I think we can make something out of this fellow." The game was to train him. Or should I say tame him? Oh my, he was the wild wolf for you. But still, I thought that if we could get our leash around him, we just might have the man to kill the Nazi brass. Got my picture? After all, he was ready-made. So they huffed, and they puffed, and they finally let me go.'

This was the spring of '43, Abbey said. The Bitch had been going great guns for almost a year. 'But who was he? That was the question of questions. Where did he come from? Oh, well, it took us a pretty penny to find that one . . .'

Return to 1936, the old man then told them. Michael Jaques was the youngest son of a Parisian tailor. 'And the boy was bright, brighter than the lot of them.' At the age of twenty-four he was a doctor of medicine. At twenty-five he had his own practice in an office off the rue Moufetard. Then came the draft, and Michael went to war against the Nazis. 'There's an odd bit to it here,' Abbey explained. 'The boy didn't serve with the medics. It seemed that his eye was even sharper than his scalpel. As a matter of fact he even set some sort of record at the rifle ranges. It was all there,' said Abbey. 'All there in the files.' So now the year was '38, and Jaques was training as a sniper near the border. 'Well, he may have taken his toll in Nazis,' Abbey said, 'but what was one gun against the *Blitzkrieg*?' When France fell, Michael returned to Paris.

To the unreality of the Occupation came the counterpoint of love. Michael, the old man said, must have fallen in love shortly after his return. How Abbey had wished for details. What, for example, had the girl looked like? Had they known each other before the war? He thought not. But then how had they met? Had they had a secret place, some garret or a tiny room at the end of a long, narrow staircase? There had been nights, Abbey said, when those two lovers had been extraordinarily real for him. He had imagined them both, perhaps in the blur of the Sabbath candles, two Jews without so much as a prayer for the future. There remained no record of a sanctioned marriage, but here too, Abbey claimed he had his visions. He liked best to imagine the dark and lovely bride as she held up the glass of wine. Then there would have been the groom, smashing the glass beneath his heel. The splinters would have glistened on the bricks, and those few present would have all cried out, '*Mazel Tov*', in defiance to the future. While outside in those crumbling hours the glass of Jewish shops was also crashing down to the pavement.

By the end of September the Sixteen Laws for the Final Solution had been posted. Xavier Vallet became the Vichy's commissioner general for the Jewish question. Then the registrations began, then the roundups, and most went willingly to the trains. Because they did not believe, not France, not especially in *Paris*.

The old man knew little of the rest, and was digressing now, rambling, mumbling on about the long strings of stationary trains and how the doctor and his bride must have marched to the cattle cars. Humphrey had been toying with the sleeping dog's ear, now he was gently pulling on the tail. Kristian was smoothing the feathers of an enormous stuffed owl. The jet lag was pulling her down into the sofa. All the while Abbey was still droning on with his recital of horrors, describing how Jaques and his wife had been taken to Mulhouse. 'Slave labor . . . women in one camp, men in the other. Pretty much what you'd expect. Men dying left and right. Women raped

135

and beaten. There was everything going on in that potash factory in Mulhouse – '

At which point Kristian sat up with a jolt. She nearly sent the teacup flying. The sugar went spraying onto the serving tray. 'Mulhouse?'

'Why yes,' the old man replied. He must have told this story dozens of times.

'But the factory . . . who owned the factory?'

The old man's eyes went sly. 'Oh, I see.' He was smiling like the little gray fox that he still might have been. 'Oh yes, now I see.' He had one finger bent up to his lips. 'Well, you played this very well, didn't you? Ha, but I'm onto it now, aren't I? Because it's as plain as day. Why, you two aren't interested in Jaques. You want to know about Kurt Kohl, don't you?'

Kristian cocked her head for her most guileless smile. 'Well, yes. We are a bit interested.'

'A bit, my dear? A bit? Well, all right. I admit it. I have often wondered about it myself. Did Kohl kill young Michael's wife? We know that Kohl took liberties with the girls, the pretty young girls. But if he was guilty, why then didn't the Bitch hunt him down? Well, you say that Kohl was well-guarded, or that much of the time he spent in Berlin. But what about after the war? You might think that such a man as the Bitch wouldn't stop. Oh no, his anger would carry them all to the grave. Well, I can't tell you the answers, because I'm fairly well lost.'

As was Humphrey. He had come in too late for any real understanding. He was doing his best just to keep up. 'Are you saying then that Kohl killed Jaques's wife? Is that it?'

Kristian could have taped his mouth shut. Dumpy Humphrey was nearly blowing it. 'Yes, of course he's saying that.'

The old man was watching his milky tea go sloshing up

136

in his cup. 'There are no reliable facts. I only know that he was born there.'

Humphrey had to frown and stretch forward. '*Who* was born *where?*'

Abbey blinked. 'Why the Bitch. Who else? And at that factory. A man loses his wife like that. It's hard to fully understand the impact. I know. I tried. I lost my Jane, but it wasn't the same at all. So that's the why for you to go on . . .'

Now Kristian had to prod. 'Because his wife died?'

Abbey's fingers went to his collar, were picking at the flannel. 'Not died, she was murdered. No doubt about that.' His voice was beginning to crack and roll out louder. 'And I think we can assume that she was probably tortured before she was raped. And what's more there's a very good chance that your Kurt Kohl was personally responsible.' Then the old man let his face fall into his hands. A minute ticked by. Then another. Until Abbey dropped his hands away. 'Funny, even after all this time, must be under my skin still. Didn't think so, thought I was over it. Well, it just goes to show you.'

Down the road from the old man's cottage the buds were bursting out of the sap-laden trees. Humphrey and Kristian walked, they'd forgotten all about a cab. The wind in the grass and the bending willows made them feel somehow frail, not to mention what they had done to Abbey. 'But don't say it' – Humphrey was panting – 'Don't think it, and don't say it.'

Kristian's skirt was fluttering at her knees, once again as though she were only a little girl. 'You don't even know what I was going to say.'

'Yes I do . . . the parallel. I mean, Jaques loses his wife and becomes a killer. Turner, it's the same thing, his girl. The killer both times . . . Kurt Kohl . . .'

They were shivering in the chilly wind. 'But it's ironic,'

Kristian said. 'Imagine . . . imagine how it must have been for Jaques.'

'How?' Humphrey felt like a straight man.

'It's 1947 and Jaques has had enough of the world as he knew it. Europe, the war, the Germans . . . he's had enough. So what? He goes to the Amazon Basin.'

'The heart of darkness.' Humphrey laughed, and didn't like the way it sounded.

'No,' Kristian persisted. The wind was tangling her hair. 'Imagine how it must have been for him. He's just traveled halfway around the world. He's gone as far as anyone can go. And then who should he meet up with but Kohl. Can't you see what I mean, Humphrey?'

'See what?'

'Christ! You really are a stupid dolt sometimes.' She whipped her hair from her eyes.

'I'm not at all, I'm simply not surprised, that's all. I've seen it coming from the start. That's right, from the very, very start. Because I've always asked myself what Turner and Jaques had in common. Well, they've both suffered at the hand of Kurt Kohl. Now it's confirmed. So what? I don't believe in fate. I don't believe in magic, or God, or fairy tales, or even happy endings.'

'Well, I do.'

'You do, what?' Humphrey stepped in cow dung and cursed.

'I believe in all of it.' She tried not to sound apologetic. 'I can't help it, Humph. It's just too weird, you know? Here are these two men, generations apart, and both with the same story. Well, it's weird. And then there's Turner. I can't seem to get him out of my mind.'

Humphrey was scraping his shoe on the rail of a fence. 'Well, that's a dangerous road, that one is. You've got to learn to keep your distance with the game. Believe me, I've seen it before. I remember this one guy who became

138

totally obsessed with some Russian dancer who was feeding stuff to the Cubans on the side. Well, this poor guy just went off the deep end. Know what I mean? It destroyed him. So keep it all at arm's length, all right?'

'Yes, of course,' Kristian said, but she knew she might already have gone off some kind of deep end, now staring out to the last of the orange light, the bending grass, and all the while wondering what he was doing right now. Oh God, that Robin Michael Turner . . .

He was still on her mind that night when she could not sleep and walked out to the Kensington Gardens. Why, he could have been sitting there among the midnight roses and ferns. Here he would have been a rather dangerous Peter Pan, stalking among the snapdragons. But if Robin was Peter, did that make Kristian his Wendy? No, but for an instant there in the sculptured moonlight she felt as if she really would have been willing to fly off to his Never Never Land. Which probably meant that Humph had been right. This Turner was slowly becoming an obsession of sorts . . .

Back in Langley the sheer work load kept those more romantic sensibilities tamped down. Kristian and Humphrey were at it for nineteen hours, working away at their intelligence prospective. The conclusions surprised no one, although they sounded pretty impressive, all neatly bound and typed in the eyes-only folder.

The gist of their findings revolved around the Jaques-Kohl war, and for all it was worth the others had difficulty envisioning the scope of a thirty-year struggle, not to mention the Turner end of things.

At the second gathering of the tribes, Victor Ross went so far as to complain that the findings were presumptuous. But the facts had, at that point, not been fully presented. When they were, even Ross became a believer, emitting a whistle at the end of Humphrey's climax.

Of them all, only Watson remained cool, occasionally smoothing the knot in his school tie. His most pertinent question was, 'When do you estimate that this Jaques-Turner attack will occur?'

'We have no estimate,' Lyle replied.

'None at all,' Humphrey added, enjoying Watson's discomfort.

Watson coughed. 'Well, that would seem to leave us high and dry.'

Lyle was stirring the bowl of his pipe with a tiny silver knife. He had not felt this alive in years. 'Only if we remain passive,' he tossed off.

'Passive?' Watson was turning the gold band on his liver-spotted hand. 'Passive. Passive as in nonoperational?'

Finally Ross could not stand it any more. 'What is it?' He kept looking from Lyle to Watson.

'Well,' Watson said. 'we obviously can't compromise our situation by warning Kurt Kohl, now can we?' His elbows were planted on the table. 'Really, the last thing we want is to be implicated in whatever Turner has cooked up.' The man smelled faintly of the corned beef he had eaten at his club for lunch.

'So naturally,' Lyle cut in, 'we have to find another entry into the game. Something a bit . . .' But he couldn't say it, he couldn't drive the dagger home, not even into the heart of Ross. After all, the point might have snapped off.

But rude, scratchy Humphrey could say anything. 'We need something that will not continue to jeopardize our standing with the Brazilians, as say the Vegas affair has done.'

'All right,' Ross snapped. 'So?'

'So we have something that may get us in with a minimal risk,' Humphrey said. 'I think it's nice.' You could even see the dandruff on his collar today, the stuff was flaked all over the shoulders of his crumpled jacket.

'Well, I think that's Harlon's decision.' Severson smiled. It seemed his role that he would be permitted to pass the buck.

Ross's index finger tapped on the oak. 'Oh, I see now, I see it all very clearly. Well, gentlemen, you don't seem to need me. You've already got it all worked out, haven't you?'

Watson tugged a little at his sleeve. He couldn't have enjoyed his work any more than now. 'Yes' – he finally smiled – 'we do actually have something worked out. Let's just say we have something like an entrance to the crux of the matter.'

'Oh Jesus!' Toby Pitt just couldn't hold it back any longer. He had promised Ross he'd keep cool, but this was too much. 'What the hell is going on? I can ask that? Or isn't it the polite thing to do? God Almighty! What is it with you people?'

And then Severson, as the sly fox once again, said, 'Well, it's really very simple, we're going to put an agent in.'

But as the night wore on Lyle became less the fox and more the congenial uncle. Particularly when asking Kristian if she would care to spend the evening with him. For dinner, of course, and one was to understand that the event would eventually come around to business.

Still, Kristian hardly knew what to expect, or even what to wear. She must have spent an hour before the mirror, slipping into dresses and then peeling them off and tossing them back onto the bed.

Lyle picked her up in a chauffeured car driven by some Langley novitiate. As they sped through the wide boulevards of Embassy Row, Lyle told stories of even more

141

glamorous years. After all, he had always been a mixer within the circles of the seriously rich. He may have even been consciously trying to woo this girl when he told her about the now-gone elegance of top hats, monocles and ebony canes. While the women, he said, wore silk and strings of perfect pearls.

They dined at one of Washington's best. There were tiny mounds of Belgravian caviar, and oysters in half a shell. But Lyle seemed most impressed with the service. The waiters in starched red coats, nodding; he could not take his eyes off them. 'Have you ever noticed the art of a good domestic?'

'Uh, not really.' She had begun to wonder about the motives of this supposedly clean old man.

'There's a good deal to be said for a man who knows his trade. Or a woman.' He was still watching the sweep of silver platters at another table. He seemed particularly to focus on the glinting knives as they eased through rumps of red lamb. 'Which all has something to do with why I asked you out.'

Kristian dabbed at her sherbet. She felt a bit exposed tonight in her simple frock. 'Is that so?'

He nodded. 'And I thought that perhaps you might feel a bit more free to express yourself away from Langley. I know I often find the place somewhat inhibiting.' He was fingering the tiny monogrammed coffee spoon. 'On important issues I like to get away.'

Kristian's eyelids fluttered. She was fast becoming the pretty imp. 'I wonder' – she laughed – 'I wonder if I already know.' Her lips were glossy from wine and sweets. 'You want me to go in, don't you?' She waved her spoon, like the tart she sometimes was. 'Which is what all this is about.'

Severson returned with his most paternal of smiles. 'Yes,' he said. 'I thought you might go in.'

Kristian ran her tongue around her mouth. Then her pretty hair shook. 'Well, then let's have it.'

'We have a chance to get a young lady placed inside the Kohl home. That would be his villa in the south of France. The opening is fairly reliable. As a matter of fact, it's absolutely reliable. It comes from one of Harlon's people, someone who has kept an eye on Kohl for a long time. We can get you in as a domestic. It's a very clean, a very neat little placement.'

'Why me?' Kristian was gazing through the blur of silver and china, the swaying furs and cascading hair. She could not tell where the mirrors ended and the light really began.

'Well, you know the case better than anyone. Beyond that you're a capable girl. What's more' – and he laughed – 'we couldn't find anyone else.'

Kristian reclined in her chair, abruptly the sultry Mata Hari. 'Oh, I see.'

Lyle was growing pale and moist from a brandy, the smoke of his own cigar reaching to the coffered ceiling. 'I can tell you a bit.'

She patted the melting sherbet with her spoon. This salon of Lyle's definitely brought out the worst in her. She truly had the urge to shock them all. 'Yeah, all right, tell me.'

Lyle's ash broke prematurely, sizzled into his saucer. 'The target is two-fold. First we want to know what Kohl is up to. There's that Amazon business, you know. Then too, there's a very good chance that our boy Turner might pop in. Well, you can imagine what we need along that line.'

Kristian swept up her napkin. The spoons and knives went clattering across the tablecloth. 'Really?' Her voice was ringing, her heart had begun to crash. 'You really think he might show up?'

Severson shrugged. 'He's in the area. I managed to get some people from the French contingency to look about. Well, they haven't actually located him, but they tell me he's been around.'

Kristian was nibbling on the end of her napkin. Her eyes were set high up. She might have been gazing at nothing but the spray of gold light, while the clatter of dishes echoed around them. Then she let the easy smile spread. 'I'll do it.' Of course she would . . .

Lyle could have taken her hand just now. He had grown fond of this girl, now especially. He was particularly touched by her fragile profile, those delicate fingers clutching the linen cloth. 'I want you to think about it. I don't want an answer just yet.'

She bit her lower lip. 'Okay, I'll think about it, but I'm sure. It's what I want.'

Lyle dropped his eyes. He was swallowing, staring at his hands. He couldn't help thinking, what the hell am I doing? This wonderful girl. Then he lost control entirely, and the glass tipped. Water and ice poured over the table. 'I'm sorry, please forgive me . . .' But the waiter was already descending with a stiff, red towel and all was soon back in order.

Or so it seemed.

Sometime within the uncertain hours after midnight, Kristian stood in front of her mirror to undress, to slowly peel the dress from her shoulders. A pale scarf had been spread on the shade to dim the light still further. Cold notes of a distant piano sounded through her open window. She had even propped the photograph of Robin Turner against the glass, wedging it in tightly with a vial of perfume.

7

There were days in the passing weeks when Robin Turner nearly lost awareness of the jaguar-man, bent on death. Possibly spring had lulled him, spring and the easy afternoon along the wharf. Then too there was Jack Sweet, who had become a friend, and Robin's first real touch with humankind in a very long time.

Together they worked the boats, caulking seams and repairing leaks in the garboard. Sometimes they even had to dive beneath the oily water to reach a rudder or repair a screw. But what Robin had come to like best were the days spent high in the rigging of the sloops. There, rocking slowly in the web of rope, cooled by a breeze, soothed by the view of other flapping sails in the blue bay, he truly became the boat-boy that everyone assumed he was. And so as spring settled in, his cover nearly eclipsed his essential self.

Further, you do not maintain cover, said Langley tradecraft, you live it. On Fridays or Saturdays Robin and Jack often set sail in some absent client's boat. Usually they merely eased about the bay, and the beer and the lapping water made them drowsy. On other days, however, the sea was skittish, and then they went keeling off the edge of the wind, leaning into the glassy wake, pulling hard on the lines.

The women came and went. Jack knew them all. There were American women, naive and wicked at the same time, with money to burn. Sometimes Jack and Robin took them sailing and stuck them for the rental fees while the tins of cheap caviar and bottles of champagne drifted in the wake behind. Most of these women were undone in the cabin. Jack said he only serviced them for big tips nowadays. He probably hated the American women most of all.

The local girls were smoother. You could almost love them. Even Robin took one, a thin pale girl with long braceleted arms. Mostly these were the daughters of the upper crust who came to the coast to gamble and tan . . . or was it to bathe in just the sort of low life that Jack Sweet offered for a price?

Very few were generous beyond the night. They told you, 'Thanks a lot, and I'll never forget you,' but they were always gone in the morning. They were young, but they had been around the block. Most saw Jack for the flimflam stud that he was. He didn't mind. He agreed with them.

Best of all, as far as the game went, were the itinerant women of the old Continental guard. These were the gigolo's staple, they were his meat. They did not expect anything more than what they got. They didn't ask for some bullshit story. They didn't give you one either. They had no illusions. Jack didn't have to play the Huckleberry Finn with the ten-inch cock. These women took only what they paid for and not one penny more.

Sometimes Jack brought one for Robin Turner, because he thought that his friend was also in the game. And so Robin, in a different game, was obliged to play Jack's. When the women were drunk and had had enough sex, then the whole party would tumble into a hired car and roar off to the clubs. In tow, Turner and Jack became the questionable pretty boys, but even with the most jaded ladies they were always admitted into the ranks of high society. They would hang around the green tables and watch Lille textile tycoons and Marseilles shippers throw away thousands of francs an hour. One night an older

146

woman had Jack lay down dozens of blood-red chips. The wheel flashed around, and she began to giggle. But he lost. The chips were raked away, and she nearly slapped him. 'You little dog,' she snapped.

But even in his lowest moments Jack kept a loser's pride. 'If I could win every time, honey, then I wouldn't have to stoop to hustle wasted cunts like yourself.'

The woman laughed at him and ran her rings across his cheek. Which probably proved what Jack had always said. They loved the abuse, or they wouldn't pick up his sort of trash in the first place.

To the fragile days among the boats, and the harder nights in town, finally came Turner's mark – Frau Ingeborg Kohl. She came from the north in the first grip of summer heat. By chance Turner even saw the caravan of limousines snaking through the white hills above the city. Next came the bustling from the Kohl villa. Servants were sent out to lay in stores of bread and cheese and poultry. The gardeners arrived. Frau Kohl was seen in her Lotus along the autoroute. Then again she was seen dining with her younger friends at La Pignata. All this Robin heard from his loose string of watchers. Some passed on the word for nothing. Maids especially liked the thrill of spying. Others, the delivery boys and the urchin from the pool service, Turner had to pay in cash.

On the eleventh day after her arrival she made an appearance at the dock. Turner saw her first from aloft – he had been hanging high in the rigging all morning. She was a slender woman but tall. He guessed she was in her late thirties. She had tawny brown hair that fell just past her neck. Her features were sharply cut but smooth.

To inspect her yacht she wore a beige skirt and a striped sailor's top. She had a stiff gait to her walk.

Jack pulled the woman aboard, and Turner saw the

muscles of her calves stretch as she went swaggering about the deck, laying her hands on the varnished teak, giving the rigging a husky tug. Under sail he imagined that she liked to play the red bitch of the sea while her crew of boys played galley slaves.

But when Turner actually shook her hand, he was playing her obedient gallant, though smiling a bit impertinently to let her know that he could be the sexual rogue if only she dared ask. He had also shown a little flair swinging down the ropes to the deck. For her own part, however, she seemed stiff and Germanic, each syllable coming out with a guttural edge.

When she left, the two men stood on the bow and waved her off. 'She likes you,' Jack shouted above the squealing of Frau Ingeborg's Lotus. 'Yeah, I can tell. She definitely had the hots for you, sport.' The wharf was suddenly quiet again. There were only the crying gulls, the lapping water.

'She didn't say five words to me,' Turner said. He was watching the Lotus wind out to the distant hills, light smearing off its streaking finish.

'That doesn't signify. I'm telling you, sport, that woman has the hots for you. She wants you.' He was grinning now, a cigarette bobbing between his lips. 'Hey, you're talking to a guy who *knows*.'

Frau Kohl sailed with them the following week. She brought friends: a paunchy German and his dull American wife. Jack set an easy course with the wind, and they blew along the glimmering coast, although they might have been merely following the clouds above or even drifting aimlessly.

The hours became elongated. The only real adventure came when the German snagged a fish on his drop line. 'Oh, but it's too small,' Ingeborg squealed. So they tossed it back. Except that when she yanked out the hook, she also ripped out the fish's guts.

Several times during the day Turner felt the eyes of Frau Kohl on him. Outwardly, however, she remained indifferent.

But returning into an indigo sky, he found that she had joined him on the bowsprit. She stood with her legs spread to brace herself against the bucking chop. The wind was blasting them. The ocean spray was misting in their faces. 'Don't fall in,' she shouted. 'Then you'd be lost and I don't even know you yet.'

Robin, stomach heaving, leaned into her ear. 'I won't fall,' he said. 'And besides, you do know me. Everyone knows me. I'm just a friend of Jack's.'

He saw that the salt air was making her blink, but her eyes still fixed on him long enough to tell him progress had been made. He also noted how she licked her lips. 'He gave me this job,' Turner yelled, and he jabbed his finger at the deck. 'I help with the boats.'

'How nice,' she yelled back. 'So you'll be around for some time to come.'

Turner nodded. 'Yes, for a while,' His stomach was in knots. The bow bucked again and for an instant they fell together. He could have put an arm around her but didn't. This wasn't like killing the priest, you had to have a whore's sense of timing. You had to take it slowly, carefully. If you yanked too hard you were likely to get what you wanted before you wanted it.

In time, however, Turner came to realize that he was as much the fish as the fisherman. Frau Kohl was a hungry woman. She used her breasts and thighs in studied poses while her eyes nibbled away at Turner's buttocks. Twice that week she used the boat, and each day moved in closer to her prize.

149

Then came Sunday afternoon. They had spent the morning zigzagging under a rustling breeze. When the wind died they opened tins of smoked oysters and bottles of Burgundy. Jack and Turner played servants for Frau Kohl's guests, more inconsequential friends of her husband's. She might even have wanted to ignore them and drag her Robin below, but pretenses were necessary here. So she waited until they docked, and then, as if the thought had suddenly come, 'Robin,' she called, 'I wonder if I couldn't borrow you for an hour or so. There are some things at the house that I need lifted.'

'Sure,' and he gave them all his most winning smile.

There were, in fact, some things she wanted lifted, clay planters from a potter in town, and Turner hefted them into the trunk of her Volvo. Not that she couldn't have managed easily enough without him, but she did have the excuse of the servant's day off, which also meant that the villa was deserted.

From the village they climbed through hills until they reached the ring of scorched laurels where the villa lay. The walls of the home were rough stone. There were solid tiles in blue and red. A balustrade led down the windy steps through the garden and finally onto a lawn. The front gate was a granite arch capped with an iron eagle.

He had no idea what to do with the planters. They had served their purpose. He was here, so maybe he should have just smashed them on the courtyard brick? Or heaved them over the wall that trapped him now within this semi-palatial grotto? Frau Kohl, however, merely had him line them by a marble fountain where the water was jetting from a naked cherub and lilies floated in the rippling pond.

She asked him in for drinks. He would like something nice and cool, no? Well, of course he would, and they stepped on through the thick front door.

Within, the powdery light through the drawn curtains emphasized the seductive quiet. Frau Kohl sat Robin on a low settee, then skipped off, leaving him sitting in this moody, cream room whose corners held darker Oriental suggestions. He became particularly entranced with a bamboo screen. Faces of demons had been brushed on the rice paper panels. Even more grotesque was the stuffed parrot staring out of the gold cage. The eyes were terribly real.

He heard her footsteps on the marble. When the wind outside shifted there was also the faintly oppressive fountain gurgling at him from the courtyard. Above his head was a spray of violets in a silver vase. Their odor was even more upsetting.

She entered with a copper tray and two long glasses brimmed with wine. Now she wore blue chiffon. Her feet were bare. With her clothing her spirits had also changed.

'This is so informal.' She was sighing. 'Sundays are my favorite days.' Then oozing into the cushions, she told him that she did not really like the servants on principle.

No, he thought, she much preferred slaves. Her breasts had been perfumed. She may have even chosen this hour when the shifting light and shadow on the sea-wood and copper would help mesmerize him into submission. On another man, on another afternoon, the scent and stillness might have actually worked their charms, but Turner kept on seeing a vision of her broken neck in his hands, her pearls scattered on the floral rug.

An hour passed. Twilight, and Ingeborg got up to light a pair of candles. When the fumes and smoke had been flung to the coffers, she announced, 'My husband does not like an open flame.'

Turner was watching the sputtering shadows on the wall. 'He does not like them?' he repeated. The sudden irony was almost too much.

'No, he's afraid of the open flame.'

'I see.' Turner smiled. Well then, what would Kurt think of the incendiary bombs?

'He had an accident as a child in one of his father's factories.' A blob of stray wax caught, and the light flared up on their faces. 'So today he does not like the open flame.'

Turner lowered his mouth to the rim of his glass. 'But you like it.'

'Yes, I like to play with fire.' She tossed down a slug of wine. 'It's one of my few pleasures.'

'But what about the money?' He threw it out so she would know where he stood. Naturally she could relate to the pretty-boy gigolo.

'The money!' She yanked a ruby off her finger. 'Take it,' and the ugly little ring went bouncing off his chest. 'I don't care a damn about the money.'

Turner brushed it away. 'You don't care because you have it? Always had it?'

She held up a bony white hand. 'Not true.' The light was winking off her other jewels. 'Once I was an actress, and I starved, I assure you. There was no industry in Germany after the war. And the theater! Who had time and money for the theater after the war?'

Depends upon what sort of theater, Turner thought, remembering the psychodramas played out every day in the streets of Hamburg.

'So I starved. I had no money. I had *nothing*.' She stretched her arm so that the candlelight would turn her to ivory. 'But I had my art. I could act in our little productions even though I received no money.' Her arm flopped down, and in the darkness she turned back to clay. 'Now I have money, but I cannot act.'

'Oh really? So now you act only in your husband's drama.'

She squealed and scooped his hand to her breast. 'You understand! You truly understand! Here I find you on my boat and all the time you knew.' Her mouth was close to his own. 'You,' she said again. 'You,' and her lips finally plunged, and began sucking on his tongue.

He did not have to make love to her. All she wanted was to absorb him, to rape him. So he finally played the role, naked on the rug, while she, still clothed, rubbed and gnawed at his arms and legs. He even let her rake his chest with her nails, because it seemed that she wanted to hurt him. Or was it only his skin she was after? Perhaps she wanted a slice for a lampshade, a gift for her husband, the tender Nazi who was afraid of open flame?

Turner soon came to realize that Frau Kohl was fashionably mad. Not a flat-out psychotic as he had at first suspected, but certainly a little unhinged. She had a dozen quicksilver personality changes. You hardly knew when she wanted to smack your buttocks, or break down and cry on your shoulder. But as a peephole into her husband's life, she had become pure gold.

So Turner *developed* her, as the term went. She had become his unwitting agent, and how else did you handle agents, but *service* them.

Servicing Frau Kohl soon became his only real job. You had to remain at her beck and call. She liked her boys devoted. But Jack, who was in effect the case officer in this round of the game, had every move psyched out. 'You've got to keep her on the come,' he told Turner. 'Don't be too easy.'

So Turner played her as loosely as he could. They met in nightclubs, where he was supposed to hustle her away from the bar. They usually dined in darkened rooms, the rings of candlelight glowing on the ceiling. Meals were supposed to be a big part of the scam and Jack explained how he was to eat. He said that the women always liked hungry boys, 'gives them a feel of youth and health,' he said. So Turner made Frau Kohl take him to only the finest places for red fish grilled over a fire of fennel twigs, eggplant stewed in garlic, mushrooms stuffed with rice. After dinner she usually took him to some distant hotel. On Sundays there was the villa.

On the whole she seemed unconcerned that others would discover what she had been doing with this beautiful boy. Her friends, she said, understood. Half of them had young men as well. The servants were also loyal to her cause. Most of them hated Herr Kohl anyway. So as long as one remained discreet, one had nothing to be afraid of.

There were, however, moments when the weight of it all fell in around her. Then Turner, gagging, would have to console her. On one such day she had come to the botanical gardens, where he found her waiting on an iron bench. She looked especially pasty against the background of glowing fuchsia. Her purse was lying on the grass. She was crying.

Turner did not sit by her side. He knelt. He laid his hands on her knees. This was how you showed you loved her, he had made something of a study. But this morning she was only a brittle woman. Her angelic boy had to have the strength today. She didn't want him to be her gentle fawn. She wanted something with a bit more bite. Well, he could have given her a glimpse of the cat, but no, he wouldn't let her see that one until the very end.

For her opening she said that she was afraid. 'Yes, afraid, so afraid.'

'Oh?'

'Maybe we should stop seeing one another.'

So, she was testing him. 'But why?' Which was the best he could manage.

She sniffed. 'Oh, it's too dangerous.'

'Why? What's changed?' A bit too dramatic, but he had

long since learned that subtleties were lost on his leading lady.

'Oh, I don't know, I just sense things . . . I sense danger.' When her mascara ran she looked like a clown. 'I'm afraid for you, my husband can be a tyrant. There's his man Konrad, a brute. There's no telling what he would do.'

Turner risked pressing. 'But how will he find out? Your husband and Konrad are in Germany, aren't they? On a business trip.'

She began to stroke his head. 'Oh, you don't understand, dearest.' She was weeping a little. 'You don't understand at all.' She let her head drop to give the scene more strength.

Meanwhile, the dew on the grass was soaking through the knees of Turner's trousers.

'My husband and Konrad, it's as if they are in the military. Konrad was a soldier, you know?'

Turner hadn't known, but he could easily imagine the shaved head and wooden face.

'It's a matter of honor . . . German honor. Konrad would be the one to avenge the honor of his superior officer, Kurt. Honor to those two is a serious thing. It would be terrible. They do not understand the necessity of love. Especially for an artist like myself.' Ingeborg was crying openly now. 'You must understand the German mentality, it's medieval. So, what are we to do?'

If he told her she would not have believed him. 'There's nothing to worry about, dear lady.' He was rubbing her hands in his. 'As long as you keep me informed of *everything*.' He risked hitting it home, perhaps too hard.

Now she was running her fingers through his hair. 'Yes, I must.' There were cobwebs of saliva in the corners of her mouth. 'Yes, we will be secret lovers from here on out. Secret lovers.' And she pressed his face down into her smothering lap.

* * *

By the end of a month she was sharing everything with him. Everything about herself. Only he, she told him, understood the essence of her soul.

Wunderbar! he felt like screaming, but what about your damn husband?

She was far too engrossed with her own self for any insight about Kurt, but in time she at least was able to sketch the overall. The general tone was German, wealthy, and a little bit seedy. Herr Kohl, she said, was something of a rebel in his day. He grew up in Gothic austerity. Sex, in particular, was a very dirty word. Thus the more mature Kohl was obliged to go to extremes for gratification. There was something about a secret society, young boys and girls and a dungeon of revelation where he took them. This had been between the wars, she explained, and many Germans had been involved in perversity of one kind or another. As for the war itself, she said she knew very little, that Kurt never discussed it, presumably because he had suffered what she called 'a dehumanization.' For her own part, she was an open apologist. She described how she used to visit the death camps after the war. Often she would be the only native German there. The shrine at Dachau was always filled with tourists, especially Americans. Only the Germans never went there. 'But I would go. I would go as an exercise in guilt.' Guilt, she said, was important, there was guilt at the core of every German. Even Kurt felt guilty in his way, they all did, she said. That's what she said. There were times, though, when she hated her husband. He didn't understand her, he didn't understand artists . . . all he knew was business, and money. For herself, she didn't give a damn about money – she said.

As for the essential questions, though, Frau Kohl was not as informed as Turner had hoped. There were serious gaps . . . as, for example, exactly *what* was Kurt doing in

Brazil? 'Brazil,' she would say . . . of course, the jungle had become her husband's latest passion, but what did she care? Except that she would soon have to accompany him down to that dreadful plantation. It seemed that there was to be a celebration. Her husband's project was nearly complete. What project? She did not know, nor care. But imagine how it would be in the jungle. The mosquitoes alone would kill her.

'When?' Turner wanted to know. 'When do you have to go?'

'Well, soon. I don't know exactly, but soon.'

Which meant that he would have to keep on servicing her . . .

If there were times when it seemed that Frau Kohl was hardly worth the effort, there were also fruitful moments. One night, for example, he left a sleeping Ingeborg and had an hour to himself rooting about in Kurt's study. There hadn't been any momentous secret revealed that night but there was a deeper acquaintance made as he leafed through the man's papers, wriggled his toes, so to speak, in the man's slippers.

Then too there was the practical side to consider . . . A progress report had come from Brazil, an aerogram really, but coded and delivered to his post office box in the old section of town. The message was characteristically terse: All was well, the weapons had arrived, the training had begun. Morale was high. Turner felt exhilarated riding, he hoped, Kurt Kohl to the kill.

First there were rumors of Kurt Kohl's coming . . . ironic way to think of it. Turner saw less of Ingeborg, what with all the good wife had to do. And then Kohl came, suddenly and at the worst time.

Turner was down in the bowels of the sloop that

morning tinkering with the engines. Not that he understood machines but he liked the cool cylinders and smooth
tubes of steel. Topside, Jack was coiling ropes and slug-
ging down beer. Then Turner heard the voices break.
First there was Jack. Turner heard him hamming up a
welcome. Next came Ingeborg, laughing, her spiked heels
clicking on the deck. Turner was about to pull himself up
through the hatch when another voice, thicker, deeper,
bellowed out.

Turner froze, nearly tumbled back down the ladder.
'Kohl.'

While above, Ingeborg had begun to squeal, 'Where is
he?' She must have been speaking to Jack.

Well, he had to answer, there was nothing else to do, so
he called out, 'I'm here, down here,' and began to hoist
himself up.

If he remembers you, Turner told himself, then you
laugh it off, tell him he's mistaken. If that doesn't work,
you kill him, drive that blob of his nose into his brains.

Turner's head pushed through the hatch. His stomach
clinched tight. The veins stood out on his wrist. He
vaguely wished that it would all end here. But when
Kohl's enormous head swung around, there was not a
trace of recognition in his eyes.

Turner had to sag a little at this near-comic meeting. To
stand there, shake the man's warm palm, say, 'I'm hon-
ored, sir . . .'

That afternoon Turner and Jack took the Kohl party
out to sea, and the day went whirling into unreality . . .
Ingeborg sunning herself on the bow, chatting with the
wife of some French attorney, both women in string
bikinis and smoking Turkish cigarettes . . . As for the
paunchy Kurt, he might have been a mushroom, the way
he shriveled into the deck chair. The attorney was dark,
suave, on the make for Kohl. The two men spoke English,

probably because Kohl's French was poor, and the attorney's German worse. Turner caught only snatches, out of context, which only helped to warp the hours all the more.

The wind kept fluttering at them in tiny gales. Jack was a fiend at the helm . . . he must have been crashing the bow through the chop on purpose.

Turner could not keep from staring at Kohl. Even hanging over the rail, pulling hard on the last flapping luff, he kept on twisting back to see the lumpy, pale figure of the man. 'I say there is nothing after death,' Kohl was saying, 'I've come too far to believe in heaven or hell, except maybe the hell on earth.' Which, Turner thought, he'd done his share to create.

By now they were rushing through a tube of wind. Jack had found the slot, and the hull bucked on, splashing, faster and faster. At one point Ingeborg rolled to catch her Robin's eye. Robin nodded back. Jesus.

More than once he thought of killing Kohl right away. He hadn't any logical plan, but if he could just get the pig alone, break his neck, push him into the sea, then his death too might pass for an accident. But no, an accident would not do. Not this time. As Jaques had said, you had to play this one out until the very end, because Kurt Kohl's death had to be an *event*. An extravaganza, even. They mustn't be selfish . . . Kohl's death had to give satisfaction to many more than just Robin and Jaques.

Now the ocean lay flat, and the deeper blues were fusing to an indigo. The seascape might have been a still-life water-color. The foil of palm leaves were spiked against the sky. There was even a moon through the masts of the moored ships. The tide heaved gently in the pilings and lapped against the barnacles.

For an hour now the creaking wood and harbor sounds had lulled the two men. Jack especially seemed to be dreaming off into this Riviera night, as though he might have been happy if nothing ever changed, if this were life ticking forever. 'Anyway, I'm too blown out to hustle,' he finally said. 'I'm just going to sit here, I'm just going to sit here and drink this champagne right out of the bottle, and I don't give a crap about anything.'

Even Turner felt pasted into the velvet limbo. Some time had passed since the Kohl party had left.

'It sort of freaked you, didn't it, man?' Jack was gulping more champagne. 'Here you are screwing this *fräulein* and her old man shows up. Kurt Kohl, no less.'

Turner shrugged.

'You looked pretty freaked out to me.' He whistled the mouth of the bottle. 'When you first saw Kohl you looked damn *spooked* to me.'

'Did I?' Robin was lazily picking at the caulk between the planks. A whispering breeze was stirring the palms down the esplanade. 'Well, I suppose it was a bit of a shock, the husband arriving the day he did.'

Jack raised his eyes to look directly in Turner's face. 'You know, sport' – his voice was low and firm – 'you can play it straight with me.'

Each watched the other. Faint voices came from a long way off. The sky had stretched to admit the first stars. Turner let his breath out between his teeth. 'What do you know, Jack?' This simple question was like a hard, cold object between them.

'Three days ago,' Jack said, 'a guy comes to see me. He's got a picture of you. Says he heard you were working down along the docks. Wants to know where he can find you. So I say, "What's it to you?" Right? I'm playing it cool. Well the guy says that you got into some sort of trouble back in the States. He wouldn't give me details.'

Turner had gone back to digging his nails into the caulking. 'What did he look like?'

'Not like a cop,' Jack said. 'He was classy, about fifty.

160

He wore a Pierre Cardin suit, for Christ's sake . . . he might have been a lawyer.'

Turner was looking off at the solitary pines that studded the tops of the palisades. 'So what did you tell him?'

'What do you think I told him? I snowed him. I told him the only other guy I knew that worked the boats regularly was this Italian fag. I told him you were a wop.' He laughed. 'Well, what do you want? It was the first thing that came to my head.'

Turner didn't smile. 'So, Jack?'

'So what, sport?'

'So what do you think?'

Jack sloshed the dregs of the bottle around, swigged down the last of it. 'You come to me and say you want to make it with Ingeborg Kohl. So I think, "Why just one chick? Why just that one?" Not that I give a shit. I mean, if you've got some sort of fix on Frau Kohl, that's your business. But then I get to know you. We spend some time together. Pretty soon I'm getting so I think I know you real good. You know what I'm talking about here? I mean we've spent some time together, sport. I mean I consider that you're a friend of mine, and I don't have too many friends any more. So I don't take it lightly. You're not just some asshole who helps me with the damn boats. You and I, we've had some times together. Well, okay. But if you're after Ingeborg Kohl, then you're after her for a reason, because I know, man, and you're not some common nut case . . .'

No, Robin thought, to people like Jack he was certainly not too bad off. But then it was all a question of where you were looking from, wasn't it? Imagine how they felt about him in Langley now?

Jack was now looking sullen, then came out with, 'So you ask me what I think, huh? Well, I'll tell you, sport. I think you're a sight less innocent than you come on to be.

You ask me what I think? Well, I think you're out to stick Kurt Kohl. And not for money, either. I think you're out to get him for . . . I don't know, political reasons maybe . . like those terrorists or something.'

A terrorist? Turner had to smile at that. 'It's not like that, Jack.'

Sweet was nodding, his tone changed. 'Sure, I know. You're too cool to be a terrorist. But it's that kind of gig, isn't it? I mean you're playing the big table, aren't you?'

The hulls of other boats were listing with the tide. Ropes were groaning. Turner finally sighed again. 'It'll probably happen like this,' he said, and his eyes were glazed now. 'Someone will come around again, not the same guy. It'll be some loudmouthed tourist with a Texas accent. Maybe it'll be a girl, a very pretty girl. You won't be able to tell, but they'll somehow get to talking with you, to draw you out. If you slip, they'll be on you like a ton of bricks. They can get very rough, Jack, and you're right about them not being cops . . .'

Jack nodded slowly. 'I think I follow better than you think, sport. See, I've been a wharf rat long enough to get into some fancy doings that I've never told you about either. We've both been a little cute, sport. Oh, nothing now and for a long time, but I've been a stringer of sorts when I was really hard up, or down and out, take your pick. Didn't much care who was holding the money, it was a little snoop job here and there. Far as I'm concerned, sport, they all suck. Anyway, spooks aren't exactly a big mystery to me. I saw them in Nam too, believe me. I saw them toss the dinks right out of choppers. In fact, for a while there they were the meanest characters around – what the hell, they started the war, they had to prove we could win it. Don't you worry, sport, I'll keep an eye out. Guys like that are enough to drive women to boys, which, come to think of it, isn't so bad for my side.' He smiled when he said that last.

162

8

Robin Turner had by now become more substantial than any of them in Kristian's world. You are my touchstone, she could have told him, and thought of him often. In some ways he had become more *real* than all the others, but then such was the unreality of training . . .

They had moved her to the Farm. She stayed in a small gray bungalow, one in a series of many. She slept on a narrow cot under rough sheets and coarse blankets. The place was drab, clinical – a desk, a chair, a toilet. In the mornings the bare concrete walls and linoleum floors were very cold. This obscure box they had put her in might have been a prison.

Training – really a refresher course – was divided into two periods of a week each, the first a refresher course filled with all the silly stuff they gave every fledgling spy . . . opening envelopes with jets of steam from neat little burners, showing her how to seal them up again so you'd never know, teaching her how to place a bug and the rudiments of cracking safes. They even had her fire a few rounds with a semiautomatic. She thought she did okay, but her ears wouldn't stop ringing. They played tapes for her . . . she was to remember key words and phrases peppered into otherwise meaningless conversation. The principal speakers were a man and woman. The woman in particular was macabre, sounded flat, serious and vaguely haunting. The dialogue took unexpected paths. At times their voices grew distant and watery; occasionally the words were lost completely beneath a wailing horn or the drone of an engine . . . First the couple on the tapes was dining. They spoke of food, something about trout from Scotland and a tainted jar of marmalade. Next they were walking, and Kristian envisioned an aviary because of the trilling birds in the background. Soon the voices became cramped and hushed, words were barely audible over the slow slosh of water in what may have been a steel drum. For a time there were sounds of running feet on wooden floors, a breaking window, a slamming door. Through all this Kristian was asked to follow the thread of some mysterious letter. The voices kept on telling of this letter. In the end they asked her from where the letter had been sent and where it had been delivered. She guessed New York to Berlin, and flunked.

For close combat they brought in a red-haired kid named Skip. For security they used a makeshift gymnasium at the edge of the compound. As always, Lyle Severson looked on from the corner. The kid put Kristian through a quick run of infighting techniques, and if he touched her more than was necessary, once even mauling her breasts, Lyle said nothing. Nor did Kristian. She was too exhausted, too apathetic. Half of her instructors had been horny pricks who copped feels when they could.

They spent nearly an hour wrestling on the mat, and there were moments when the kid held her breathless chest to his and stretched her arms above her head. All the while he was singing out pointers . . . 'Guy grabs you.' He would snap her over. 'Don't ever try to break the hold. You go for the groin, the eyes, the nose and the throat. You go for whatever seems closest.' Then he would clamp her wrists together. 'Now you stomp on his foot. Or if you're really cool you can kick him in the balls.' When he slapped his hand to her mouth he told her how you could always tear at the flesh with your teeth. Once, during a clumsy mock rape, he told her, 'Honey, I don't care how strong a guy is, no one has strong eyeballs.'

164

But when she was finally through with him, sagging against the wall, swallowing the aromatic memory of his aftershave, she still had the strength to shatter one small crystal of a spy's propriety. 'Hey, Skip, ever know a guy named Robin Turner?' If Severson was cringing, she pretended not to notice.

'Turner?' Skip was toweling the back of his neck. 'Sure I know Robin. I studied under him.'

'What's he like?' Kristian was rubbing a bruise on her hip, thinking that she should have kicked *him* in the balls when she had had the chance.

Skip whistled, shook his head. Sweat sprayed out of his knotted hair. 'Oh, that guy is just incredible, that's all. That guy is from another planet. He can wipe you out before you even have a chance to think. I once saw him take on about five guys at once. And his kicks . . . that guy can kick through a steel door. It's like I told you, honey. The power and the speed come from the *form*, and Robin Turner has perfect form. But you don't have to worry, you'll be able to make it against any untrained person . . .'

Except that when they sent her limping off to shower, she lingered by the door and caught the gist of another verdict. 'That girl,' she heard the kid tell Severson. 'Yeah, she's got lots of spirit, but if she ever gets in a real scrape, she won't stand a chance.' . . .

They waited until the very end to teach her what she would really need. Which was traditional. They wanted to see if you made the grade before they compromised details. For whatever it was worth, Kristian was impressed. They even had the floor plan to Kohl's villa. Circles in red marked the rooms she was to bug. The wall safe was marked in black. They also had a partial list of whom she would probably meet. For cover she would go in as Kristian Miller. Miller was just a name, whereas the

Kristian was so that she would be sure to respond on reflex. Give them a bit of reality to hold on to, said the Langley trainers. Next came this Kristian Miller's story: She was a student, a bit down on her luck but more than willing to work out the summer as a maid on the Riviera. Naturally she didn't have a proper work permit, but they said that no one would care about that. They were equally precise on the objectives. First they wanted to know what Kohl had going in the Amazon. Further, it seemed that the Company had finally crystallized its feelings toward Turner. If possible she was to find out exactly what his intentions towards Kohl were. If, as all suspected, they proved to be aggressive, then naturally the boy would have to be stopped. American relations with Brazil must not be endangered, came the word from the top. To this end Kristian was told that under no circumstances was she ever to reveal that there was any known connection between the Company and Turner. She gathered that 'no circumstances' meant torture, but of course no one spelled that one out.

In the last days before takeoff Kristian's status became vague. Yes, they explained, you were one of them now. You even half expected to be shown a secret handshake. But there were also moments when she suspected that she may have become a symbol of sorts to this quirky gaggle of old spies. Oh yes, now they had a real live agent to drop behind the enemy's lines. Well, of course, Severson and Watson had been running these sorts of shows for years, but Kristian guessed she may have been a little special to them. Possibly she just fit the bill of some slightly archetypal spy. Here then would have been the mythological cycle that stretched back through the war. Didn't they always send out lovely blond girls to be tortured by the Germans? You only heard about the tortured ones, and like Joan of Arc the stories had definite mystic-sexual overtones. But if they really meant to sacrifice her, she was still unsure exactly who would hold the knife. Technically Lyle Severson was to play the high priest case officer. Yet Harlon Watson also seemed to want the role. Then too, even Andy Aston may have read for the part, although no one took him too seriously any more since he was the one who had passed on Turner.

Toward the end someone threw a party, and all the dotty old ghosts showed up. By midnight the whiskey was spilling onto the Asian rugs. The hostess was tossing out tarot cards, sliding them across her sandalwood table. Whenever she laughed she threw up her arms for a flourish of brocaded sleeve.

Finally Jenny Rice arrived. Kristian found her weaving through the smoky gallery. The poor woman was hopelessly drunk on sweet sherry, sometimes crying, sometimes bitter. Eventually she collapsed on Kristian's shoulder. 'Now you've done it . . . now you've really gone and done it . . .' and she went coughing off into the clouds of brier.

Now and again the rapture of the old boys was broken by the less romantic strains of Victor Ross. No one seemed to know exactly where Ross stood. Clearly he was out of the doghouse for blowing the Julia Vegas run in the first place; some even claimed that he had gotten himself a place on the roster of this new operation, though just how large a part he would play was still a mystery. Kristian rarely saw him and when she did he was brusque. Obviously the man had his own ideas about the making of the very model of a United States Government Spy.

More and more Kristian felt caught in the ebb of the old school and the flow of the new. There was Severson and chums, apparently trying to dazzle her in a show of classic gallantry. Then there was Ross with his precise survival factors and cool intelligence. Kristian hardly knew which side she was supposed to entertain – particularly since she didn't believe in either camp. For all their clever humbug-gery, you really had that horrible feeling that everyone was only fooling themselves. No wonder Robin Turner had been able to screw them against the wall.

Only Humphrey remained untouched by the operatio-nal fever, still his scratchy self, Kristian's hound dog, true blue and loving. On the last day she made a special trip to say good-bye and found him nosing through his cluttered den, brooding a little, nibbling on stale chocolate cake. He seemed more upset than he let on.

Finally, though, she got him out to stroll with her along the leafy paths of the public park. The wind had shifted around to the north, the air had become quiet. The gardens might have been encased in a bell jar. The steaming foliage was very still. The warm damp promised summer rain.

Kristian and Humphrey were moving through the white sculpture of eucalyptus trees, sometimes speaking, some-times not. Finally she said, 'I'm going to miss you, Humph.'

'Me too.' The soles of his Hush Puppies were slapping on the flagstones. His sweater was inside out. He had to swallow. 'Everything's going to be all right.'

'Sure.' Kristian nodded. Except that they always told you that. She turned to him. 'But what's it like, Humph. What's it going to be like?'

'Oh well.' Humphrey kept rattling the keys in his trouser pocket, and sometimes his voice sounded just as rattled. 'I suppose in a way it's just like starting any job. I imagine they fly you to France, put you on a train, and then you'll just be knocking at the door. "Hello, I'm the girl from the domestic agency." Come on now, Kris, you've been through worse than that.'

But she was fighting against a knot in her throat. 'I don't know what's going on. It seemed like such a good idea at the start . . . but now it's like I don't even know why I'm going . . . do you know what I mean, Humph? I don't care about the Company, or Lyle Severson, or any of it. This is crazy. It's not me, it's someone else.' And she screwed up her nose. 'You know, I don't even believe this is *happening*.'

'It's always like this before you go. It's always the weirdest just before. You just got to take the plunge. The water is never as cold as you think it's going to be, right? You'll probably even like it. It's going to be an adventure, Kris . . .'

'Hey, Humph, I don't need that kind of shit from you.'

His face crumpled. 'Oh, come on, Kris, you know it's not like that, I'm just saying things, I'm just saying anything. I guess you know how I feel.'

She looked quite frail there on the path. She stood in the crosshatched shadows where the sun streamed through the limbs of trees. 'Yeah, I know, I know how you feel.'

'Hey.' Humphrey smiled, brushed a strand of hair from her eyes. 'You take care of yourself.' His fingers were still hovering above her forehead. 'And . . .'

'And what, Humph?' Although of course she knew.

So he let it out, almost. 'And I like you, Kris. A lot. That's all.'

And she allowed the tears to finally break in her eyes, allowed herself to feel like the child that she sometimes couldn't help being.

Takeoff. They put her on an Army transport and for a good part of the flight she slept, wrapped in a woolen blanket. It had been dark when she had boarded and dark when she woke again. Maybe they were following the moon. There were others in the plane. Severson and Watson, of course, but also the half-shadowed faces of men she had never seen before. For some reason only the feeblest light cut the inky night in the fuselage, while below she saw vast sheets of ice and cloud.

Touch-down came on a desolate stretch of Tarmac cut across a grassy field. The fog was still with them, waving and undulating inches above the earth. Dawn had not yet split the violet sky. The whirring jets of distant planes sounded from across the airstrip. The passengers descended single file and waded through the fog. No one spoke above a whisper. Someone was coughing. Lyle, she thought.

The remainder of the night they spent in a corrugated way station. Globular neon lights hung from steel rafters. Kristian was given a room to herself – a cot, no sheets. Now and again clipped young men passed through the hallway. One came in and brought her coffee, but he must have been ordered not to speak. The sentries were all Marines.

At dawn she was led by two Marines out to the field, where a waiting van sat in the dewy chill. Severson, in his greatcoat, stood in the misting exhaust. His skin was pallid, his eyes red. He couldn't seem to stop shivering. When they finally stood together he took her hand and said, 'I want you to know that we'll be with you every step. As soon as you plant the transmitters we'll be a word away. We've got the best team imaginable backing you up.' Then his mouth cracked for his best father's smile.

But was there some more escaping from his eyes? Kristian could only guess. Maybe the man had gotten his years confused now that this particular passion play had finally come to a climax. Maybe he was frightened too. Here in this windy stretch of France, it was impossible to say . . . so she gave him a few throwaway lines, ending with 'Thank you, Lyle.' Then she climbed aboard the

170

van, wide-eyed and numb, and the door thumped shut behind her . . .

Impressions were jumbled for the rest of her journey as she rode a lurching train across the milky landscape. The porter kept eyeing her calves. Suntanned women in straw hats and flowered shifts hemmed her in with chatter. Cameras clicked through the rattling windows. By the last stop she was dazed, tired and scared . . . not at all the gum-popping good-natured American kid that they had settled on for her cover.

They brought her in not long before nightfall. A car had been sent. The driver's name was Paul, and he hardly spoke to her. She sat in the back seat, very still. The road wound up the white cliffs above the feathering breakers of the Mediterranean.

The butler met her on the drive. He was a tall, thin, self-denying man. She was told to call him Goulart, and to keep her eyes lowered, and to curtsy, and not grow too familiar with Herr Kohl or his wife. So much for the cocky back-street girl she had always envisioned herself playing.

Days passed, and the Kohl house soon absorbed her, sucked her down actually. It hardly mattered who she was. For a while they had her in the kitchen, where she would sit cutting vegetables into shapes. Sometimes they had her scrubbing floors, or they made her polish the silver, or beat a rug, and once she had to bring Goulart his tea. 'But look, love,' another maid told her, 'you'll never make good as a waitress. You're too slow.'

As if Kristian really cared. In fact there were days when the whole game seemed so ludicrous that she forgot why she was there and hardly gave a hoot whether they fired her or not. But if they fire you, she then reminded herself, you might never get another chance to play cat and mouse with that incredible Robin Turner.

171

At the end of a week she had a fairly good handle on who was a friend and who was not. Goulart, for example, was definitely an enemy. He may have had a servant's charm with the Kohls, but to the lower staff he could be a tyrant. The others called him skullface, probably because he had black eyes and his skin stretched tight against protruding bones. That was the Arab in him, they said, or maybe he was some sort of Gypsy. For friends there was Tanya, the cook, a classic by any standard. Kristian guessed she was Old French, but there was also a maternal hint of Bavaria there. She loved to feed you, especially a pretty but too-thin waif like Kris. She also liked to sing above the clattering bowls, her voice going to a mezzo, the flab on her arms quivering. The others were fairly neutral. There was the upstairs staff, which never let you forget that they had seniority, and the downstairs staff, which had their own peasant pride. On the fringes were Paul, the driver, and several nameless gardeners. The commander of them all was Konrad, half beast, half machine. It was whispered that he had been a real jackbooted Nazi in the war. But then there was also Herr Kohl, so Kristian wouldn't have been surprised if she had opened a pantry freezer and found Hitler in cold storage all ready to be thawed out for the new Reich.

Konrad mostly kept to himself. So did Goulart, although once or twice he gave her the eye, nothing serious, just a glance at the hem of her swishing, starched skirt. Generally, however, the servants were ignored by all but themselves. Which was fine by Kristian. Except that when she got to meet Kurt Kohl, and gave the old fart her loveliest curtsy and smile, the bastard only nodded and grunted back. So much for the dramatic first encounter between that archfiend Kohl and Langley's finest.

But then there was Frau Ingeborg. Kristian hardly knew what to make of that one. The woman was weird. Mistress and maid met first in the scullery. Goulart presented the purposefully demure Kristian. 'Come closer, dear,' Frau Kohl commanded, but smiling, flicking those mascara eyes. 'Oh my,' the woman said, and nudged Kristian's chin with her knuckle. 'Aren't you the pretty one,' and for a moment Kristian felt like the Anglo slave child before the barbarian queen.

It wasn't long, though, before Kristian came to believe that perhaps Ingeborg was somehow trying to reverse the relationship, that this Brunhilde was actually out to woo her. Well, what better entry into Kurt Kohl's life than his ridiculous neurotic wife? Still, what if Ingeborg were a dyke? Wouldn't that be some luck? Kristian doubted she could run *that* gauntlet. She had to draw the line some-where . . . after all, it was only God and Country at stake.

The simple truth, however, almost made her feel ashamed. Almost. The woman, it turned out, mostly wanted a friend. She even spelled it out one day. Kristian had been dusting when Ingeborg cadged up behind her. After a time they fell to talking and the woman said, 'I really do get lonely sometimes.' Kristian's heart had been thumping away. 'But from the moment I saw you, from the very moment, well, I knew. I knew I could *trust* you.'

Kristian knew she would blow it if she didn't pick up on the woman's plea. 'Yes, ma'am, I guess I felt the same way only – '

'Only you didn't think it would be proper. Yes? Well, who cares what is proper. We are discussing human relationships here. I don't care what is proper.' Her tone came down to a whisper. 'We can be friends! Yes, you and I. We can be friends. Secret friends if you want. I don't care one hoot for this proper business. We're going to be friends!'

173

Kristian stood there, nervously swinging the feather duster, tugging at the hem of her uniform until she could finally get out, 'Yeah, sure . . . that will be great.'

Sometimes Kristian was virtually alone in the house. The cook would retire for a snooze,. Goulart would run off to the town and Paul was almost never there, what with driving Frau Kohl about. So there were times when Kristian was left in the ticking silence of the vast house, free to probe around for niches and cracks where she could place a microphone. This sort of thing seemed a bit melodramatic and phony to her. She was more comfortable, in a way, with the Ingeborg end of things. After all, she would tell herself, you've always been a devious kid. If it wasn't one thing, it was another. Besides, Ingeborg was easy.

For example, once Kristian was sent out to the garden to gather fresh flowers for the bedroom vases. They even gave her this little basket, so she was the little flower girl. She had hardly begun to snip off the stems when Frau Ingeborg sidled up beside her. For a while the German woman stood with arms crossed, and spoke with a jutting chin about such and such a party, names were bantered about. During this chat, as with others, Kristian tried to gently steer the conversation to Kurt, or the Amazon, or business in general, but Frau Kohl never wanted to discuss her husband. Her husband was just Kurt, if you got the picture. Besides, business had nothing to do with real life. Oh, but what was real life then to Ingeborg Kohl? Kristian had asked this question a dozen different ways with no results. But this time, there in the garden, Frau Kohl let the truth slip out.

'Real life,' she said, 'is love,' and with that came the first scrap of hard intelligence. 'Yes, I have a lover. I have a beautiful, lovely, blond-like-you lover.'

And then Kristian knew. Deep down she knew. 'Do you have a picture of him?'

Frau Kohl frowned. 'He doesn't like his picture taken, but I will describe him to you.'

'Yes, please.' Although Kristian hardly needed any more confirmation.

'He is not too tall. He is thin, but not skinny. And as I said, he has hair like yours.'

'Oh, he sounds just wonderful,' Kristian gushed.

'And he's such a gentle, sweet boy,' Ingeborg went on. 'You wouldn't believe it.' . . .

'Oh, I'd believe it,' Kristian said. She was fingering a velvety petal. 'I'd believe it.' . . .

That night from the servant's parlor Kristian called the number Lyle had given her for a crash meeting. At the end of the line a voice said, 'Yes, this is the residence of Manon Alarie.' Kristian hung up, as prearranged. Later Severson met her at a corner in the old quarter. There were no lights, no moon. Few pedestrians passed through these twisting streets at such a late hour. Lyle stepped out from the shadows. Kristian followed him into the alley. Both ends of the block were covered by his watchers. She had seen one smoking on a wooden stoop. But even with the team behind him, Lyle would only give her fifteen minutes. He was careful.

Sunday came two days later. This time Kristian met Lyle by the sea, where they were hidden from above by a jagged cove of rock. Around them lay the curling fog. Far out to sea there were breakers on the jetty. To the south in the calm lay Robin Turner's marina, though Lyle said he hadn't been able to confirm it. 'I'd say that you're *probably* right. It's very much in keeping with his style. And it's impressive. No denying that. But as of yet we've had no luck.'

Kristian was shivering. She was hugging her sweater to

her sides. 'But Ingeborg hasn't a clue. I mean, really. She's been completely taken in. She loves him. She's mad about him, and I use the word advisedly.'

'All the more reason for us not to interfere. He's obviously part of her life now. So we can't very well pick him up, or terminate him. That would disrupt the existing situation, wouldn't it? Cut us from more information we're after, put them on the alert.' The breeze was toying with the strands of his gray hair, squealing gulls were diving through the mist.

'Then what should I *do*?' She had suddenly grown oddly frightened. There were sharp slabs of black rock around her. The fog was blowing in from the sea. The damn gulls would not stop screaming.

'Continue,' Lyle said. 'Fall into the life. We've only just begun.'

Before they parted he was kinder to her. He had an old spy's touch to handle nervous agents, calm them, reassure them. He had played the game in Prague, in Berlin, in Istanbul and Paris, and nothing had really changed. The art of lying was a high one. And there was no useful substitute for it.

So Kristian fell into the life, or perhaps was dragged in by the undercurrents at the villa, the strongest of which, she realized, was fear. She felt it most in the evenings and early mornings. Footsteps outside her door made her hold her breath. Lyle had said that fear was part of it. You couldn't help being afraid, it was normal. Always lying, always waiting, watching, praying that the moment never came when they found you out – no one could take it for too long. Langley doctors had whole programs for untangling knotted agents. An apt expression, she thought. Inside she always felt a little knotted.

Still, Lyle had lectured her well: A good spy works to

the rhythm of the run; regularity will be your most important security factor; keep to a schedule, same thing day in day out . . . So she tried to keep it regular, serviced the dead-drop on Mondays and Fridays. It was a fairly easy job, the dead-drop lying as it did in a chink of the garden wall where vines had run a little wild and there were tufts of high grass and coils of thick ivy. A lemon tree with shriveled fruit cupped the grotto so that others could not see. The roots of a spreading oak had cracked the stone and so formed the vital hollow in the wall. She had no idea who serviced the other end of the drop. Obviously Lyle had his team of runners. Or maybe there was a schoolboy who threaded the hillside every evening. The drop could have been serviced by anyone – what you had to do was pay them enough, or apply a bit of pressure.

Through these days there was a tangle of forces at work. First there was Herr Kohl. Kristian sometimes saw him knifing off roses in the garden, or lounging on a lawn chair beneath the green veranda. He often met with men on the patio; most were stiff and foreign; some were German, some French. Usually they came in limousines, the drivers of which, she guessed, were armed. When the pattern seemed to be set Lyle had her slip a tiny bug in the leg of the lawn chair. She had to do it at night, prying off the plaster caster and then gumming the mike inside the aluminum tube. The whole job took about twenty minutes. She thought she would die.

Next in Kristian's world there was Ingeborg. Lately the woman had been playing the desolate lover, while Kristian was conveniently cast confidante. The latest was that Ingeborg's boy hadn't called her. He hadn't been around the docks, and since she did not know where he lived she couldn't get in touch with him.

Then the boy returned, and Ingeborg told Kristian how he had said he had needed to get away. He'd gone off to a

177

little place he knew in the Alps, apparently there had been a few things he'd needed to think over. Well, that was fine for him but Ingeborg was livid, had even been all set to break it off . . . except that he had brought her back a gift.

'Come, I will show you,' Frau Kohl whispered. She lay sprawled on the crushed velvet sofa. Kristian had ostensibly been summoned to the boudoir to gather up dresses and stockings, but in reality Frau Kohl had wanted her there to listen. It was always like that . . . Kristian would be given some excuse to enter Frau Kohl's bedroom, and then together they would chew over her life of love.

Now the woman was fairly panting. 'Here, look here.' She was holding out a small white box.

Kristian took the gift in the palm of her hand, then she was pulling off the lid, peeling back the folds of cotton, and there – her throat tightened, her breath caught. 'Oh, it's just lovely.' She was turning a tiny china jaguar in her fingers.

'It's a tiger.' Ingeborg beamed.

'Yes.' She couldn't take her eyes from it. She thought of the tape they'd listened to that they'd found in his drawer back in Virginia . . . the native ceremony . . . she thought of the transcription of his debriefing and his reference to the face of the jaguar he saw on the wall in the jail . . .

'I know it isn't much,' Ingeborg was saying, 'but it's not the gift. It's what the gift says to me. It says that he loves me.'

'Yes,' Kristian said dutifully. 'It says that he loves you.' But what is it supposed to say to me? She wondered. *I know you're here?*

Odd, but Kristian somehow felt safer now that Turner was definitely out there. Yes, he was *out there*, a presence, however spectral. And nights he would become real to her. She could lie in bed for hours while the household slept, when there was only the scraping of boughs on the

178

shingles, the distant barking of dogs. The window of her tiny room opened onto a green tunnel of shaggy ferns. On bad nights when she could not sleep she would sometimes sit by that window until the light turned pearly with the dawn, and all the while there was Robin Turner . . . out there, and they couldn't catch him no matter how much they tried. Which, of course, was *not* the way she was supposed to think . . . which was even counter to her mission. Whose side was she on . . . ?

As the days passed and the nights grew worse she found herself thinking of him more and more. She couldn't help it. He was simply there, hovering between waking and sleeping, between fear and worse. He seemed to help.

Which was more than she could say for Lyle Severson. In all fairness though, Kristian knew that Lyle was trying his best. Still, there were times when they met that it was all she could do to keep from breaking down completely. There was one night in a grotto of bamboo at the edge of the park that was particularly bad. Earlier that evening she had left the pantry door unlatched and Goulart had screamed at her. At the time she had played it contrite and controlled. When she met with Lyle, however, all she could do was cry.

She told him that she wanted out, that she was not making it. She even begged him. For close to an hour he held her in his skinny arms, told her that they all had bad days . . . 'But it's going to be all right, everything will be all right.' When it was over she made her way back through the warren of unlit streets, feeling like the walking dead.

Then, one day when she was certain that she could not go on any longer, the mood of the house began to change. There was a bustling excitement about the place, rumors circulated, and finally Goulart made the announcement that the Kohls were going to Brazil. Naturally the tempor-

179

ary staff would not accompany them, and so Kristian was given notice.

To Lyle Severson the move was a disaster. Kristian sensed his frustration immediately . . . he began to run her harder, he had her plant more microphones (by now nearly every room in the house was bugged). However, the breakdowns had to be replaced. In a harried meeting by the seawall Lyle told her he was having trouble maintaining a tap on the Kohl phones. Could Kristian get to the wires? No, it was too risky. So they compromised – Kristian placed an internal tap in the mouthpiece, which, because they sometimes buzzed and echoed, was considered a most chancy way to go.

Back at the seawall on the following Sunday Lyle pressed for even more. Langley, he said, was demanding details while the electronic surveillance was only returning generalities. For example, on one transcript made from a meeting that Kohl held in his study a seven-digit number had been mentioned in connection with the Amazon deal, but whether profit or expense, the transcript did not reveal. The mention of large sums made Langley all the hungrier.

Finally the reason why the bugs had only yielded paltry scraps came out: Kohl had been ahead of them from the start. From the moment he took up residence in France he had counted on the likelihood of surveillance. During one telephone conversation he had even gone so far as to warn a caller outright . . . 'This instrument cannot be trusted.' he'd said.

Langley was furious. They wanted results, and in their frustration they kept on hammering at Severson harder. Follow Kohl, they told him, bug his car, his driver, his damn underwear.

To which Lyle replied, and later repeated to Kristian, 'How do they expect me to monitor his bloody jet in

180

flight?' That morning Severson had also learned that Kohl had his cars electronically swept clean on a regular basis.

And when it came down hard from Langley on Lyle, it came down harder on Kristian. If Kurt Kohl was shut tight, he told the girl, then we'll just have to prod a bit harder at his wife.

'I don't see what else I can do,' Kristian told him. 'The woman doesn't know, she doesn't *know*.' By this time Kristian, worn raw, had been ready to pack it in for good, and not just this run either. She felt she wanted to quit the whole Mata Hari spy business completely. It wasn't worth it.

Before the meeting ended Lyle even yelled at her, told her that he was sick and tired of her hysteria. 'You are going back and you're going to push it home right down the wire. Is that clear? Bloody hell, I don't need such nonsense from you.'

He had never yelled at her before. In the end he left her standing there in the sand. The wind was blowing the spray off the waves, the air had turned cold. She wished she were a rock, or a lump of brown seaweed. Treading back along the seawall, she still couldn't stop crying. Her knees were weak, her shoes were filled with sand.

There had been Sunday nights when she had dawdled about the old quarter. She liked to browse at the shop windows, maybe wander into the lobby of a big hotel. Now, however, she walked in a quick line back to the villa. If you don't return now, she had told herself, you never will. Because it was going bad. It was going very bad.

Midway up a steep, cobbled street she had to pause to catch her breath. Below were slate roofs fading into a slate sky. You too could fade away down there, she thought. Get yourself a room. They might not find you for weeks . . .

181

She entered the villa through the servants' door, went down the pantry corridor and into the kitchen, but there were only the piles of gleaming copper pots and the tap was dripping. Next, into the dining room, and there were still no sounds, no voices from anywhere. Well, you might as well go to bed, she told herself, and headed for the servants' stairs. She felt a little better running her hands along the wall. At least the plaster was warm and dry. But what about the bedroom light? You didn't leave on the light. Then the door was open, and she nearly screamed.

Konrad sat on the bed. Goulart had taken the chair. Kristian tried to speak, but her tongue kept sticking to the roof of her mouth. Konrad kicked the door shut behind her. 'Kristian,' he intoned, 'Kristian . . . Who are you? Huh? Who?'

Her fingers went up to touch her face. She was shaking her head, she couldn't stop it. 'Listen to me . . .' and she was stumbling back to the door.

Konrad grabbed her, took a clump of her hair and wrenched her back. 'Who are you?' and yanked her head down to his fist. 'And what is this?' His fingers uncurled, and there in his palm were the shattered fragments of a microphone.

They took her to the basement. Here there were only the four concrete walls and a concrete floor. Light fell from a naked bulb, and there was a little bit of moon through a window some fifteen feet above.

They pushed her face down on the concrete. Konrad kneed her in the small of the back to clip on handcuffs. One of them had hiked up her dress; now he was alternately smoothing and pinching her thighs, all the while saying, 'Who are you, little bird? Who are you really?'

Konrad ripped her dress from the neck. Now Goulart was kneeling above her head. He pulled her face up to his.

182

He held a hypodermic needle to his lips. Konrad nodded, threw her over his knee. She felt her panties ripped away, the needle stinging in her buttock, then a blazing in her veins and a pounding in her head. She was reeling, her throat raw from choking screams.

They trussed her over the seat of a discarded wing chair. Goulart crouched, held her face up to his. 'So princess, what? Is it bad? Good? What?' He cupped a hand to her breast.

Konrad had drawn off his belt, was winding the end around his fist. He turned away, ran a knuckle across his mouth, and the belt cracked down on her buttocks.

Kristian arched back, crying out. The belt swung down again. Goulart had his mouth against hers so that she was sobbing right into him. Then he pulled away, crooning, 'So, princess, tell us a story.'

The fallback, she kept trying to get it out. 'Okay, okay . . . we were going to rob you – '

Konrad whipped her again. Now the pace had begun to change. Goulart was softer, his voice a singsong voice, lilting, his lips very close to hers. 'Tell me, princess, are you Catholic or Protestant?'

Kristian squeezed her eyes shut. 'I don't . . . Protestant.'

Goulart bent in and kissed her on the mouth again. 'Oh, that's good, then you believe in telling the truth. Because this is vital. Tonight you must tell the truth. All right with you?'

She nodded, tears streaking down her cheeks.

Goulart was tracing his finger around her jaw. 'So you do admit that you spied on us?' She half-nodded. 'Now, that's better.' He had begun to rub a nipple. Konrad was running his hands over her legs, wedging his fist between her thighs. She shuddered.

Now Goulart's mouth was at her ear. 'So you're a thief,

183

huh?' His tongue kept probing in. 'But not a very good one. Here we find the microphones, and who else would have done such a thing? Tanya? Oh no. So now we have you. Now tell me, who's your partner in this crime?'

A moment passed. The she blurted out the name they had given her. 'David, my husband . . .'

Goulart was smiling. 'Well, he must not be such a good husband to let this happen. Here we're going to punish you, and rape you, and what's the point of having such a husband like that?'

Whatever they had shot her with was still simmering in her head. Her skin was growing raw. Whenever they touched her it burned.

Goulart pulled slowly on her nipple, then wrenched hard. 'I said what's the point of having a husband like that, princess?'

Kristian could hardly breathe. 'I don't know, I – '

'No, no,' Goulart was saying, 'if you're merely a thief, then why microphones?'

All she could do was scream out, 'I don't know.'

Goulart raked his nails across her stomach. 'Konrad was in the Army. Every day there was nothing to do, so he would sit and think of things to do with women. Maybe he'll take a bottle and put it inside you, and then kick until the glass breaks.'

Now they were dragging her across the room again. Konrad had her by the hair, was shoving up her thighs, so that she had to kneel, then bend over a galvanized washtub of water. When she finally understood, she began to thrash about. His weight came down, and her head went plunging under water.

Konrad couldn't stop. Water was flying. The front of his shirt was drenched. But he must have appreciated her, the way she kept trying to twist up for air, while Goulart lashed at her back and thighs, or kept mumbling into her ear.

At the end they were now pulling at her thighs, now sucking her breasts. One of them even clamped his mouth to hers so she had to draw in his breath too. Oblivion . . .

Konrad was sprawled on the sofa. Even Goulart, usually stiff, was reclining into the cushions. Now and then they sipped dry wine. Sometimes they spoke, always in German now.

The doorbell was chiming, and Konrad looked at his watch.

Goulart held up a hand, now his formal self again as he moved briskly down the hall, out into the entry room. The doorbell was still ringing.

Such a bad night, he vaguely thought, and here the servants were coming home early . . . He turned the latch and the door slid in. The black night was pouring through the door. Goulart had to lean around the jamb, and call out for whomever would be standing there. His hand was cupped around the knob.

While outside, just off the brick step to avoid the wash of light, interwoven in the hanging ivy, Robin Turner was reaching out, his arms stretching through the leaves, his fingers clamping down on Goulart's arm. 'Who is this?' Turner yanked him forward, whipped him with an open palm and threw him face down on the bricks.

Goulart was wheezing, spitting out blood. His teeth had been smashed on the edge of the step. Robin's knee was against his back, the crook of his arm around his neck.

Turner's mouth was close to Goulart's ear. 'You have a girl. Who is she? Who else is in the house?'

Goulart's throat was backing up. As he answered he also had to tongue out blood and spittle. 'Are you the girl's husband . . . is that it? . . . are you the one – '

Turner shifted his knee. 'Sure,' and wrenched back suddenly until the man's neck cracked.

Now Turner was a shadow, moving through the bluish

185

rectangles of gloom. Ahead were the subdued sounds of clocks. He brushed past tall drapes, leaving them trembling.

Now in the den he was full centered, moving directly from the stomach, which kept one low and stable – form above all else. At the hearth, though, he couldn't resist the iron poker. It was not part of the empty-hands tradition, of course, but now he was a little less the pure karatica, a little more the simple killer.

Yet even so he had some style, waiting in the fold of curtains, nudging a crystal vase off the shelf that smashed on the parquetry. Konrad's voice came up from the hallway. 'Goulart? . . . Goulart?'

A door eased shut. Turner marked the double click of the latch. Next came the creaking of slow steps, then the bobbing shadow on the wall, and now Konrad's head and shoulders were leaning out, watching, saying again, 'Goulart?'

'Here,' Turner answered. 'I'm right here.' When Konrad spun he met the crashing arc of the poker full on. The blow wrenched him back. Plaster broke away as he went down.

Turner was padding faster now, hardly slowing to round the corners. He had thrown the poker away, it took two hands to deal with all these doors. One was only a closet. Another led to a servant's washroom. He hadn't recalled that the house was so devious. Every room seemed to be taunting him.

At the end of the hall one door did give way, and he descended the flight of stairs so that finally he was hanging just inside the basement while across the blotted darkness, through the dust, he made out the prone, bunched up figure of a naked girl . . .

Time had wound down on Kristian. Only seconds were left. All around her loomed the junked-out furniture

– the sagging chairs, the battered lampshades. She was not asleep, but she was moving in and out of dreams just the same. She might have been flying, tossed high up on the wind above the sea. In the distance lay an island, and there was also something about that Robin Turner, only you couldn't make out what he was saying. If only he could speak a little louder . . . So she called to him . . . 'Robin?' And tried to twist free into his arms.

While he, her fantasy man, only bent down closer to see her face, then said, 'Who *are* you?'

9

They had been bad hours just before Robin had decided to go. He had thought, wait until the morning comes, give it until then . . . except that he had also kept on seeing visions of Lyle's wonder girl blowing everything from start to finish.

He had suspected the girl from the beginning. Frau Ingeborg's pretty little American maid – it was such an academic plant. At least his move into the Kohl home had showed a little imagination, but their placing a servant, well, you would have expected more from the famous Lyle Severson.

As it had gone, Robin had seen trouble immediately. First there had been Ingeborg's tossed-off remarks. Konrad, she had said, hadn't liked the girl. Then it had been Goulart, the butler, hadn't trusted her much either. Next he'd gathered that Kohl had stepped up the electronic sweeps, and finally he had met Frau Ingeborg in the botanical gardens . . . she had been sobbing into the tulips, telling how they had caught her beloved maid with a hand in the cookie jar. Well naturally she didn't know all the details but she did know that Kurt had chased her out of the house, which only meant that Konrad was about to handle the girl himself, and you could imagine the screams that would come through the floorboards. Clearly he had to move quickly, before she told what she knew and ruined everything . . .

There was really nothing else to do but hold the girl gently as he could. An hour ago, moving out to the house, he had thought he would not only have to get her, perhaps he would even kill her, depending on what she knew, what she had told them. Now he was cradling her head to his shoulder, because the pretending was over. After Julia there had to be a limit to this business.

A quarter of an hour passed. There were moonbeams through the glass, and Robin was stirring, whispering to her. She would not respond, so he had to do it himself . . . free her hands, guide her arms into the sleeves of his long leather coat. For the first few steps she had to lean on him but outside she seemed to be moving more easily.

Once beyond the villa walls he was pushing harder, faster. He wanted the distance. All throughout the city a false dawn was breaking. At these hours the town looked plastic, too perfect for real life. Turner led, sometimes even pulling her along. They kept to the back streets and unlit edges of parks and courtyards. Once she asked him, 'Where are we going?' but he only said that he wouldn't hurt her. Sometimes cars rushed past. Sometimes the slapping of their feet made the only sounds to be heard.

Jack Sweet lived in a tiny cave of a house perched on a hill above the harbor. He came to the door bleary-eyed, wrapped in a bedspread. 'Oh, sport, it's five in the fucking morning. What is this?'

By now Kristian was only hanging on to Turner's sleeve, huddled into his coat, squinting at the porch light. He thought she might have become delirious because she wouldn't let go.

Soon, though, Jack was bumbling about in the kitchen, dropping coffee grounds into his pot, throwing matches at the burner. Turner ran a bath for the girl, and coaxed her in with mumbled, self-conscious words. Outside, dawn was lighting the sky.

With Jack again, Turner became still. He was facing the picture window. The sea was deepening to a translucent green. 'Don't ask us any questions,' he said. He held his mug of coffee in both hands.

'Sure, sport, no questions.' Jack was watching his friend against the blue glass. Blades of clean, steely light had stuck between the slats of the blind.

'We'll be leaving soon,' Turner went on. The pipes were still rumbling from Kristian's bath.

'Yeah, well I know that much. Come here at five in the morning, I can see there's trouble.'

Turner kept looking at the city and sea below, at the cliffs and the shore and the red clay tiles of villas encircled by trees. 'I'm wondering,' he said, 'if you might have something for the girl to wear?'

'Yeah, I think so.'

'And what if we borrowed your car? It would just be to see us out of town.'

'That bad, huh, sport? Sure, you can have the car.'

Turner looked round slowly. For an hour now he had been his gentlest self, as if something inside had shattered. 'I appreciate this, Jack.'

'Hey, sport, I've been through it. I know how it gets.' From the bathroom they heard the girl draining the tub. 'She's pretty,' Jack said, 'she's got a pretty face. You dig her?'

'I don't know, I just met her.' Which was only what one man said to another. The truth was more complex.

'Well she definitely has possibilities,' Jack said. 'Not that I know what's happening. I guess you're mixed up in something heavy, but now you got this girl, maybe you'll be able to dig her. Know what I'm getting at, sport? You take a girl like that, get her out of town, and then say screw to the whole world. To all the heavy stuff that's supposed to be so important.'

Which was close to what Turner had been thinking himself . . . until he clenched his teeth against it.

Robin and the girl left shortly after dawn. A light breeze was blowing steadily from the south. A few small sails were already riding this wind across the bay. Turner wound down through the hills to the marina. In the jetty by the edge of the sea he fetched what he would need – money and an escape passport bundled in thick plastic and wedged deep into the rocks. They followed the coast out of town, drove for an hour, hardly speaking. Robin asked her how it was going. She said better. 'They hit me with something. I thought it was acid or speed but it wore off too quickly. Anyway, I'm better now . . . thank you.'

Later, rounding a bend beneath a wave of trees, she suddenly asked him why had he taken her with him?

There were several cruel things he could have said, but all that came out was, 'I'm not sure.' He even managed a weary smile. 'Maybe I just couldn't resist it,' and then was sorry he'd said it. It wasn't funny, though he was afraid she would think he meant it to be.

She didn't react. 'So what happens now?'

'We'll talk about it later,' he said softly. This girl was wasted, he told himself. It was in her eyes, in her voice. He was off a little himself, but they definitely had wasted her.

Well beyond the city and into a wooded grove, Turner left the main road and they bumped along for another mile, then pulled off the shoulder into a flowered meadow. All around them were young beech trees, some white, some gray. He led the way without speaking, treading carefully through the knee-high grass. Kristian walked behind and a little to the side. Halfway into this lake of purple flowers Turner said, 'How much do they know?'

191

Kristian rubbed her eyes. 'We know about Jaques . . . my guess was always that you were planning to move against Kohl. I thought it would be his plantation. I don't know if the others really bought that . . .'

'I see.' Turner sighed.

'It was all in the files.' She was looking up into the ring of leaves and glittering green light. 'Two of us were hunting . . . myself and Humphrey, Humphrey Knolls. Did you ever meet him?'

'No.'

'Well, he's all right, you know? He respected you.'

She was wearing a pair of Jack's trousers with the bottoms rolled. She also had one of his shirts, the collar of which kept falling past her shoulder. 'God, Humph . . . if you could only see me now.'

'And Lyle,' Turner was saying. 'What about Lyle? How much does he know?'

But the girl suddenly seemed to be going vague on him. Then, 'Lyle's kind of a twit. I don't like him. I don't like any of them.'

'They can be bad, I've seen what they can do too.'

She gave him a weak smile. 'So I've heard.' She was careful not to mention that she knew about how they had sent in Julia, and what happened to her. 'Well . . . yes, you're Robin Turner . . . I've heard all about you, I cracked your case, Humph and me . . . God, I never had days like this before.' She sank down to her knees in the grass as she said it.

Turner was also kneeling down in the grass. 'I have, I've had quite a few days like this.'

'Well, look how you turned out.'

Good point, Turner might have added, except that he couldn't help smiling now, smiling at this girl in her ridiculously ballooning corduroys.

So Kristian gave him a small grin too, then actually was

192

able to laugh. 'Oh, screw it! It's Robin Turner. It's himself in the flesh.' Then their eyes met, and each was breathing more deeply, and when the tears finally came from her eyes she slowly bent over and kissed him on the cheek, so that they were both surprised . . .

The air was cooling. This might have been the first of autumn. They lay in the grass, having finished the bottle of wine and the sandwiches Jack had given them. Gray light was breaking through the circles of the beeches. Kristian had been speaking freely now for nearly an hour. She spoke slowly, first of those disquieting days in the archives, then of the hunt. Turner was able to confirm much of what she had already guessed, but this, the two of them together, this seemed wholly unexpected . . . or was it, really . . . ?

At some point she had even fallen into his arms, collapsed onto his shoulder. He saw no reason to shove her off. So they dozed with their arms intertwined, and when they woke the sun was a flimsy orange ball beneath the trees and the wind was hissing through the grass.

'I've got to get going,' Turner finally whispered. 'I've got to put some distance between me and them.' It sounded logical.

'What about me?'

He had been afraid of that one for close to an hour now. 'I don't know.'

'Well, I *do* . . . I'm going with you.'

He had thought as much. Still, he couldn't help resisting with one last line. 'But you don't even know where I'm going.'

'Oh, yes I do, Turner. I told you, I know all about you.'

'It could be bad. You've never been in a jungle. I have, I know what it can be.'

She was staring into a tiny jungle of grass. 'I don't care. I've hit the bottom. Anywhere will seem like up to me.

I'm going, Robin Turner. It's there and I'm just going to take it.'

'It's that bad?'

'It's not bad *or* good. It's there, and it's just too late for either of us to turn back now.'

That night they caught a train for Paris. They were running now, flat out. Turner said that all France would soon be coming down on them. First there would be Kohl, and what with Kristian's shabby fallback, you could only expect the worst from him. 'And people like Kohl have all kinds of connections. You wouldn't believe the places he has them. He might even put us together, it depends on what Ingeborg tells him.'

In equally determined pursuit would probably be Severson. 'Maybe he'll think you've kidnapped me,' Kristian offered. She rather liked the notion. 'You've dragged me off to your lair.'

But seriously, they knew, Lyle was CIA, and the CIA could easily enlist, no questions asked, their French sister. And then they'll be coming from both sides. And the French are real s.o.b.'s.

Except Paris, Turner said, might throw them all off. 'They'll be expecting us in Marseilles, and then out to the border. So Paris might give us cover for a few days.' There was also Kristian's passport to consider. Robin said that he knew a man in Paris who did very good work.

At midnight they shared a narrow berth. Kristian lay in his arms, while his head on the pillow faced the dark glass. For a long time neither slept. The train rattled on, the poles along the track bending and snapping out of the night. Now and again there were lights in the distance, but no stars and no moon.

They spoke a little, Robin saying that he was worried about how Kohl would react when the bodies were found.

'I think he's going to be scared, he might even cancel his trip to Brazil,' which would ruin everything. Beyond that he was concerned about the Company's reaction, that Severson might panic and even try to warn Kohl for the sake of good relations with those Nazi-loving Brazilians.

But Kristian said that Lyle would never contact Kohl. 'He wouldn't want Kohl to know that the Company knew anything about you. There could be too many implications. Yes, the Company wants to stop you, but only because they're deeply concerned that they'll be held responsible for a plot to kill Kohl.' She also said that not much had really changed inside the Company since Stansfield Turner's takeover. 'The same crap still goes down.'

For her own part, however, she may not have cared about any of it. Brazil, the Amazon especially; she said that none of it seemed very real. 'I've always been a city girl, you know, so I can't even imagine this terrible jungle of yours. I'm afraid you're the only thing that's real to me, Turner. Can you stand it?'

And that night in the rumbling berth they made love, a little desperately, as though trying to shut out any thoughts of what was to come. Afterwards there didn't seem much to say, but Kristian had to tell him. 'You're just the way I imagined you would be.' She didn't apologize for the school-girl sound of it.

Paris in the morning was blanched with an autumn sun. The crowds were milling, women were loaded down with packages all along the boulevards. Turner and Kristian hurried north along the Saint-Michel closer to the Seine and the Latin Quarter. They took a room, one of six above a bakery. The place might have been run on the sly for fugitives just such as themselves. You had to pay extra for discretion. The bath was down the hall. The wallpaper hung in strips and threw shadows on the warped floorboards. But the sheets were clean and here among the castaways, the thieves, the washed-out painters and thin students, here they could believe they were safe.

Mornings were the best. Usually they would sleep late while the white muslin curtains flapped inwards. Outside, the steady rush of traffic also seemed reassuring. Afternoons they lunched in a basement café.

On the second day they shopped for things they would need in the south. Also Kristian bought a skirt, white with a pattern of green turtles.

Next came the passport. Jocko was the only name that Turner had for the forger. He knew him vaguely from his last pass through to Hamburg. There were records of this Jocko in Langley, but the respectable community no longer used his sort so the plump Corsican was always on the come. They said he serviced the nicer side of the underworld, political criminals but not terrorists. Apart from that he always called Turner 'child,' and had seemed to like him.

They found Jocko on the riverfront, unshaven and sweaty in a sleeveless undershirt and grimy black trousers. His shop was a hovel, squeezed into a back street among sheds and factories.

Robin made him happy this night. 'Sure, I remember you, child. Hey, and now you got a match. Blond on blond. So what else is new?'

Kristian, reluctant to step into the light of the naked bulb, stood by the door with her arms crossed. Turner leaned on the workbench. He had even slapped the Corsican on the back. 'Uh, what can be done for her, Jocko?'

The forger shrugged, then tapped a dirty finger on the bridge of his nose. 'From scratch, I got to work from scratch?'

Turner gave him a sheepish smile, playing the innocent

kid again. 'Well, yes, I'm afraid that she's misplaced the original.'

Jocko began to shake with laughter, his belly flapping over his belt. 'Oh I see, child, I see. Well, in that case, sure, sure I can help the children. What else do you think? I'm the big daddy. But you've got to make this big daddy a little promise.' The forger laid an arm around Turner's shoulder. Their faces were very close. 'I think maybe you have to be a very good fellow. I think maybe you got yourself in a lot of trouble, and now maybe there's some big fish after you. Know what I'm saying, child? They say you're in trouble.'

'Who says, Jocko?'

'Oh, you know, the word passes around. It's a small world. Me, I happen to mention that I know you, and then they tell me to watch out. Not that I care, not for a friend, but just the same now you've got to be a good boy.'

Turner had begun to bob his head, slowly up and down. 'Who's after me?'

'Everyone, child . . . the cops, the crooks, everyone's after you.' He pulled Turner to him. 'Hey, don't look so sad. I'm not just giving you bad news. I just thought you should know. So you can be careful, okay? If I do the work and then they catch you, it's my neck too.'

Turner and Kristian sat on the edge of the bunk while the forger worked. Moths spun around the dangling bulb. A plastic radio blared out Nana Mouskouri. Through it all Jocko rambled on, claiming that the world was dangerous for Turner. 'They say you killed a dozen people, killed them with your hands. Is that true, child?'

'No,' Robin answered, 'it's not true.' He and Kristian were drinking bad wine from tin cups, nearly down to the dregs. Now and again horns sounded from the river. Once they heard cats screaming in the alley.

In the late hours, Jocko grew melancholy. He was sweating heavily, going at the Burgundy straight from the

197

bottle. But his work was flawless. Even Kristian couldn't help smiling when she thumbed through the pages. At the door the forger threw his arms around them both. 'God's luck to you,' he said, and laughed, and then kissed them out to the night along the Seine.

Sometimes in the evenings when their room became too constrictive they took to wandering the streets. Later, alone in their room, they had to face that they had each other, and nothing else. They would lie on the bed, and once Turner told her, 'I don't want you to be afraid.' He had spoken out of the blue.

'I'm not,' she told him. 'What's going to happen is going to happen.' They were both still, while the water kept rumbling through the pipes above and below and the stray horn of a car sounded. Finally tears glinted in her eyes. 'We're crazy. All day I've been trying to figure out exactly what I'm doing here with you. Then I realized that it doesn't need an answer. I mean, this is no weirder than working for the CIA, or IBM, or going back to school and getting a teacher's credential, for God's sakes. So I don't care about the logic . . . I also think I love you.'

In time she came to see that Robin's reasoning was also innocent of analysis. Once, bent over the balcony of their window ledge, he told her that he did not believe he was the fanatic that Langley thought he was. 'It's just that I've started something and I can't stop it. I'm committed. I've got to ride this out until . . .'

She understood. 'Sure, I've been through this before. We don't have to talk about it. We don't need *logical* reasons. We're just going, okay?'

But he couldn't just shrug it off today. 'I just want you to know where you stand.'

Well, she knew where she stood, all right. She was

caught in the middle of two different Robin Turners. There was the soft one and the hard one. Sometimes she could hear them fighting it out at night.

Below them came a rasping voice now, some reeling drunk. Kristian leaned to peer down at the black slate roofs, the sooty bricks, the warren of streets. 'I'm like that guy down there,' she said.

'No, you're not.' Turner smiled. 'You're like me.'

'Yeah? Well, sure I am, but wouldn't it be great if we both wound up in some suburb with two kids and a recreational van?'

Now came the other Turner, slinking out very dry, very cold. 'We'll wind up in the jungle. That's where we're going, that's where it's taking us.'

Beyond the rooftops another drunk was howling away, the traffic was sounding, dusk was beginning to destroy the day.

Yes, there definitely were two Robin Turners – both, she decided, oddly innocent. He could say the simplest things and mean them from the bottom of his heart. Yet whenever that second Turner spoke, the one who was going to kill Kurt Kohl, she always felt he was also speaking from the bottom of his heart.

As though to make it seem more logical, he told her that they could run to the edge of world, but there was no place in the world they could hide. He said that any train they rode to the end of the line would only wind up in the jungle anyway. He said it by rote, because to him it seemed inevitable.

On that particular afternoon she may not have understood him completely, but by the close of the following Sunday she knew. He had told her everything while they lay in the sleepy calm of their room. For a while he fenced, then it all came out. He spoke of the prison, his voice flat. He lay by her side on his back. A hurdy-gurdy had been playing all morning, and you could hear the children shouting. Once when the chimes of the cathedral rolled on in, he paused. When he resumed he was describing those lost weeks after his escape.

From the start he said he had known that Jaques was the man to see. Even the priest had told him that Kohl was afraid of Jaques. So there was nothing else to it. 'I knew that the Company would bury everything, so it was just a matter of getting down to Jaques.'

He recalled only the starkest impressions of the trek south . . . money he had stolen from a man in the streets of Belém, a drunk. He'd caught him in an alley. For drama he had held a bit of lead pipe, but he hadn't used it, even though those kinds of scenes went on nearly every night at the mouth of the Amazon River. Down along the docks was the worst end of Belém, Robin said. They would rip you off soon as look at you . . . every other guy you saw had a piece missing from some fight . . . the man who had finally taken him in, for a price, had a glass eye (someone had snapped him across the face with a length of barbed wire).

This shantytown, though, was home for survivors. The law did not search you out in the docks. It was a thieves' code. No one talked. Besides, the law was fair game. Kids would pelt them with bottles and rocks from the rooftops. The older ones would drag them into doorways if they got the chance. So Robin had kept to the docks.

Finding Jaques was the hardest part. Those who knew wouldn't talk, or worse they led him astray. But he kept at it, prodding, begging, bullying. In the end the halfcastes came to trust him, because he was clearly alone and on the run. They had also heard that he had killed a couple of guards escaping from prison. This made him one of them. All of the doctor's men were outlaws.

From Belém it was down the river on small boats. Sometimes all he could get were canoes. He passed through mud towns filled with *garimpeiros* – the gold and diamond hunters; most only lasted a year or two, some were shot for their claims, some for their women, some for no reason at all.

There was also disease. Robin told her they had strains that weren't even in the books, but they killed you all the same. Most people lived in sagging shacks of corrugated tin, or rotting logs, and everything bred in that filth. Cut your finger and it could kill you, because an undressed wound always festered. Gangrene was rampant. Then there was the dysentery, the malaria, and the slow death from parasites. Down in the jungle the pharmacist was king.

But through all this he had managed to pass untouched. Some even believed that he was charmed, maybe because he had blond hair. Indians have always been obsessed with blond hair, he told her. Also, there could have been that jaguar thing at work, had taken over . . . unsummoned but there . . . He didn't dwell on it with her. How could he, he had never wanted to face it himself . . .

That he arrived was enough for Jaques to accept him. To describe the doctor to her, Robin painted a large barrel-chested man in ratty khaki, hair grizzled and white. The Indians might well have believed he was some sort of god. Either that, Robin said, or else they were afraid of him even though they also loved him.

Robin had stayed on with Jaques for seven days. He ate what they ate, mostly lumps of fish, and the bread they ground out from a plant. Sometimes they would kill fresh game, and there was always alligator meat. In the afternoon everybody slept, except the guards. Robin shared a hut with Jaques; he had a bunk in the corner under a tent of mosquito netting. In the nights they often stayed awake and talked. Which was how it all started. At least the plan . . .

They made charts and maps by the light of an oil lamp. Jaques was keen on his charts. He had timetables, graphs, but when Turner left he was still not altogether sure about the doctor's motives. Jaques said he was doing it because one must preserve one's dignity, and the dignity of one's people. A man should die, or even kill, for dignity if it came down to it. But Turner felt there was more. For himself it seemed that there were at least some other forces at work. He had never known a man who was able to hate as fully as Jaques. Not even himself.

As for the rest, Turner said that there was probably little Kristian did not know. The Company got him out of Brazil on a Navy transport. He stopped in Florida for a night, but no one would touch him. By this time Andrew Aston was already on the line, and Turner was out of bounds for anyone else. Apparently they all felt that they owed something to Robin's father . . . there were the years between them and the tradition that one must help the son of a friend . . .

Of those months in Langley, thieving, lying, putting Go-between into the existing machinery, Robin said only that he was frightened almost every moment. If they said that he was a gentle boy, occasionally even meek, this was because at least the conscious part of him fell into the role naturally. When you're afraid, he said, you want to please. Every kind glance, every kind word could make your spirits soar. Now he realized better that spies all over the world went through that sort of trauma. You ran on hate, but the hate was laced with fear and need. Strange.

Fall settled in. All along the grand streets the leaves had turned, and chilly winds blew them into the Seine. Robin and Kristian would walk beneath the fluttering awnings.

Once he bought her a tiny gold bangle from a market stall and gave it to her matter-of-factly. Generally she thought that they were happy together, even if they were often so very quiet.

They worked the escape route together. Kristian made the calls to airlines. Turner drew up the timetables. Direct flights, of course, were out of the question; they'd be watched. But from Paris to Milan to Madrid and out . . . they thought they might have a chance that route. Touch-down would be the tricky part, but Robin believed that this nine-day hiatus in Paris might well muddy the airport checks. 'They can only keep on their toes for so long,' he told Kristian. 'They'll get a bit lazy.' He hoped.

Once or twice he made attempts to follow up on the Kurt Kohl end, even phoned Jack, who said that some people had been around but they didn't get shit. Every day he would ramble down to the stall by the river and pick up the papers, usually reading them in the shadow of Notre Dame. There was never any mention of Kohl, and in these timeless mornings when the white light was reduced to green or the fog heaved up to the cathedral's spires, Turner sometimes wondered if he even cared.

But that false peace never lasted, not even for a day. Because even in the calmest moments all he had to do was turn to a glass, catch his own reflection, and there would be that damned cat, maybe even whispering, *Who do you think you're kidding, friend?*

10

Lyle returned from France to a Virginia that lay in the cusp of an early winter. Each day began with gray folds of clouds in the sky. Drizzle dampened the leaves in the mud. Spirits were also dampened now.

The days following Lyle's return were lost days. His status had become unclear. Rumors circulated that the director was displeased. He was displeased with Lyle's product, and displeased that the girl had been lost. Victor Ross, said those in the know, was now running the show. He had the committee mandate, and the director's ear. Still, no one gave the Severson group any conclusive word one way or another. No one wanted to be remembered as the ax that felled the oak of the old generation.

But Lyle hardly felt like an oak these days. How long he had been alone in his house, he hardly knew. In the afternoons he would walk from room to room over carpets that failed to muffle his footsteps. As time passed he took to creeping up on doors as if some ghost were waiting at his side. Except maybe there really was a ghost of sorts tagging along behind. Since his return from France everywhere he looked he saw the face of the girl.

His only real line into Langley became Humphrey Knolls, who also led a lonely life now . . . with the decline of Severson came the decline of Severson's staff. Humphrey still kept his hours in the office, not really working, but there all the same. Occasionally the junior staff would see him about the grounds kicking at the crisp red leaves, or find him brooding in his office when they made the morning rounds.

So it went for a week or more. He was not to be included in any Victor Ross operation, but at least he was welcome to watch from the sidelines. So he did watch and listen and in the evenings he would drop by on old Father Lyle's because there was nothing else to do. The two would sit in Lyle's conservatory among the ferns and ratty white straw lawn chairs and Humphrey would provide the latest gossip. Ross had become a toady, he said. The silly fool was blowing himself up every day and croaking through the halls. He had a man in training. All was very hush-hush, but Humphrey had checked the Operation roster and found that the man of the hour was, God help them, the guard dog Toby Pitt . . .

'Oh,' Lyle said, 'so it's going to be a picnic in the Amazon.'

'I'm not really sure what they're planning.' Humphrey was sipping Lyle's sherry, drilling his finger into the soil of a monstrous potted orchid.

'Oh, it's going to be the Amazon. I know Vic Ross.' Lyle's own sherry kept sloshing up the sides of his glass whenever his hands began to shake, and his tattersall cuff was stained from other nights. 'Vic Ross is going to send that bugger down in the jungle and have him tramp around on Kohl's doorstep until he uncovers a plot. The idiots.' Whereupon Lyle knocked back the last in his glass, and coughed loudly. How else did a gentleman display his anger? . . .

Two days later Humphrey returned with a sort of confirmation of the old man's theory. Ross really was sending Pitt to Brazil. An Army shuttle would get him down. Final landing was supposed to be on a very secret base a few hundred miles south of Belém, so secret the maps didn't even show it.

On this particular evening the two men had stepped out into the garden, into the cold dusk. They were walking along the brick path under the boughs of sycamores. Lyle had torn off a supple twig, swishing at the air as he walked. Humphrey's head was bumping on his shoulders. 'Do you think they'll find anything?' The round man was breathing hard.

'Of course they'll find something. Probably get a fairly good catch. But it's the Brazilians, the larger picture, one worries about. Will the end justify the risk? It's that sort of situation.' He was moving crabwise where the moss had run over the bricks. 'Then, too, Toby Pitt might get his head blown off.'

'I don't know,' was all Humphrey could contribute to that. For a while their shoes made only oily sounds as they were squelched over the mossy path. The damp sky above was growing blacker. The first trill of crickets broke and echoed across the garden. Finally Humphrey rolled his shoulders back. 'By the way,' he said, 'I saw the report on the Kohl situation. There were definitely two men killed the night we lost Kristian. It's positive. And one was killed the same way as Simeon.'

Lyle's neck went rigid. He twisted to face Humphrey. They had come around to the porch again, and the shadows of the vines were fluttering above them. Humphrey had reached out to pluck at the vines of ivy. 'I have my own ideas . . .'

'Sure' – Severson smiled – 'so have I.' His hands were fists in his pockets, his back was humped, his head was down. It was only last night that he'd dropped onto the sofa, feet on the comforter, and while Chopin had drifted through the house had tried to come to terms with *that* Robin Turner. 'But he's harder to pin down than one would think.'

'What makes you say that?'

'Well, I mean that, yes, in one sense Robin Turner is a sort of traitor. After all, he secretly used us for his own ends. But somehow traitor doesn't satisfy. It doesn't completely explain it. Perhaps it's too strong a word. Yes, he's gone dirty, but not for the usual reasons. Harry May, Kim Philby, I can account for those two. They believed in *history*, which is the Communist's substitute for God and man. But how do we account for a Robin Turner? Can we say that he was morally justified in lying and stealing because of the pain, the loss that he suffered? Can we say that? Can we say that because Kurt Kohl is an evil man Turner is justified. I would think that these are questions worth considering.'

Humphrey's face had pulled itself into a frown. 'I don't know.' He felt a pang, though, because after all Robin in a way was his discovery . . . his and Kristian's.

'Still,' Lyle said, 'there has to be a Robin Turner that none of us ever saw firsthand. He was always a model boy, always all things to all people. But what, as they say, made him run?'

Humphrey allowed himself to say what he'd been thinking for some time, and it paralleled the old man's hints. 'Yes, they can say that Turner is a monster, or a traitor, or whatever, but I'll tell you one thing that I know is true. I just know it.'

'Go ahead.'

'If Kristian is with Turner right now, if she's actually running with him, then it's because she *wants* to. She wants to be with him. And that makes him truly something else . . .'

First light, and a flat brown Ford met Toby Pitt three blocks down from his apartment. At the Langley gates Vic Ross himself was waiting. Vic was always there for the send-off. Coach and player; there was even a locker room feel to the waiting room with its drab green walls and tiled floor. Coffee brewed on the hot plate and if you wanted, they could do you with some eggs and a Danish. But Toby could never eat before a run. Too many butterflies in his stomach.

Johnny Short from Technical Services was another early riser, flitting about, swinging a flight bag, singing out, 'Here we go again, Tob.' His end was the Nikon and the telephoto lens. There were three forms for Toby's scrawl. One was for Johnny, one for Victor, and one for Uncle Sam.

Five minutes before the go, and Vic cleared the waiting room. This was pep-talk time, and Ross put a thigh on the table. Casual, nothing to get uptight about; that was the way to send them off. 'Next time the door opens, you go.' Just like Vic to keep a run on schedule, must have been the Navy in him. He also liked maps, but map-time was over. 'Severson screwed it up' – he grinned – 'now it's our turn. You know the target. You know the stakes, and I can't think of another goddamn thing to say.'

Trotting out to the chopper was the best part. Toby played it like a player taking the field in the first innings. Sure it was corny, but what the hell? He was looking good, flight bag flapping at the shoulder, slapping the hands of the guys he passed. Happy Jack was shouting out the same old gag: 'Keep a tight ass, kid.' Then the whole damn crew was waving him off, and they kept on waving as the blades went revving, and the chopper wobbled up, and finally sailed out over Virginia . . .

All through that gray day and into the following night Toby was shuttled through an operational fantasy. The route was secret. They just took you places. The chopper dropped him off in some sterile base east of Langley, where only barracks broke the landscape of green hills and the distant mesh of cyclone fencing. From here they hustled him onto a waiting plane. The pilot was a chatty Southern boy, called himself Butane Dempsey, said he'd

208

been flying out the Special-Op guys for eighteen months now. He also claimed he knew 'every trick in the book,' and the only way to go down this route was to go down stoned. So Dempsey blew himself out with bennies, and Toby took some grass . . . But even that couldn't provide an easy way to the jungle, not when the end of the line was this shaggy, half-lit strip at midnight, right in the midst of the rain forest.

In this gorge between the waves of vegetation, the Company service broke down. When the plane backed off again into the night, there was nothing. All real life was huddled in an iron shack at the end of the strip. Inside, Toby found a couple of listless stringers in drip-dry suits, tossing out cards on a rickety table. No one seemed to be in charge. They couldn't, it appeared, have cared less about Pitt. There was only the slap of blackjack cards, and the air conditioner rattling uselessly away. 'I'm looking for a guy named Alverado,' Toby said.

'Alverado?' The bleary, unshaven wreck of a man hardly seemed alive. 'Now where the fuck is Alverado?' The other laughed.

So Toby laughed too, not understanding but needing to be one of them. 'Ah, give me a break.'

His sour host only laughed harder. So Toby poured himself a tumbler of gin and lay down on the ratty cot. Headachey, dizzy . . . finally one more gin let him crash into sleep. When he woke up the stringers were gone, but slouched against the wall, smoking, watching him, was Alverado. 'Call me Danny,' the lank mulatto said. 'I'll call you captain. Fair?'

Toby wasn't sure. Here was his guide, half Indian, half Black, a grubby junglebunny with rotting teeth and a whiskey smile. His lips had recently been split in a fight. 'Well, I'm all you got,' the guide told him. Which was true.

They breakfasted on fried pork sizzled on an open fire in a pit at the back of the compound, and sour coffee. 'Who were those guys last night?' Toby was still a bit numb, milling over the mud and black ash, watching his guide and the spitting fat in the pan.

'Those guys?' Danny shook his curly hair and whistled. A bird was screaming from the circle of palms around them. 'I don't know those guys,' Danny said. 'They're gone.'

A hungry dog, roped by the neck to the shed, had caught the smell of meat and was beginning to strain for it. 'Well, are they Company?'

Danny sniffed. 'Yeah, sure, Company, same as you, Captain.' He began to pluck out the wads of fat from the pan and toss them to the dog. 'Mean,' he mumbled on, 'you don't want to fuck with them,' and lobbed more meat to the dog.

'And this place? What's this place?' Toby was tamping a crumpled cigarette against his fingernail.

'This place is a . . . what you call it? . . . a way station? Yeah, it's a way station for all you tough guys passing through.' He even smiled when he said it.

Alverado had a jeep, fairly new, but the hot damp was already beginning to eat away at it. There was nothing you could do about the jungle, he said. If the animals and the natives didn't get you, then for sure your friends would. So Danny had a couple of M16's and a government issue .45 automatic. The rifles he wrapped with oilcloth and kept in the well of the jeep. The .45 he always carried on him. There was also a submachine gun, some German model. Apparently he had a thing about it, because he wouldn't let Toby see it. He said the gun had sentimental value, that he'd taken it from a buddy who had died of snakebites. Toby wondered what the hell he was talking about.

They took the jeep along a beaten trail some eight miles into the heartland, where the trail died and the jungle became all-consuming. The canopy of leaves was the only sky. They were following a stagnant river or sometimes threading the edge of a bog. Ferns and creeper vines grew in the sodden hollows. The creeks were red from tannin leaves. Macaws and kingfishers called from above. In the groin of buttress roots from an andira tree they saw a swarm of ants feasting on a litter of new-born pigs.

By noon the heat and steaming air had pretty well wasted Toby . . . he had to keep on sucking to catch his breath. Finally, they rested in a mango grove, propped themselves against the trunks and stared up to the forest roof and the shifting net of light. 'Kohl,' Toby began . . . 'Kohl. How far from here?'

Danny was spitting out the sap of some wild gum he had begun to chew. 'Not too far, Captain. Tonight we spend in a village. Tomorrow night we spend in Kohl's asshole.'

'And this village?'

'Just a village, Captain. It's a *garimpeiro's* village. How do you say it? Prospector. These guys come down for gold, then they all go bad on booze and *maculo*.'

A monkey began to scream. '*Maculo*?' Toby said. 'What's that? Is that the shits?'

Danny popped a shriveled gourd. 'Yeah, it turns your guts to water, eats your stomach away. Everything kills the *garimpeiro*. The Indians shoot him, the ranchers, even Kohl kills him. He doesn't like him on his land. So these guys are a dying breed. Pretty soon you got big companies coming down here. You got Exxon. You got IBM. You got . . . I don't know, a few years back you got the Brazilians yelling, "Amazon for the people only!" But money yells the loudest. So the prospectors are kaput. In fact, everyone is . . . the Indians, the ranchers, the homesteaders, me, you . . .'

Toby could believe it . . . tramping through the compost of decay, tearing at the strangler vines, warding off sucker flies and huge mosquitoes. By now the earthy red glow was flushing to an unearthly copper haze. Before full darkness the veils of trailing lichen broke suddenly away to the slashed and burned clearing of the village. Here lay the tilted plank shacks, some thatched with palm leaves, others roofed with iron sheets. Most of these sagging hovels were unlit, but there was laughter spilling from the trading post at the far end of the muddy road.

The trading post and bar sometimes doubled as a dance hall. But no one wanted to dance with the prostitutes tonight. The locals were happy enough to loaf at the wooden tables or sprawl on the floor. Alverado had boasted that he was a regular here but all he got for banging through the rusted screen were a few nods. Even the hookers weren't on the make tonight.

Warm beer was a dollar a bottle. Also available were hunks of gray fish in soup. The bouncer wore a Smith & Wesson. A sawed-off shotgun hung above the bar.

Pitt and Alverado nudged their chairs into a circle of dark faces. An Indian with a bandaged head and puffy jaws was groaning, pointing to the brown gauze above his eyes. 'He says there was a fight, two guys got it,' Alverado said, 'but they were creeps and no one gives a damn. In fact everyone here is celebrating. Now the bodies are being eaten in the river . . .'

A radio was blaring out the tinny strains of a clipped steel band. One drunken Black began to rock himself back and forth. 'Where do we sleep?' Toby finally asked. He was picking the bones off his tongue.

'They got a room.' Danny shrugged. 'Best place in town.' The moths were smashing against the windows.

That night they shared a tiny room above the store. There were filthy mattresses on the planks. Mosquito netting hung from lines and for an hour the rain hammered off the corrugated roofs. After that there was nothing but the whining insects and the jungle.

In the morning Toby wandered out to the street, where he saw a thin girl crying on the porch of a shack. She had cut her fingers with a broken bottle, but when he tried to help she told him to go away. For a meal they made do with moldy bread and tepid Coke. They moved on by mid-morning. Further still the jungle became devouring again. Through the morning and well past noon the two men hacked into the curtains of hanging bush. A downpour broke in the afternoon, and they sat it out in the roots and fallen logs. Once, not far above them, the foliage came alive with shivering frenzy . . . something howled and they saw a dark shape crashing through the trees and scampering away.

By the fading light and longer shadows they were climbing higher ground where the vegetation was not so thick and the steamy heat was falling behind. Dusk came at the mountain's summit, and they even saw stars through the broken patches of trees.

Toby would have stopped and spent the night in the relative calm of the jungle hilltop, but Danny pushed him on until they were slithering down the other side, plunging into darkness. Thorns tore at their clothing. Vines pulled at their legs. When they finally sank to the rotting leaves, they might have been at the bottom of the sea.

When Toby said as much, Alverado shook his head. 'You can't tell because of the night, but what you want is down there . . . down there is Kohl's land.'

'Where?' Toby saw only the blackness.

'There,' Danny whispered, 'there, through the trees. Wait until dawn, then you'll see.'

Toby's wrists were already swelling from insect bites. 'Wait here? All night?'

Danny was sucking his palm. 'You'll see,' he breathed, then rolled on his back and began to thread the mosquito netting through the brush above them. The net was becoming their cocoon, but all around them the bugs were gnashing and humming.

An hour passed, then another. Toby was crimped up in a sticky trance. Whenever he closed his eyes he saw snakes uncoiling, the jungle began to heave and vibrate. 'Be still,' Danny kept whispering. 'Be like the Indians.' But Toby couldn't keep his muscles from jerking. The insects alone were tearing him apart, and then some howling noise would shatter him completely. He couldn't stop digging his nails in his thigh, couldn't stop clenching his teeth against this whirling jungle.

Dawn came to a thundering silence. Even the birds seemed stunned. First there were long tubes of violet light breaking through the upper reaches. Below, the cobwebs and flimsy strands of moss were glowing purple. Toby, dazed, feverish, hurried down the hill, crawling on his knees through a flood of low vapor that rose from the forest floor. Alverado rolled down to his side, and now both men lay in the fingers of rising mist while vague sculptures became substantial in the breaking light. And when the watery jungle grew solid again, they saw that there was no real jungle at all. 'What the hell?' Toby was muttering. 'My bag, man. Get my bag.' Then he was fumbling with his camera, fitting on the lens, winding, and finally clicking away.

'What is it?' Danny strained to see. 'Hey, what?' He was tugging on a green mesh of canvas, not real leaves at all. 'He's tricked us,' Danny said. 'Look at this. He's tricked us.' But he still couldn't understand the steel forms, like sawhorses that stretched out below.

'They're *oil derricks*' – Toby coughed – 'he's got himself an *oil field*.' He was rocking back and forth, snapping

214

the shutter. Further back there were sausage shapes of more equipment, bits of pipe sticking through the camouflage and branching off with valves beyond a row of prefabricated sheds. Directly ahead lay a pyramid of steel barrels.

Toby, his camera over his back, had begun to crawl forward, but Alverado was trying to pull at his ankles. 'No,' he said tightly. 'Listen. Hear that?'

Overhead the sky had begun to rattle with a shuddering wind. It was growing louder, closer. 'Chopper,' Danny said, 'we got to go.'

Then the light was glinting off a swooping Plexiglas bubble and Danny had spun back into the bracken. Toby was clawing at the roots, but the chopper was dropping, hovering right above them, the blades sending up a storm of leaves.

Toby's boots kept slipping in the rippling soil. Spears of dwarf palms were exploding up. Then above the wind came a burst of fire. Toby twisted to watch as a man leaned out from the cockpit and fired from his hip. A slash of air cut the side of his head. He tasted blood, and tumbled deeper into the bush.

Now they lay in the mottled shadows beneath a skin of trembling moss. Toby was moaning, hands clamped to his ear, rocking back and forth. There were ribbons of blood on his face, more soaking through his collar. 'Oh God, they shot my ear off!'

Danny only touched his finger to his lips. 'Shhh, you got to be cool, Captain.'

Toby's legs were balled up to his chest. 'Well, *God*, they shot my *ear* off.'

Danny began to tear away blue paper from rolls of cotton gauze. He too was groaning, but also laughing. 'Yeah, Captain. But listen, it's an improvement. Don't sweat it. It's an improvement.'

Toby was puffing out air and spit, his bloody fingers reaching for the gauze.

'No, Captain . . . really, now you'll be looking good, you'll be looking cool,' and he kept right on as he knelt by Toby's side to press the wads of gauze to the wound.

Toby was growing quiet, spellbound with shock. He seemed to be watching a dangling spider. The creature was twirling in the stagnant heat, while the shimmering mandala of the web hung quivering from a taut fan of leaves.

Alverado too had become silent, although his fingers kept uncoiling long strips of gauze. Soon the entire crown of Toby's skull was wrapped in bandages. 'Okay, Captain,' Danny sighed. 'Okay, okay. Now you'll be good as new.'

'What do you mean?' Toby was ripping off clots of blood from his hands. 'I'll look like a fucking idiot without my ear. I want that fucking ear.'

Danny slumped to the soft mud. He laid an arm across Pitt's shoulder. 'Ah now, Captain. What's a fucking ear, anyway? Besides you still got one left.'

Toby's face was rubbery. Finally his cheeks were streaked with tears. 'Why?' he was gasping. 'Why? I'm going to look like a dope. They're all going to fucking laugh at me.' ·

Danny's fingers clutched him tighter. 'No one's going to laugh, Captain. You're going to be a hero. They're going to think you look good. The women especially. They're going to think you look real good.' He started tugging at Toby's hair. 'See, all you got to do is grow your hair long. You grow it long right around here. You grow it nice and long, then no one can see you don't have an ear. But even if they do see, they're going to think you're cool. You just say, "Yeah, I had the sucker shot right off. It was shot off by the richest man in the world." It'll be like having a medal,' and he tapped Toby's chest.

Pitt was now breathing deeply, slowly. 'Yeah? Well,

maybe you can go back and find that ear of mine. Yeah, you go back and get it, man. Then I can have the thing laminated, or maybe even bronzed. I'll wear it around my neck. Imagine, having that baby bronzed and wearing it around your neck on a chain?' He was laughing into his fingers now. 'Wouldn't that just be the funniest thing you ever saw?' But his voice had already begun to crack, and he was whimpering again. 'Oh God! It hurts. It hurts and I can't even believe it's happening.' He sagged back and began to cry, this fierce guard dog did . . .

Infection set in. There were hard jokes along the route back to Langley about how they would have to amputate poor Toby's head. 'Or else we can cut off your other ear,' said someone, a tanktown doctor on the Army shuttle. Then there was an awful muddle about security. Toby's guide had orders for only Company medics, but the lout they sent didn't know anything about this CIA stuff, didn't want to know. Finally a compromise was reached, and Toby's wound was properly dressed.

Once in Langley, Vic Ross's boy received the best. The medical office even had a specialist flown in, and for several days there was some talk about plastic ears and tricky skin grafts. But then Toby's ear was pretty much forgotten as the enormity of his find was realized.

The intel breakdown project was now headed by another Ross staffer, the bird-boy, Lewis Dixon. Running next to Dixon was Norva Baugh, a sparky readhead with a bent for soft science and hard industry. Along the route the two team leaders picked up several helpmates, specialists in imagery analysis and photographic interpretation. Everyone wanted to join the party. There was no end of jealousy.

At the center of the storm were the seven Pitt photographs, as they had come to be called. In all, Toby had actually taken more than a dozen shots of the Kohl land, but only seven were useful. And what a tale these seven told.

Dixon supervised the analysis group that clearly identified the sausage-shaped blur as a separator tank with a capacity of eighty to one hundred thousand barrels of oil per day. There were also several wellheads, each capable of passing thirty to forty thousand barrels per day. A large booster station was deduced to lie underground and one photograph even showed a line of pipe for big-load oil.

Equipment inventory estimates were tallied for cost. Dixon took the conservative line and published only the base figures, but he calculated that Kohl could have picked up a separator tank for a quarter of a million, maybe more, certainly not less. The wellheads went for ten to fifteen thousand. The pipe was indeterminate, because there was no way to calculate length, but Dixon added in another million to cover meters, water lines, power plants and other miscellanea. Dixon felt that given Kohl's easy route out along the river, plus what he guessed would be a light drill, the complete per barrel cost would not exceed thirteen dollars, a figure that allowed for substantial blunders. A realistic low was far less than that. All this taken into consideration, along with the amount of oil indicated by equipment handling capacity, Langley went on critical alert.

For three days the Ross team toiled in the murky depths of statistical estimates. Scraps poured in from every area, but still Dixon demanded more. Send a satellite over, he said. Send over 'Blackbird.' He was finally appeased when research turned up the Radar Amazon project, RADAM. This aerial survey from Litton Industries turned out to be a bonanza, and RADAM kept Dixon and team busy for another three days.

Yet for the broadest perspective of them all, Harlon

Watson brought in the old oil hand, Jeffrey Boyal. No one, said Watson, knew more about the oil world than Jeff. Dixon and the others might have taken odds, but there wasn't time. So the shaggy gray Harvard man entered the ranks of Ross's team, and soon proved himself the most valuable mind of them all.

Like Lyle, like Harlon, like most of his own generation, Jeffrey Boyal favored the historical approach. After all, the man was also a part of the history he spoke of. Stories varied . . . some said he had been a loyal British Petroleum boy, others that he had always played both ends against the middle, which meant that he had always been an agent in the stable of Harlon Watson. Either way he had seen the industry and truly lived the life of the shambling oil dog from Baghdad to Bangkok. They said that Boyal began in the baroque days of oil when the world had been divided between Henri Deterding of Shell and Walter Teagle of Exxon. Both were old-line oil aristocracy, Teagle by way of his grandfather who served with Rockefeller in the early Pennsylvania days. Watson recruited Boyal. London trained him, and the probable target was the wayward Henri Deterding, who by that time was living in Germany as a full-fledged Nazi. At the war's end, however, Jeffrey was still only an irregular spy, whereas his place in the oil world was firmly established. They still talked about his Middle East days, how he knocked around in Iran and Kuwait, how be bought and sold the weaker tribal heads and kissed up to the stronger ones. There were supposed to have been all those starry desert nights under the billowing tents of emirs when Boyal sucked on hookahs and his dreamy eyes saw petrodollars. For a time he went completely native with a camel and burnoose. Some said he very nearly qualified as a latter-day Lawrence, but those who knew him better said that old Jeffrey actually detested the Arabs.

For two decades Boyal watched the dance of the Seven Sisters. There was Exxon, Gulf, Texaco and Mobil, Socal, Shell and British Petroleum. Sometimes they fought among themselves. Just as often they fought as a team. He remembered days when they cried out for God and Country, and other days when they kicked up prices hand in hand with some cocky Arab sheikh. But next to Kurt Kohl, even Texaco was as pure as virgin snow. So choosing between Kohl and any one of the Seven Sisters to control a substantial source of Amazonian oil was damn near like choosing between Hitler and Santa Claus.

For explanation Boyal drafted a forty-two-page brief as an amendment or commentary to the Dixon report. The main thrust of the Boyal brief naturally dealt with the viability of Amazon oil. Conclusions were based upon projected oil reserves and operating costs as determined by the Dixon team.

All felt confident in the accuracy of the projected figures. Not only were there fairly detailed geological studies of the Kohl region, but they also had a bottom-line equipment inventory. So Boyal's report was no mere 'think piece' on a theoretical situation. The numbers were real enough. Dixon put the Amazonian reserves at twenty billion barrels – certainly a figure worth fighting for.

Boyal went on to argue that the Amazon oil was particularly important in light of Mexican and North Slope Alaskan oil status. The Mexican reserves, he said, although sizable, could not be considered a reliable source for some time to come. Development was moving slowly due to Mexico's insistence that the goods stay in their hands. Obviously, Boyal explained, they've learned a thing or two from the Arabs. So the United States could not realistically hope to sit in on the Mexican game unless she was willing to meet a stiff ante. But Boyal could hardly blame the Mexicans. Oil friendships, he said, were always greasy.

As for Alaskan oil, the Great White Hope, Boyal was even more pessimistic. 'Here is a project,' he wrote, 'that lies squarely on high-barrel floor.' He claimed that the project's selling point – reduced foreign dependence – may have been a valid argument, but to anyone who really knew the game, the Alaskan project was just one more energy crisis scam. North Slope oil was never intended to compete in a buyer's market. The stuff just cost too much. If the market ever dropped, the pipeline would go bust, and every taxpayer in the country would know that the president wore no clothes.

'But the Brazilians,' Boyal wrote, 'are whores.' With pressure, Exxon, Mobil or any of the Sisters could move in and pick up Kohl's concession for a song. And there was a source for you. The oil was cheap and plentiful.

As for Kohl himself, Boyal said that there had been mavericks before. Armand Hammer had been one. J. Paul Getty had been another. But wild as those two had seemed at the time, they had still been inextricably linked with American interests. They had been far less interested in rocking the boat than climbing aboard. Kohl was different. Kohl had nothing to lose. He was an old man, an old crab wedged too tight in foreign rocks. You couldn't get him out by conventional means, legal or not. He couldn't be bought, bribed, or burned. 'Nevertheless,' Boyal wrote, 'it is out of the question as regards our interest that such a figure remain in control of these twenty billion barrels of Western Hemisphere oil.'

The paper was released in the morning. The screams began in the early afternoon. Harlon Watson was besieged with queries. Everyone wanted something. There were requests for confirmation. (As if the facts were not enough.) Alaskan backers demanded apologies. There was no end to the ruckus.

In an attempt to keep the lid on, Harlon decided he

would put the outspoken Boyal on stage, so that evening he called an ad hoc meeting of all concerned. Not surprisingly everyone and his brother tried to crash the gate. Guest of honor was Jerry Crundle from the National Security Council's Special Coordination Committee. Jerry was no Kissinger or Brzezinski, but he was major league all the same. For the NSC meant the president, which also meant that Victor Ross had finally made the big time.

For this final round, this beginning of the end, the party was held in the large north conference room – the baron's room, Lyle had always called the straw-brown hall. The walls were matted with laminate strips of knotty pine. The table was oak, but the chairs were covered with Naugahyde. A bowl of dried flowers and gourds sat on the marble mantel, as a hint to the passing autumn, while beyond the triple glass lay still one more view of the Fairfax country, a spiked and black tangle of bare branches on the rolling lawn.

There were twelve in all around that thick slab of oak. Ross and his people took the head. Watson held the center chair across from Jerry Crundle and his aide. On the flanks sat two Special Operations hounds in charcoal gray. David Kluge from the Energy Department was a latecomer to this party, and he wore what he always wore: the polyester of a hard-nosed civil servant. Cross-grained to the polyester, the charcoal grays, Vic Ross's plaid and Watson's country tweed was Norva Baugh in prim twill skirt and a little lace at the cuffs and collar. Like Kristian, she was thought by the others to have a touch of the pixie. Today her hair was done very thirties. Sitting down she had attempted a joke as the electronic baffle hummed a scale. No one had laughed, and now she sat still and tight as the others.

Crundle had a gap in his front teeth that gave him a vaguely predatory look. Now, however, he was giving them all his winning political grin. 'Well, I'd like to say that first of all this is one hell of a way to start the Christmas season.' Laughter all around. 'Next I'd like to say that the president *has not* been informed, because no one wants to look like an ass in case you boys are wrong.' More smiles.

'Oh hell, if that's all you're worried about,' Boyal said, 'then I'll tell him.' Some laughter.

'I think we've heard enough from you, Jeffrey.' Harlon's tongue was bulging in his cheek.

Crundle was now leaning forward, the folder in his hands. He was gently rapping the bound sheets on the tabletop. 'Now people, now really? How serious is this? I think that's a pretty fair way to start the play.'

Boyal met the challenge. 'That depends on how badly America needs oil.'

'Oh for God's sakes, Jeff.' Watson could have elbowed his friend in the ribs.

But Boyal was pleased with himself. He hadn't held the spotlight in years, not like this. 'All right . . . now we know that Kohl has got the oil, and we know it's cheap, and we know there's plenty of it. But to give you the whole picture let me digress to the technical side for a moment.' He turned to Norva. 'You'll help me out, dear?' He clasped his hands beneath his chin. 'It's not the easiest job in the world to determine how much oil is in any given patch of ground. Even when you've got a strike, and the old pump's going at it madly, it's a difficult question. How much oil? You'll hear that question from every direction. What you usually get are only rough estimates. So from here on out, people, everything is going to be in estimates.'

Kluge had bunched himself up to listen. His arms were knotted at his chest. 'What's your variance factor?'

Boyal threw up his hands. 'I don't know. Norva?'

'It's just a straight estimate,' she said. 'If you want the statistical base, I can get you that.'

Boyal nodded too. 'All right then, from the top. Kurt Kohl goes into the Amazon Basin to plant trees – ' Someone started to interrupt. 'Yes, I know there's more, but let's just keep it simple. All right. He goes down there for wood, and one day he decides to make a geological survey. Maybe he's looking for gold, maybe Eldorado. It doesn't matter. He hires out to a firm and they do the survey for him. In all probability the survey is the first thing he did down there. Surveys are always the first step to drilling. You have an idea that there's oil down there because of the lay of the land, adjacent wells, or what have you. But in order to pinpoint a source, you've got to do a survey.' Boyal stopped, scratched his head. 'I really think Norva should take it up from here. Norva?'

She began in her clipped schoolteacher's voice. 'All right, basically there are several ways to survey. We suspect that Kohl took the common route, which consists of seismic tests. Our own little survey' – and here she smiled at Boyal – 'was a little less direct, but I can cover that later if you like. Let me first tell you about the probable Kohl test. We suspect that he used a standard method . . . You have modest explosive charges set into the ground about eight to a mile. When the charges are detonated, seismographs record the echoes from under the ground strata. If you saw a graph this next bit wouldn't sound so silly . . . What you get are sort of ripples and bumps which indicate the presence of rock structures likely to provide suitable traps for oil. It's a fairly quick and inexpensive job. You can run off maybe twenty or twenty-five such shots in a day. At the end of the line you return and repeat the shots down a parallel line a mile or so to the left and right. Follow me, gentlemen?' She flashed a sly smile down the rows of heads.

'Carry on,' Watson returned.

She bowed her head and took another breath. 'Eventually after all those shots you end up with a broad area of grid.'

Suddenly Crundle shook his head, and raised two fingers in the air. 'Uhh, has anyone thought of trying to contact the fellow who actually made the test?' He let his glasses slip down his nose, peeked over the rims.

Ross tensed. He was glaring at Watson, rapping his thumbs on his thigh. 'Yeah,' he snapped, 'we've thought about it.'

Crundle flicked his hand. 'What? Hit a sore spot?'

Watson's tongue was clicking off the roof of his mouth. 'Tell you what, Jerry, after all this you and I will have a little chat.'

But the nervous Ross was still trying to smooth it over. 'Oh, come on. There's nothing mysterious. Yes, we have made extensive efforts to locate the party responsible, and yes, we have had some success, but let's just take this one step at a time, shall we?'

So Norva took it again. 'Exploration is the only really unpredictable aspect of the operation. Once you know there's oil down there the rest is relatively easy. You've all seen the photographs so you know how far Kohl has taken it. He's virtually all ready to go. He's placed the valve systems, the flow lines.'

Boyal patted her wrist. 'Why don't you just quickly run through the sequence?'

Norva began to rattle off the words on her fingers. 'The oil comes up through the wellhead, flows through a gathering line past rock traps which remove sand and other debris. Then it passes through various separators – those are the sausage shapes in the photos. They strip the water and salt from the oil by means of electric plates and the gas by means of baffles. The oil then moves through further gas-oil separators and finally into a large-diameter crude oil pipeline which either takes the oil directly to a tanker or an intermediate station. That's pretty much all there is to it.'

Boyal picked it up. 'Gentlemen, if I may continue.' He stared at the chewed end of his ballpoint pen. 'I had Norva run down the drilling process only so that you would have some appreciation for my next, and very critical, point. Money, gentlemen. Money.' He looked at Jerry Crundle. Then, still turning the mangled end of his pen, he continued with, 'There are very finite costs to an operation such as Norva has just described. The figures are broken down in my memo, but to summarize let me bring up the concept of the daily barrel cost. This would be the cost to produce a barrel of oil a day. Now the average well runs about a half a million, and there are two vital factors which will really determine the cost. One is the depth of the well, and what sort of rock formations the bit has got to pass through. The other is how far you must pump your oil to get it to market. If you have a terminal operation wherein you have to pump it to a station and then onto a ship your cost is even higher.'

Dixon had to throw in, 'Terminal operations are a bitch.' He was trying to sound knowing . . . 'it's like herding too much baggage onto a plane.'

Boyal could have rolled his eyes, but his nod said it all. He hadn't liked Dixon much from the start. 'But in a nutshell,' he began again, 'Kurt Kohl has it easy on both scores. We managed to piece together a geological profile of the areas that he was drilling in, and I can say pretty conclusively that he's had a fairly shallow and easy drill. As a matter of fact he's got places where the oil is just about breaking ground on its own.'

A Special Operations voice rumbled out. 'Then why the hell haven't we discovered it before?'

226

Boyal blew out air. 'I was, of course, speaking figuratively. Oil doesn't actually leak to the surface. More important than the easy drill, however, is the proximity of the fields to the river. You can load a barge or sink a line, so you're looking at an absolute maximum daily barrel cost of two hundred dollars. And my guess is that even that's too high.'

Harlon, playing off the lead-in, said, 'Which means, Jeff?'

And Boyal, who must have had his line prepared, rattled off: 'Which *means* that we cannot afford to let Kurt Kohl control what is potentially the ninth largest oil source in the world. Especially not at those prices, we can't.'

Adjacent to the conference room lay smaller, cozier chambers. The walls were darker, there were maple turns to the chairs, the legs of the table were claw-and-ball. Time was less exact here. The carriage clock chimed imprecisely. But one came to love the gleam of crystal and tinkling brass, even if the ruffled shag, a languorous maroon, sometimes made the older men a bit drowsy.

Harlon liked these rooms – indulgent, yes; pretentious, yes; but you had to appreciate the thought behind them. So he came here now with Ross and Crundle, and they sagged into the Chippendales and grumbled into their Scotch.

Crundle was toying with the bric-a-brac on the mantel. 'Tell me,' he said, 'how would the Brazilians take to all this?' He was fingering a horn of scrimshaw. Outside lay the fading landscape of a Virginia evening.

'They'll be obliging,' Ross answered. He was rolling his brandy around in his snifter. 'They like Kohl because he's got money, but if he was out I think they'd be more than happy to dance with us.'

On the wall behind them hung a meaningless still life of fruit in a silver compote. Harlon had always fancied the rococo frame. 'Now and again you'll hear a bit of saber rattling, a bit of old "Brazil first" talk. It's nothing, we can get the oil and get it at a very reasonable price. There's no problem on that score.'

Ross rose into the light of the graceful porcelain lamp, his hands moving across the furniture. 'What remains then, Jerry, is simply this. How far do you want us to go?'

Crundle was rolling the wand of scrimshaw between his palms. 'Oh, is that it? Well, I think there's also the matter of how far you've already gone.' He was watching Harlon. 'I asked you about the possibility of tracking down the geologist who conducted those tests for Kohl. And you blushed, you distinctly blushed.'

Ross began to twist the tassels on the floral lampshade. 'We happened to find the man in New Orleans. So yes, we've already had some direct contact with him.'

Crundle slapped the scrimshaw in his hand. 'Located him, huh? And approached him covertly, no doubt. And pressured him into talking, no doubt. And that's why you're both so willing to swear from here to Jesus on that twenty-billion-barrel figure, isn't it? And what's more that's why you're both so goddamn sneaky with me . . . because you've just broken your charter up, down and all around. What are the counts? Bugging a private citizen? Undue pressure? What else? Anyway, as if I give a damn what you did. So you want to know how far I'll go? All right, I'll tell you, get me the damn oil, but *don't* blow it. And that, gentlemen, will be the word from above.'

Watson, however, would not be outdone. He even risked a wink at Ross. 'If it's unorthodox you want – '

Crundle leaned against the maple edge of the library table. 'Now don't go testing me, Harlon.'

'Not testing, simply giving you the current situation. And it's a rather interesting one at that. I'm going to speak and wash my hands of it.'

Ross had suddenly begun to look glum, his fingers pale and thin among the crimson tassels. 'Sure, tell him.'

So Harlon did. 'There's something happening down there, Jerry. Kurt Kohl has made enemies all along the way. He can be a real bad guy. You know that, but now it seems he's taken a step too far. Ah, now it seems that he's going to be in a *lot* of trouble – '

'Simply tell me that we're not involved, Harlon,' Crundle interrupted.

But Watson only shook his head. 'A rather basic story of revenge. I can hardly come to terms with it myself. It involves a young man who was deeply hurt, emotionally and physically, by Kurt Kohl. Nice boy, really, from a good family.'

Crundle had begun to trace the maple border, his index finger following the swirls and grooves. 'And this boy is one of us?'

'Was one of us,' Watson said. 'He's gone renegade, and now he's about to launch his *own* little war party, without regard, of course, for the niceties of our relationship with a friendly government . . . You *know* how sensitive our superiors are to that sort of thing these days . . .'

Crundle began to dig at the maple even more intently. 'Spell it out. Is this boy about to move against Kurt Kohl?'

Watson hunched his shoulders. 'I would have to say something like that. And I would also have to say that we have been painfully aware of the danger from the start. One of our people runs out and terminates Kohl. Even though he's not officially with us now, it still would sit less than well with the White House. What if he were caught and he pointed the finger at us. We'd be the same old naughty boys, fishing in troubled waters at the expense of our government's international image, and so forth. You see how simply I'm laying it out.'

Crundle nodded. 'You're in the clear from here on out.'

'Very well then.' Watson sighed. 'Let me also say that we have made several attempts to abort this boy's plans.'

Then still pressing his fingers on the table so that his knuckles were white, still not looking up, Crundle finally said, 'But all that's changed, hasn't it? I mean, you're no longer sure that you *want* to stop the boy, is that it?'

Watson's breath whooshed out from between his teeth. 'It's a question of calculated risk versus potential gain. As I have suggested, in the beginning we felt it important to stop this boy because he might very well endanger US relations with Brazil, a friendly country with Latin sensitivity about its sovereignty, and so forth. Yes, we did not like Kohl, but we could not allow his death to occur under circumstances which might prove to be, well, embarrassing to the administration. In short, the gain was not, we judged, worth the risk.'

'But now,' Crundle said, 'now you feel that this risk of embarrassment is worth the potential gain . . .'

Watson snapped, 'We are talking about a good deal of oil, are we not?'

Crundle was smiling, nodding. 'Well, let's say for argument's sake that I too feel that it's now worth the risk. What then?'

Now Ross stepped into the lamp's shower of light, his cheeks seeming especially round in the shadows. 'As I see it we need only have one good man down there to insure our interests, to get us a foothold, if you will. I believe we have a man who cannot be easily traced back to us in the case of a problem. All right then, we send this man down with a laundered case of weapons. This will insure his place in the attack party. I was thinking we might even give him a howitzer. I'm sure this jungle party could use a

230

howitzer, and a West German model would be difficult to trace. Furthermore they break down easily, so we can drop it in with an un-marked chopper.'

Crundle's mouth began to pucker. He disliked these sorts of details. 'I think I understand,' he said quickly, then slid to his feet. 'But I'll have to check it out. There's the committee, and I'll want to speak to a few people.'

Watson too was livelier now. 'Test the water?'

'Mmm,' Crundle said. 'I hate the shock of the cold.'

Ross was already moving to the door. 'Oh, I think you'll find it warm enough, but ask around if you like.'

For some days thereafter Langley stood by while the powers above conferred. There wasn't much else to do but wait. Even Harlon Watson had no place in the upper reaches of Washington. Once, like Lyle Severson, he had known and loved that special sense of belonging . . . at least the final decisions had been closer to home. Not now . . . now they told you that you were not quite trusted, so there was nothing else to do but wait for word to trickle down.

Typically the first news was ambiguous. The barons are considering your proposal, said the rumor line. Another hollow day inched by, and a favorable word came through. Washington is pleased. Then the tidings became altogether more dramatic. Crundle, went the word, had met in absolute, so to speak, secrecy with some unnamed but very important figure within the secular oil establishment. Would you be interested in developing a certain petroleum concern should said concern become available through some unforeseen event? This was what Crundle was supposed to have asked. There were those who believed that Crundle's man was a certain Mr B. from Mobil. Others said that Jerry would only have gone to Exxon. In any case, regardless of who it had been, the response was said to have been a careful but clear yes (provided that Washington would cover in the event of a problem). 'Oh,' Jerry was supposed to have answered, 'we'll cover for you all right.'

So the end of the game became a shadow play. Nothing would be written down. Crundle met with Harlon Watson at his home. The old colonial place lay in a bower beneath gray limbs of trees, but the two men chose to saunter off toward the grass paddock beyond for their chat.

As they passed a crumbling sandbox now overgrown with weeds, and then a child's swing, tilted and rusting, Crundle asked, 'All grown up now?'

'The children?' Watson's eyes were watery in the cold. 'One teaches college. The other, the boy, he's working out West.' He felt a bit silly standing ankle-high in the frosted leaves. 'He's an anthropologist. Peculiar subject.'

Crundle looked up at the blue, glazed sky. 'Oh I don't know, would you rather have had him follow in your footsteps?'

Watson coughed. 'Good point.'

'I mean, it's not the same any more, is it?' Crundle said. He was running his hand along the rusted pole of the swing. 'The world's changed, the Company's changed.'

'Some say for the better.'

'What do you say?'

The old man was breathing hard in the crisp air. Leaves were cracking under his shifting weight. 'I miss the old clubhouse feel, if that's what you're driving at,' he said. 'But I suppose we are less . . . insular now, more . . . responsive to the mood of the nation.' He coughed again. 'Whatever the hell that means.'

They had wandered further along the ragged path, and now stood at the top of a windy hillock. Below lay dark tangles of rosebushes and a litter of frozen petals. 'I assume you know that there has been a decision,' Crundle was saying.

'We guessed.' Watson smiled. They were two bent figures on the rise, and just now the sun was blazing golden in the ice around them.

'It's the oil,' Crundle said. 'Nothing has really changed. It's the old energy crisis . . . no one is about to sniff at such a source.'

Watson's teeth had started chattering. He felt stiff, cold. Frost had gathered on his brogues. 'What we're about to do is let a bomb go off. I hope you fully understand that, because no one can ever tell exactly where the pieces are going to fall.'

'But you're going to have one reliable man down there. One of Ross's people, isn't that right?'

Watson nodded. 'He's been down there recently. He knows the ropes. Although last time he was shot up a bit. God knows why he wants another crack. But then they're all crazy, those Special-Op people.'

'And that boy,' Crundle said abruptly. 'The one who's after Kohl . . . what's he like?'

Watson bowed his head. 'I can't really say . . .'

'Well, he must be a tough one.' Crundle was squinting into the last streaks of amber light.

'In some ways I suppose he is, but in others . . . well, we'll never really know, will we? . . . There was a time when we all spoke very well of Robin. Now I expect we're obliged to consider him a traitor. But it's really a question of semantics, isn't it? By his lights he's embarked on a labor of love, or rather hate, if you see what I mean . . .'

Crundle pressed his heel into the patch of hard mud. A soft wind was blowing through the open land, bending the grass. 'You realize that afterward we can't possibly let him . . . continue. The boy, I mean. As has already been pointed out, he could cause us no end of difficulty.'

Watson puffed his cheeks, sighed. 'So I've been given to understand.'

Crundle squinted, turned to the old man. 'I know that this is the most difficult part.'

Watson nodded. His face was flushed. 'These sort of things are always very sad. All the way around they're very sad.'

'But I've been hoping that you'd be able to see beyond it,' Crundle continued. 'Harlon . . .' He almost reached out to touch the old man's elbow. '. . . We're very close to something that's going to prove vital. I've been hoping that perhaps you'd find it all, well, like the old days maybe?'

But, Harlon told himself, this part *is* the old days . . . tramping out through some desolate field so that the microphones don't pick you up, plotting a man's murder within the fabric of a guarded chat. No wonder Robin Turner *turned* out as he did. We have shown him all the moves.

11

Soon the days were tumbling over one another. Robin and Kristian were wholly together by now. Some deepest part of their beings had merged, and as they flew on into the southern latitudes they saw their pasts dissolve behind them.

They reached Belém before hard rain and landed in the afternoon beneath a slate gray sky. The old stone quarters were baked to earth colors, pale raw or deeply burnished. The palms along the esplanade were knife-edged and very green.

They took a room along Mango Street. Birds had nested in the eaves beneath the purple-tiled roof. More birds, even rare parrots perched in cages that swung from the crossbeams of thatched market stalls. But the air was hot and moist, and Kristian felt terribly alone unless she stayed very close to Robin. They were knitted together, and they did not regret for a minute what had been done.

For three days they lived in the torpid sway of the town, sipping coconut and rum on planked verandas, browsing down cobbled alleys where sly natives tried to sell them boa skins and all that other tourist claptrap. At night they could hardly sleep for the hiss of steel bands, the sound of natives leaning on the horns of their pickup trucks.

Then came a friend of Gabrial. Robin met him in the hotel bar. Kristian covered the entrance in case they'd been set up. For the first round Robin played the boy at a distance . . . he was cautious, stringing out the swarthy mulatto . . . and then it became pointless because the kid was nothing more than he claimed to be and Robin could be straight.

The boy was called Arujua, and he said that he would be the one to see them down the river to the doctor's camp. He was a little like Gabrial, squat and muscular. He said that Robin had come at just the right time. 'So me, I'm real glad, everyone is going to be glad. Because we love you, we love you for what you've done for us . . .'

Turner was still a little brittle. 'I have a girl with me,' he said softly, then twisted in his cane chair to nod through the fan of leaves that sprang from the potted palm. 'That girl sitting at the bar.'

Arujua craned to see. 'Oh sure, she can come. Sure, we'll treat her like a princess.' He reached and patted Turner's arm. 'Maybe she would like to meet me right now, you know? Maybe it would put her at ease.'

So Robin called her over, and they all sat drinking at the bamboo table among the shiny flat-backed rubber plants. 'Got to live for today,' the kid kept sing-songing. 'Live for today, for tomorrow we could be dead.'

Kristian was dipping her finger into her rum, bemused by the feeling of what it must have been like for old decadent colonizers . . . there was enough rococo gilt in the plaster moldings, enough varnished teak and rosettes of tiled parquetry to inspire anyone to such fantasy. Robin would have been the planter's wayward son while she the sultry blond, hanging from the arabesque windowsill. This was not the Brazil she had figured on. 'Anyway, I'm drunk,' she announced.

Later that night they wandered out along the esplanade. They walked arm in arm, Kristian between her two cavalier adventurers. A warm breeze from the sea kept stirring the mango trees. A flute was trilling from the shantytown below.

236

'Everything is settled,' the kid was saying. He was weaving on tiptoes across the balustrade. Then he leaped down and slapped Turner's knee. 'Don't be scared' – he smiled – 'everyone loves you, like I told you. The doctor loves you, Gabrial, everyone loves you, because you've given us everything.'

Turner sniffed at the air, he was biting his lip.

'We got the guns safe and sound,' Arujua was saying, staring out to the shacks of the slums below. 'Down here you're a hero, just like I told you. It's all settled, Kurt Kohl's been on his plantation farm for five days now. What do you think of that?' He stole a look at Kristian, who had been holding up her hair from her neck to catch the breeze.

'It's all there, waiting . . . all settled, just like I told you.'

They left the next morning, down the brown river beneath the proprietary banyan trees buttoned to the muddy banks. Naked children hooted them off, but an old woman on the bank blessed the low flat-bottomed boat for its mission. Further on they passed mauve trumpets of unfurled flowers, violets and blooming liana. Then the walls of vegetation that rose from the water's edge became dark and thick.

For the first day Kristian stayed below. She felt safer here in this cozy plywood cabin with an oil lamp and a ticking brass clock on the bulkhead. Even when they bumped off shoals and skirted through tiny wooden islands she could remain centered on the axis of her own world with Robin.

Lying on bunks, sipping more rum, watching the lantern sway from the overhead beam, she could honestly tell him, 'Don't worry, everything is going to be all right, it's all *settled*,' and she smiled.

Not that she felt Robin was worried. Now well into the jungle, she had never seen him so calm, almost . . . complacent. Often he would just lie there on the bow in the sun. But she had to reassure herself . . .

They had drowsy days, and the mornings were steamed with ground fog. Sometimes Kristian spent hours stretched out on the deck. Once, when gliding through a patch of rush, a flock of ashen parrots wheeled off around her. Often the river grew narrow, the lips of foliage nearly blotted out the sky, but only the softest fronds swept across them. Kristian liked to pull them off, she liked the way you could strip the leaves. Or else she would just lie back and stare into the almost solid shafts of light through the trees.

Toward evening the wildlife emerged. They saw pompadours in the trunks of great moss-bound trees. There were even red howler monkeys swinging from boughs. Once Arujua shot a wild cock and they roasted the bird on an open fire. He also knew where the best fruit grew, and where the turtles laid their eggs.

One night the Indians came down to the shore, carrying flaming brands, and as the boat neared the lights began to waver back and forth and a gentle chanting rose. 'Listen to them,' Arujua said. 'They're singing to us.' He was leaning out from the railing, bobbing with the chant.

Turner and Kristian lay on a bed of canvas, passing a bottle of warm beer. 'What are they saying?' Robin asked, sucking on that bottle of warm beer.

'I don't know' – Arujua shrugged – 'but it's good, it's always good when they sing to you like this.' The voices still echoed out across the river.

Usually at night they would loll about the deck if the mosquitoes weren't too bad, or else they would drink and smoke in the rocking cabin. Outside, flower petals almost seemed to burn and glow. With the engine off there were only jungle sounds and the brush of reeds against the hull.

Arujua had all sorts of stories about the Indians. You couldn't talk about this place unless you talked about the Indians, he said. They'd always been here, were probably prehistoric. You had your myths of how the first man was born from a turtle in the silt. Then there was something about the moon, which was also this woman, and how she made men crazy because she was so beautiful . . . On other nights the rain fell, boiled in the river, drummed on the decks, slashed reflections out of the dark green bush. Arujua would wipe himself out with rum and rattle out the Indian's horror story . . . disjointed pictures but the point was always the same. You had your Indians getting it from the first day. Twenty thousand were killed in the legendary Moon Pond by the Portuguese. More were taken as slaves and sold on the coast, but Arujua said that the Indians didn't make such good slaves. Most of them died on the way to the markets. The others died in the cane fields. In Bahia no one could believe that so many Indians had been used up in so short a time so they brought the slaves from Africa. Then there was the legend of how six escaped into the jungle. 'Now you've got a tribe in the upper Xingú that still sings with Bantu melodies.'

Worst of all Arujua hated the missionaries. 'You had them in here since the seventeenth century, they came in on the heels of the soldiers, and they're still here today. If you talk to them they'll tell you that they're here to save souls, which is just a lot of crap. They try to get the Indians to live by the clock. You know? They try to get them to work the same hours every day. Then on Sundays they all got to go into the church and pray. Big deal, huh?'

But Arujua said that the Indians were a lot smarter than most people figured. 'Once there was this priest who said that you could live forever if you took the Sacrament. Live forever, I always loved that one. But anyway, this chief, he says, sure we'll take the Sacrament. We'll eat you, okay? You're God, right? So we'll eat you. And there was this other chief who told me that his people were partly converted. So I asked him what he meant. And he tells me, "Oh, yes, my people are partly converted. On Fridays we only eat fishermen." God, that just kills me. They only eat fishermen.'

After the first wave of missionaries, Arujua said, there was a sort of peace in the jungle for a while. Then in the nineteenth century more missionaries came, more soldiers. This time it was the rubber boom. The natives called it the weeping wood, because everyone cried during the rubber boom, except maybe a few people who made all the money.

The trees were slashed and potted by the *seringuerios*, most of them poor Blacks, descendants of all those marginal races. Arujua said they fought it out hand-to-hand with the Indians. 'Lots of them got wiped out. But most died of beriberi, which eats your nerves. And *that* was your rubber boom.' As the *seringuerios* pushed deeper into the forest they had to hire killers to get rid of the Indians. '*Pistoleiros*,' Arujua called them. 'They got paid by the head. It was big death, big business. You had the government involved in the covering up. They would even give the Indians blankets filled with germs.' Nor had much really changed. Arujua said that eventually enough spoke out so that the Service for the Protection of Indians was founded, 'but the SPI is a joke. You got these guys who just use the Indians. They get them to hunt for skins, then they sell them down the river. Anyone who wants their land just takes it.' Arujua said he knew of a club in Belém that used to hunt the Indians every year for sport. In the Mato Grasso there were still *pistoleiros* for hire. The ranchers used them to clear the frontiers. 'There's this one,' Arujua said, 'his name is Gomez. This guy claims to have personally killed about fifty Indians. And the guy's proud of it, he's really proud of it.'

As for his own story, Arujua said that he was the only son, and his mother had been of Indian blood. His father was a *fazendeiro*, a wealthy rancher. 'They sent me off to school in São Paulo, then I went to college in California. Yeah, I went to San Diego for a while, but I couldn't dig it so I left and beat it for Mexico. Then it was Guatemala, and I was a real radical there, you know? I was in love with Che. But that was all just bullshit. I'm not really an angry young man any more. I'm just playing it cool. I'm playing it real cool. Oh yes . . .' And the lines in his young face made a liar of him.

There were days, mornings especially, when the curling mist and shroud of overhanging leaves seemed to tranquil- ize Arujua. He could stand at the helm for hours. Sometimes the jungle would also leave Turner and Kris- tian feeling detached. They would lie about on the deck and dream into the slow passage through brown water. Now and again they saw trappers. Occasionally Arujua stopped to trade. Once an old man in a red canoe drew alongside to sell them fish, but before he cast away again he left Kristian with a monkey's paw. 'This is good,' he told her, smiling. Arujua later said that all the natives believed that the monkey was charmed, that you could see the future in their eyes.

Kristian decided not to look.

Finally one afternoon Arujua said they were nearing the doctor's camp. They moored in a shallow cover at the river's bank. Arujua fired several shots in the air but no one emerged from the bush. Finally he decided to lead them in himself, and they tramped four miles through a warren of jungle trails. It was dusk when they reached the clearing, and all the more surreal . . .

The first vision would always remain, Kristian was sure of it. She was hanging onto Turner's arm beneath a fringe

241

of leaves. Ahead lay the muddy track. Two dozen planked huts and a few less canvas tents lined the little road. Nets had been strung across the open patches and leaves had been knitted into the rope for cover. Apparently aircraft still hit this area. Sullen men milled around in groups, smoking. Others sat on the tilted porches, cleaning their M16's. Now and then a gunshot cracked from behind the far trees, but no one seemed bothered. Nests of AK47's had been dug into the ends of the clearing. There were two fresh graves along the main road, and a plump dog slept in a ratty straw chair.

From this passive still life, the night sucked in Robin and Kristian. First it was the men who could not get enough of them. Everyone wanted to shake their hand or clap them on the back. One skinny kid, loaded down with grenades, even knelt to kiss Kristian's fingers. Next came the formal celebration. Gabrial arrived from the bush with two dozen men. Someone cracked a case of whiskey, and there was plenty of the native stuff besides. Arujua played pop songs and a few local tunes on an old guitar. Another boy banged out rhythms on the bongos. Eventually the women came, mostly the portly wives of older men, and they all wanted a dance with Turner.

Finally, two hours into the heat of the night, Jaques himself arrived. He came with his entourage, nine men all armed to the teeth. By this time the ring of torches on the bamboo poles had been lit, so that when Robin and Kristian first saw the doctor in that flickering light he looked like an effigy of himself. Except that he seemed larger than Robin remembered, larger even than Kristian had imagined. You could believe in Doctor Jaques tonight, especially there, just inside the circle of burning pitch, hands on his hips, rocking back on his heels, laughing, saying, 'Ah, so you've come. My boy has come at last.'

* * *

The cocks crowed. The morning was cold, colder than Turner had imagined the jungle could be. He woke to find the camp nearly deserted. Only a few dogs lolled along the muddy road. Someone had left coffee and bread at the door of their hut. Up the camp he saw three men slouching on the steps of the supply hut, chatting quietly. One kept glinting the blade of his knife in the sun.

Arujua was gone. So was Gabrial, and when Robin went to the doctor's hut all he found were two hung over guards, who smiled at him, offered him limp cigars, but they didn't understand what he wanted.

So Robin took Kristian down to the stream, and they bathed while children giggled from the bush around them. Then they went along the path into the muffled thump of mortar fire. Half a mile on they passed two boys fooling with a rocket launcher. Still further they saw children dragging ammunition boxes into canvas tents.

Then they found Gabrial. He was kneeling by a dismantled mortar. Three sleepy kids were trying to hammer the tube to the plate. They couldn't seem to get the thing to fit. Rockets lay scattered about. One of them was seething at the others. But Gabrial was almost casual. Robin had noticed it last night too. The Brazilian was no longer the timid savage battered in Europe. He was home now, swigging from a bottle of Coke. 'You two sleep good?' He winked at Kristian.

Robin was frowning. The kids had given up on the mortar, one of them was whispering into the tube. Finally Robin said, 'We saw a rocket launcher back there.' His voice was dry. Two buttons had been torn off his shirt.

'Oh yeah.' Gabrial grinned. 'Yeah, we got a few of those. Nice, aren't they?' He took another swig from the bottle.

'Where'd you get them?' Turner asked. He was glancing around. Kristian was toeing the mud, her hands shoved into the pockets of her trousers.

243

Suddenly Gabrial got to his feet. 'Hey, why don't I show you around? Okay?' He motioned toward the path. 'Wait until you see the main force. They're a real rough bunch. Hector has really wiped them into shape.'

The path grew narrow. Leaves kept slapping back at them. They were winding into a danker grotto. In the clearing a few yards ahead lay several men stretched around a smoldering fire. The carcass of some rodent was turning on the spit. Behind the soldiers, strung with leaves, hung the barrel of a howitzer, a fairly new one. Robin nodded at the gun. 'Where did you get that, Gabrial? And where did you get that other stuff?'

'Huh?'

'I *said*, where did you get the gun?' They were standing on the slope above the clearing. The men below were watching them. 'Where?'

A soldier below rolled off his back, tipped his cap from his eyes, and shouted, 'I gave it to them. Me,' and jumped to his feet so they all could see him.

Kristian began to reel back, staring. 'Pitt . . . ?' Then pulling at Turner's arm, 'I know that one. It's Pitt, Toby Pitt . . .'

'Sure it's me, honey.' Pitt was swaggering up the slope. Once he slipped, but still kept grinning. 'Yeah, it's me all right. And you're Robin Turner, yeah? Sure, you're Turner, and you're Lyle Severson's little girl. Well, *okay*, it's Robin Turner and Severson's little girl. Well, well . . .'

For an ugly moment Turner's head fell, he couldn't seem to lift his eyes. Gabrial began to rub at his neck, whispering hurriedly, 'He just came here, I was going to tell you but it doesn't make any difference . . . It's still the same, the guy just came here and gave us all this stuff.'

Pitt had squatted to his haunches. He was rubbing his own neck now and grinning even wider. 'Yeah, Robbie boy. We're on the same side now. I came down here with my man.' He flung back his arm to where Alverado lay. 'Yeah, it's all real nice, we're going to be friends, no hard feelings . . .' When Robin didn't respond, he turned to Kristian. 'Hey, babe, what do *you* say? We've been worried about you. Where you been?' His cap was down to hide the slash where his ear had been.

She looked at Robin. 'I've been with him, all the way.'

The next days were static for Turner. Some of the men, though, seemed afraid and carried amulets or monkey paws. One kid – it was not uncommon in that country – wore the dried heart of a jaguar in a leather pouch around his waist.

Now and then Robin would see Toby Pitt, usually smirking from the shade of his peaked bush hat, but Robin could only gaze back silently, thinking, one day he's going to try to kill me.

In the fourth day Gabrial called Robin and Kristian into the large hut. It was going to be a war party. The doctor was there. So was Arujua and their field commander, Hector Gomez. Out of deference to Turner, no one had asked Toby Pitt.

Rain was pouring past the slatted windows and hissing on the palm-thatched roof. Faces were distorted by the shadows from the hurricane lamp. Kristian lay on a rope hammock that had been strung from rusty eye hooks. Arujua and Gabrial sat on makeshift chairs that had been hammered from packing crates. Jaques was in a sagging planter's chair.

Hector had spread his maps out on the wobbly table, the curling ends held down by blocks of wood. Black and jagged arrows marked the prongs of the attack. When Robin had been shown the oil fields, he had only been able to shake his head, again and again. Now he was slouched against the rough wood wall, arms folded across his chest.

Gabrial was picking his teeth. 'Sure, the United States needs oil. That's why Pitt is here. You think we didn't know that? You think we were born yesterday?'

Turner dropped his head, brushed his knuckles across his nose. 'Once you let them in, there's no getting them out,' he said quietly.

Now Hector was stirring. He was a heavy man, the only one with real battles under his belt. They said he fought with Che in Cuba, and lesser men in Guatemala. But now he seemed morose, toying with a leather thong. 'It's one shot . . . is that how you say it?' His vowels were clipped with Spanish accent. 'We got one shot, so we take it. Mother, you think I am in love with the Central Intelligence Agency? Me? Me, I saw them kill all my friends. But now, what is the matter. Maybe afterward I shoot Pitt, okay?'

Thunder pealed and lightning lit up the hut for an instant. The crossbeams lashed with jungle twine seemed to be straining. Curtains of water were washing off the thatch. 'This is going to be the last battle,' Arujua was saying. 'We're going to give them something to remember . . .'

Jaques interrupted. 'Tell him, Hector. Tell our friend the plan.'

Hector leaned out over the table. 'We're going to attack in two prongs.' He held up his hands like pincers, and their shadows flickered on the wall. 'One goes for the oil, the other goes for Kohl's plantation. If we cannot light the wells, then we blow the tanks. As for Kohl's place, it should be straightforward.' He handed Robin a stack of grainy photographs. 'They are not too good, but they will give you an idea.'

Robin began to leaf through them. They had been taken at a distance with a wide-angle lens. There were long shots of the white colonial mansion. Some had caught

246

figures silhouetted on the veranda; in one there was a slender woman leaning out from the columnar porch. Gun emplacements were clearly visible along the outer garden walls.

'Clay tiles,' Gabrial was saying. 'You know what happens when you hit clay tiles with mortar shell? Fragmentation. Hector says there's nothing better for clay tiles than fragmentation.'

Robin seemed not to have heard . . . he was still staring at the vaguely formless woman. In another shot she was strolling along the graceful portico. Some sort of veil was floating behind her. Maybe she was sneaking out to the stables and bachelors' quarters. Yes, that would be Ingeborg, all right, stalking love, invigorated by the dove-gray evening and the smell of those shivering roses.

Jaques had begun to stretch. 'Much will depend upon the mortars. I've seen them as an important factor from the very beginning.'

Gabrial loosed a quick burst of Portuguese as his hand chopped at the air . . . 'pow, pow, pow.'

'No, too fast.' Hector frowned. 'The men are not that good. They can shoot a shell every three seconds. If they are nervous, then who knows? Maybe five, maybe six. They'll be sighting on the flares, and the flares only last twenty seconds.'

'Oh that's plenty of time,' Arujua said, and then edged closer to Robin. 'We have one real good edge.' His hand was cupped on Turner's elbow. 'Yeah, it's going to be a real, real good edge,' and gave them all an awkward smile. 'We got silence. Our men can move so silently in the jungle that no one will hear us.' He touched his heart, then his wrist. 'It's because we have Indian blood in our veins. We can move quiet because we have Indian blood. Can you dig that, Turner?'

Robin turned to exchange looks with Kristian. More

thunder sounded and the room was shot with light again. When the rolling boom had passed, Kristian was saying, 'Oil . . . oil, don't they realize, for God's sake?' She was speaking only to Turner. 'They don't have a chance any more. You'll have everyone down here now, and they're not much better than Kohl.'

Robin, in his hoarse, fragile voice, said, 'She's right.'

'So?' Jaques had gotten up from his chair. 'So they come? You think that we're romantics here. We're not. We don't believe in fairy tales. You know better too. We can't be concerned about the future any more. We do it now . . . for now. It's the best we've got. Value it for what it is.'

Toward evening the night had begun to rock with the storm. Lightning fractured the landscape. Bits of the jungle seemed to be flying off all over. Robin and Jaques had come out on the porch of the largest hut. A bluish dark was pulling all around them.

For a while both men were silent, leaning out on the railing. Then the doctor said, 'You think I'm crazy, don't you?'

Robin rapped his fingers on the shaven log. 'I never said that.'

'But it is what you think.' Jaques had started to sway a little. His hands were shoved in the pockets of his dirty cotton trousers. His shirt was tied across his belly. 'I wouldn't hold it against you, Turner. I think maybe I am crazy, always have been.'

Robin's face tightened. 'You're fine, Michael. You're a good man – '

'Sure, fine and good and crazy.' He started rooting about in his pocket. Now there was a shabby home-rolled cigar in his mouth. 'I'm going to tell you a little story now. This story starts a long time ago. It was when I thought you could still make the world understand something. It was when I thought that you could bring a Kurt Kohl to trial and everything would be written in the newspapers and the world would be shocked at what had been done. So this is the story, and it began with the war trials. Remember the war trials? Well, I went to those trials. I thought to myself, "I will go and testify against Kohl and the other Germans." So I went. I went to this large government building. Inside there was this long bare waiting room. All those who had come to testify went into this room. They sat us on this narrow wooden bench. Then they gave you a number. So I took my number and I sat on the bench and I didn't talk much, but I drank plenty of the free coffee that they gave us. So there I was on the narrow bench, and I was happy to be there along with all the other men and women who had come to testify. We all waited very quietly. Then late in the afternoon they called my number and I went into another little room where there was a thin man with wire glasses, and a woman. I remember that she was not particularly attractive. Maybe she was bored with all the ones who had come before me. But still she had one of those machines that take down everything you said. So I began to tell them my story. I told them how Kohl raped my wife, and I told them how he also tortured. They asked me if I had actually seen these terrible things, and I said that I hadn't, but I did see her lying on the floor afterward (and Robin had his own memory to go with that). When I finished my story they gave me a form which had all these little boxes where you had to write your name and address. Then you had to write a little bit more of what had happened to you. And they even had a place to write down Kurt Kohl's name.

'When I was all done I went home to my room and made myself a bowl of soup and ate a little bread. Then I began to cry, which was something that I hadn't done in years.'

The old man might have been crying now. It was in his voice. Robin did not look back to see. Around them the storm had begun to ease. The birds were calling again. Red-brown faces peeked out of the doors of shacks. A naked child scampered across the clearing. Jaques was saying, 'This is not the end of my story, Robin. Because when they did not contact me I went back to that building. I went back many times. Nothing was ever done. Maybe we wouldn't be here now if it had been . . . And that's a little story too. How it was when I first came to the jungle. When I first came here and then learned that Kohl was also here, I thought to myself, "Well, this must be a sign from God." Why else would He bring us together so far from anywhere? Here I had come to escape from a world that I no longer could tolerate, and who should I find but my only enemy. So I believed it was a sign from God. And so I prayed to God. I petitioned Him to tell me why it was that I had come all this way only to be haunted again by Kohl. And do you know what God told me, Robin? Nothing! God told me nothing! Why? you ask. Why didn't He speak to me? Well, I'll tell you, Robin.' He was raging now. 'Because you can't petition the Lord with prayer. It's a myth.'

Jaques was still for a moment, his words lingering. Random drops were sounding on the thatch, someone was sloshing through the mud behind. Then the old man sagged back to the railing.

'So maybe you're wondering why I never tried to kill him before. Maybe you're thinking that there are easier ways. You, for example . . . you could sneak into his home and kill him. You're a silent killer. Well, let me tell you something, Robin. What we're about to do is worth all those years of waiting. Nothing has happened like this in the jungle for a very long time. I told you that you couldn't shock the world. Remember? Well, it's not quite true. What we're about to do will shock them all right. And these boys of mine, they don't care if they live or die. They don't care if they get shot in the stomach and bleed to death. They're all just like me. They don't believe in myths either.'

Now with the end so close Robin sometimes saw himself as living through a fantasy. Time moved slowly in the forest. In the mornings he and Kristian woke to the columns of light falling through the dome of trees. Beyond lay more green light feathering across the jungle hills.

In the afternoon Robin was now teaching the rudiments of unarmed combat. It helped pass the time. He lectured from the porch of the large hut. Gabrial served as translator. Together they would pantomime the basic moves. Their pupils were around them in a semicircle, some kneeling, some squatting. They all looked hard and angry in their denims and webbing, but most were young, eighteen, nineteen, twenty years old. Yet Robin had also seen them in the field, and yes, he thought they would fight pretty well. Gabrial, though, said that they were the toughest force in the area. He said that everyone fought close to the bone, which was a term he must have picked up in either Hamburg or the States.

As for Robin's other self he hardly knew what to think. Once, he remembered how he had enjoyed the image of his slinking persona, moving through other people's lives. In Langley, for example, he had been the bemused Siamese, rubbing against the gentlemen's hose, licking scraps off the bone china, purring to their rarefied tastes. In Hamburg he had been the city cat, mean and shabby. And so it had gone, month after month, city after city. But here, now, he wondered. Sometimes he thought that he even no longer hated Kurt Kohl. When he tried to tell Kristian some of this she could only smile, ask him why, then, was he going through with it?

But how did you explain what it was like to be totally locked into the purity of a killing run? All he could really say was, 'Don't think love is any more logical than revenge.'

But more and more in these last hours he was thinking of her. Often he felt as if he had known her before, or at least a girl who had looked like her. Because there was something in her face, some mystery in those still-brook eyes that he never had been able to unravel.

He thought he loved her best in the mornings when she was sleepy and vague. Once he had had a dream, something about her body lying on a bed of soggy leaves. He had tried to wake her, but she was lost, in the perfect stillness of death. When he woke he had not wanted to let her go. He no longer loved her at a distance, they were well intertwined by now . . .

In the early evening of the final day Robin went to her and they walked out into the forest and sat in the cooling sculpture of shadows. He told her that they would be leaving soon. 'Arujua has a plane. It's a few miles south down the river. He said he's going to fly us out.'

She bit her lips, nodded. 'Where?'

'I don't know, somewhere probably over the border. It's just important that we leave. It won't be safe here after tomorrow.' He became silent, tracing the veins beneath her wrist. He loved her arms and wrists, he loved the way she laid them over the ends of things . . . 'and if something should happen to me,' he said suddenly, 'if something should happen, you'll go anyway, all right?'

'Sure.' Her voice was dry. 'But nothing's going to happen to you. It's not in the cards,' and she smiled.

252

Around them leaves were sounding with the falling drops of an earlier shower. Robin now stopped feeling her hands. They seemed too fragile to touch. Then he had to ask, 'What about Pitt? Is he in the cards?'

Kristian glanced up to the still trees high above. 'I don't know. I don't know about Pitt . . .'

Pitt . . . the meaning of him plunged them into another space. A minute passed, and tears began to form in Kristian's eyes. He reached out his fingers again. This time to touch her lips.

And then it all broke inside her. 'Oh God, Robin. I'm in love with you,' and they wrapped themselves in each other's arms.

The men assembled in the moonlight. There were nearly sixty of them. Those with lighter skin smeared their faces with sepia dye. Loose clips were bound together with masking tape to keep them from clacking. Ammunition reserves had been muffled and packed in green canvas haversacks. A stretcher had been built for the launcher and rockets. All wore combat fatigues. Some had webbing belts around their shoulders, but most seemed to prefer the light pack for silent running.

Now and then in the dull light Robin saw the face of a savage that had been painted for war. Some had pinned feathers to their wrists and ankles. Others had ocher stripes along their cheeks. One man had lashed the paws of a jaguar to the back of his hands. Robin nodded . . . Gabrial had been right, the jungle hadn't seen anything like this in years.

The men formed a ragged oval around the main hut. Hector was barking at them, first in Portuguese, then in a softer native tongue. Then there was Hector again, and his arm came up in a long, slow arc. They moved on out after that.

253

Now on the forest floor the night was nearly absorbing them. Turner walked with Gabrial, while the front column was led by the most experienced jungle stalkers. You could barely hear them move. There was only the *brush-brush* through the leaves, and once Robin saw a long knife flash. Further on he passed a severed snake hanging from the vines.

No one spoke. There was no light. Robin couldn't figure out how they saw.

It was a ghost walk in time to the breathing, and maybe to some less tangible instinct. They were cutting a line right through the heart of the jungle, and he was with them, and it felt very real, natural . . .

Now the pace was changing, one column was breaking off. Blackened shapes of men were scampering around him. It was quick time, and Gabrial was nudging him up a tangled slope.

Belly down, and he had to drag himself with elbows. His rifle kept catching in the brush. The ground was damp and the scum was soaking through his clothes. Vines tried to strangle him, thorns tore his hands, the stench of leaf mold came to his nostrils. He was part of it, locked into the night and the heat . . . and what was to come.

They stopped at the top of the rise. Now there were only panting voices and the soft scrape and click as the mortar tubes locked to the plates. The Kohl estate lay some two hundred yards below. A short pull, Hector had called it. When you hit the rise you'll know everything. Well, he had been right, because there it was. There was the main house, and there the two long branching wings. New white stone rose through the trees. The sloping roof was dark red tile – perfect for the fragmentation. Behind lay the bungalows. 'That's where the guards will lie asleep,' Hector had said. 'We must blow the bungalows first.' The entire compound was encircled by high walls that the jungle had not yet covered. To the south ran black water, and boats lay tied to the long wharf.

Waiting would be the worst, they had all known that. But Robin was too knotted, too stuck in the ticking seconds to notice. Down the ranks the others were frozen still. Some kept glancing at the luminous dials of their watches, others just kept staring ahead. 'When the flares start,' Hector had said, 'you go. You go with the first flares.'

Now and then soft voices rippled through the line. Then they were rolling through Robin. Gabrial's fingers were smoothing the stock of his rifle. 'I'm dying for a smoke.' He rubbed his nose on his sleeve.

Turner had lost the count, so the buildup was gone. He did not really hear Gabrial. There was the whistling high above. The white light blossomed over the red tile roofs. The low *thump* of mortar came rolling up from behind. The blast rose squarely in the garden walls. Now the fireballs were flashing up all over, walloping out long, trilling screeches. To the north more shells were falling, the oil fields, Robin guessed. Well at least they had the timing down, and then a terrible column of flame roared up out of the black carpet.

Running, or falling through the thicket, there were hallucinations blinking out of the night. Robin couldn't be certain if anyone was shooting back.

Coming through the last of the bush, the walls lay straight ahead. The first waves were already lobbing over hand grenades, and mushrooms of brick and tile flew up from behind the walls. An automatic started cracking from an upper window, but the M70 launchers blew the entire wall away.

Now there were whole portions of the wall crumbling down and figures scampering over the rubble. Robin fell in with the last of them but had to reel back from the

255

blue-black gusts of smoke that came billowing out of the stone.

Inside the courtyard lay several twisted bodies. One man hung over the side of a wishing well. Another had been blown through a picket fence. Those still alive kept sniping back from the balcony. Robin turned and saw someone toss up his arms and spin down beside him. He rolled and fired from his hip in a trance of kicking cordite, but the trance broke when he actually sent a man sprawling over the railing.

A reddening aura was glowing up from behind the house. Showers of embers were flying off. Windows kept bursting out. Shards of glass were tinkling down. Robin nearly stumbled over a balled-up body while a headless form hung from the smoldering trellis.

A lull was passing over the courtyard. Farther on they were storming up the colonnade, through the double doors. Robin was only weaving through the smoke and debris. Once he heard his own name called out weakly from not too far away. He turned slowly, crouched, and finally was sinking to his knees, down where Gabrial lay. The boy's face was shiny and dark. He had collapsed into a line of bamboo chairs. But he was grinning now . . . 'This is good, Robin. This is fantastic . . .'

Robin's hands were already smeared with blood. 'Listen. Gabrial, listen to me. I've got to get you back.' He was feeling for the pulse.

Gabrial's eyes kept blinking. The whites were flat and glassy, but that grin was still on his mouth. Robin was trying to pull away the matted strips of Gabrial's tunic, but it was pointless. He could have stuck his fist in the hole. He sagged down closer to Gabrial's ear. 'I'm sorry . . . I can't seem to stop the bleeding . . .'

Gabrial smiled. 'I don't care. It doesn't even hurt.' His mouth was beginning to go slack. 'We've really done

256

something here, you know.' Now his hand was stretching out to Robin's, their fingers were laced together. He stiffened, and his eyes rolled back.

Robin let the head fall, rose, and moved up the lawn. The courtyard lay in shadows and flaring light. Only stray shots still sounded. Through the colonnade, past the shredded canopy, Robin was now limping stiffly, wavering into the blue marble hallway. The stillness here was so complete it seemed as if the place would blow apart. Every object looked too real . . . smooth porcelain lamps, gleaming candelabra, an open book with a broken spine lying on the parquetry. Only the muslin curtains were alive, billowing out through open windows.

Well into the long hall Robin heard the crystal needles of chandeliers tinkling faintly. Woolly threads of smoke were twisting through the passages. One only had to touch the knobs to open the doors, or brush the drapes to set them rustling.

Now, climbing the curving staircase, he heard the hacking sob of a woman from up the corridor. He would have recognized *that* sound anywhere. He stopped, pressed in the door with his fingertips. 'Ingeborg?'

She rose from the bunched-up quilt. 'You!' Her eyes were ringed with red veins. Her knuckles were white. 'You, you tricked me, you bastard . . . bastard . . .'

So much for love, he thought, but he was beyond irony. He just backed out and let the door snap shut behind him.

It would have been so easy just to turn around, step back down that hall, make it through the jungle. Kristian would be waiting. The boy has a boat, and further along he's got a claptrap plane. Then you both go sailing out over everything.

Except that everything was congealing around him now. His head jerked to the side, cocked, better to hear those voices brewing from behind the half-closed door. Well, go

257

ahead, he told himself. Ease it back, step inside. You've at least got to see the climax.

So he went on in.

Kohl lay in one corner of the room. His knees had been slit from behind. His legs were twisted at terrible angles. But he was watching, breathing.

Hunched at the end of the bed sat Jaques, his rifle cradled in his arms. Two ragged Indian boys were leaning against the windowsill. On the floor lay another body, a nameless servant.

Time moved so slowly, Robin couldn't help sagging.

Only Jaques wasn't dazed. He even gave Turner that wizened, leaky-eyes smile of his. 'Thought you'd get here too late. Thought he'd bleed to death.'

'What are you doing, Michael?'

'Doing this. What else?' Jaques lowered his head, sighting along the stock of his rifle into Kurt Kohl's belly.

Kohl's head began to move in spasms. 'Who are you? Tell me who you *are*?'

Which started Jaques's laughter. 'He doesn't even know who we are, Robbie. What do you think? It didn't do any good to explain. I told him I was once the Bitch. Nothing. I told him you were the jaguar-man. Still nothing. Oh, I see it now, the giant-man walks on us, but he doesn't even look down to see. Well, you're looking down now, aren't you, Kurt?'

Turner was sagging now against the plaster, growing still. Even if he could roll back his eyes for a close look inside his head he was sure he would not find a trace of the beast. The jaguar had departed, slipping away in the night, in this room . . . ? He couldn't be sure how or when . . . but he was sure it was gone. In its place was a waiting Kristian . . . but in front of him was Jaques, still fingering the stock of his blue-steel rifle, still murmuring, 'So,

258

Robbie? What else did you expect? You thought perhaps you'd hear the angels sing? Or all your sins fly off. Or, I know, you thought that your old girlfriend would come back to life. Well, I'm sorry, but there's nothing more than just this. Bang, you pull the trigger. Bang, he's dead. I learned that in a war.'

Kohl's eyes were beseeching. He might have started crying, but all that came out was a gurgle.

'Just like him to do that.' Jaques was indignant. 'Come over here, Robbie. Come here. I want you to help me squeeze off the shot. You should experience this. It's you too.'

But Robin couldn't.

'Suit yourself,' Jaques mumbled, and leaned back into his rifle. 'Let me show you, Robbie. Here.' Then the rifle kicked, and the blast went through them all. Kohl's body bucked back against the plaster. Blood came up from his mouth, and the weight of him thumped down.

'Now, Robbie,' Jaques was whispering into the ringing silence, 'don't you be disappointed. I told you. This is the way it always is. You just shoot them, that's all. Maybe you'll feel a little better later. Maybe not.'

Outside the courtyard was washed in steel-blue light. The dawn lay only a few degrees below the distant horizon. Everywhere Robin walked, everything he saw . . . heaps of lumber and stone, a shattered Biedermeier chair, a mateless boot, the blown-off leg of a man . . . everything lay in the blue suspension of an aftermath. He moved slowly, once stopping to peer into the face of a mangled boy, once to brush aside the hair of a dead girl. Every twisted iron rod, every dangling chunk of mortar from the shattered wall was silhouetted against the sky. And he wanted to sit down in it. He just wanted to sit down.

* * *

In the first light, Kristian's fingers curled so hard around the bamboo pole that her knuckles turned white. She could not tell where the smoke ended and the sky began. She let her head fall into the angle of her half-bent arm.

Tonight she wore a pair of boy's cotton trousers and one of the women's tunics. Not long ago she and Robbie had bathed in the stream. He had given her some kind of dwarfed but perfect orchid. Now she wore the unfurling purple petals in the band of her cap. And touched them to see if they had withered or fallen away.

How long she had waited here and watched the reddening aura spread above the jungle she hardly knew. Some had already come staggering back. She had watched them, calling out once to one who had looked a bit like Robin, only to hang for a minute in the space of no reply.

Her fingers stayed a while longer on the bamboo railing, then fell away. She scowled, kicked at an empty bottle, and pushed on through the tilted rear door of the hut.

Inside the mottled darkness had changed. New shadows had emerged. The far door was ajar. The canvas dangled away. She would have flung herself back, but her knees were already giving so she just sank down. She knew . . . now she knew . . . 'Is that you, Toby?'

Pitt stirred from the corner, and his packing-crate chair began to creak. 'Hello, baby. What's going on?'

She was kneeling on a mattress. 'Should have guessed,' she whispered.

'Sure you should have, baby. Can't leave you for the monkeys, can we?' His automatic was dangling from a finger. 'You got to make amends. Got to have a talk with people.'

'Are you going to shoot him?'

'Ah now, baby, I'm not planning on shooting anyone.'

But it was there in his eyes, she could see it.

'Yeah, I just want to talk to him.' For proof he plunked the automatic down on the packing crate.

Now Kristian was holding her sides, pressing her arms to her ribs.

Toby was back on the boxes. 'You been screwing him?'

She shook her hair away to answer. 'I've been scared,' which she thought sounded pretty good.

'I can imagine. What happened? You got blown in the Kohl place? Robbie boy comes in as Galahad, and the next thing you know you're lapping up the jungle fever?'

'Something like that.' She sighed, now well into the role of the shattered little girl.

'Well, it's time to go home, honey. I've got a line to a chopper a few miles north of here. We take that mother up and out.'

They're going to put us through the grinder, Kristian realized. Robin and me. They're going to put us in a little cage and keep us there until the world freezes over. Outside there was still, now and again, the thump of mortar fire. Another minute oozed by. She lifted up her face to Toby's. Now she was kneeling in front of him. 'Please . . . I want to talk to him first.'

Pitt still lay back on the crates. 'Sure, you talk to him first.'

'I can convince him, really. You'd have to kill him, but I can convince him to give up peacefully . . .' If she could sell it, at least it might buy Robin a little time . . .

Toby was slipping, falling into his victor's pose, waiting for her sobbing face to bury in his thigh . . . little girls liked to cry on bulky men . . .

So she gave it to him. 'I'm ripped, Toby. I'm really ripped apart.'

'Sure, I've been there. It's okay, babe. Everything's going to be okay.'

She forced herself to lay her head on his leg. She even asked, 'How's Lyle doing? How's Humph?'

They were all just great, Toby told her. 'Everyone's great. I'm great. You're great.' He was playing with her hair.

And now that he had been sucked in, Kristian's hand had begun to crawl across the packing crate, her fingers were circling around the automatic, and when she jerked away, rolled back, she was moving into the slowest fast time of all . . . trying to remember which was safety-on and which was safety-off . . . also you had to pull back the bolt on these things . . . all while Toby was coming down on top of her. But when they fell together, the whole room exploded. Her shoulder snapped back hard, and the blood flew out and away from her.

Toby was moaning, thrashing about. His fingers were grasping at the mattress. Broken glass was crunching under his hips. 'Oh God, look what you done to me.' He kept trying to suck in air. 'Well, fuck . . . look what you've done to me now . . .'

Kristian just stared. She too couldn't believe, least of all in the hunk of metal she still held in her fist.

Only when Toby died did she let the gun thump back down onto the mattress and move out into the greenish fog of dawn to sit on the warped planks of the porch . . .

Later, when Robin came walking stiffly up the rutted path, her fingers lingered again on the bamboo. When they finally came together, neither could quite read the expression in the other's eyes.

Later that day they set off again in Arujua's flat-bottomed boat. The Indian boy stood at the helm. Robin and Kristian curled together in the bunk below. Their craft slipped on past the tendrils and mossy vines. The river was still and brown.

At dawn the fire still raged, the orange disk of the sun had to rise through clouds of black-oil smoke. Robin said that one of the wells had caught, the flames might go on for weeks. At noon they had to take cover beneath the fringe of tall water reeds. Government planes had been circling. Jaques had said that no one knew how the wind would blow. When Turner and Kristian had left, the doctor was already preparing to lead his people further into the heart of the forest.

To lie here now, with him, Kristian said that it was still like a dream. She had even stopped being afraid.

Late in the day they reached the plane, a battered twin engine Beechcraft in a makeshift jungle field. In the failing light Kristian and Robin limped to the revving plane. They were bleary and tired. A gold sunset was diffracting through the Plexiglas. Then the plane was shuddering over the fringe of jungle, and wobbling out higher and higher. Night fell, and they were sailing northwest across the face of the Amazon, nodding in and out of sleep, holding onto one another.

In time the engine's drone became hypnotic. Arujua might have been flying them into the stars. Once Kristian broke the silence. 'Well, Robbie, I guess at least now everyone will know better than to fuck with your women.' Turner smiled back.

They seemed to be following the moon, and the moon finally led them down to meet the daybreak on a sloping field with only a few lonely village lights twinkling in the distance. Then Arujua was calling out, good-bye, good luck above the noise of the whirling propellers, then taxiing back into the breeze, and flying off again.

So in the end Turner and Kristian were left on a hillside in the pearly hour of a chilly dawn. They were even left laughing a little, because neither really had the faintest idea where they were. Or where they were going. They only knew who they were going with.

And for now that was enough.

12

April at last, and yes there were some violets breeding in Lyle's garden, and he decided that they were only mixing memory with nostalgia. Besides, many of the better shoots had been battered down by rain.

More and more these days Lyle had taken to his garden. He liked the accouterments . . . his cotton gloves, his pruning shears, his spade, and especially his little knit cap. Not that his garden was much to look at. It was a sort of haphazard garden. He would plant a bush with some passion, forget about it, and soon he would find it trying to take possession of the house.

Just as the house had taken possession of him. Yes, there were those awful moments of silence when he heard his own name blown out, hollow and dusty. So that his hands would tremble and his gums would ache. But worse, he often heard the names and voices of others, most now dead because they had been betrayed or sacrificed.

There was that cagey Polish stringer, for example, who used to say that living was not trusting. Well, he must have trusted someone, because they finally shot him in the base of the skull. Then there was David Player, the Oxford wit, who honestly loved those on whom he spied. But they loved him less, and Player died too. And years ago in Prague there had been the exotic Maro in taffeta and ermine, and her Oriental eyes as clear as mirrors. But they murdered Maro too, and before she died she said that you mustn't be sad, because I will be a legend. Well, you're a legend in my house, Lyle would have told her now, even if no else remembers.

Then too there were less distant ghosts. Sometimes Lyle would sit in the old bentwood rocker, gazing out to where the wind was tossing the trees into green balls, and he would hear the voices of these recent souls. If only you could understand, he had told himself.

He often thought about Kristian Badgery and Robin Turner. He supposed that somewhere there was probably a formal ending to the Robin Turner case. He, however, only learned the bits and pieces that came to him through the usual route. Now and then Humphrey Knolls would drop by. Sometimes Lyle saw Harlon Watson at the club. So by hook and by crook, by dribs and by drabs, he heard about the too-neat ending that really missed the essential questions.

First and foremost he heard about Kohl. They told him that the Brazilians only made a nominal stink, for it seemed that money, unlike martyrs, did not rule from the grave. Thus with Kurt Kohl gone, the Brazilians, as one suspected they might, were only too happy to talk up the oil rights with any responsible party. Who actually stepped in and got the land, however, was still a foolish secret. Watson claimed that even he didn't know. Not that it mattered to Lyle . . . Exxon, Mobil, Shell. They said that Jeffrey Boyal played liaison between the government and the industry, and no doubt he had his own favorites.

Additionally there were nasty titbits from the Victor Ross camp. Despite success Ross had his knuckles rapped for sending down Pitt. Apparently John Poole had an embarrassing tussle with the locals in explaining away Pitt's body. In the end it was decided that Toby could be classified as a free-lance mercenary in the pay of the guerrillas. The Brazilians grudgingly accepted this line, and Toby's mother was given compensation on the sly.

As for Jaques, little was really known. Most felt that he had simply burrowed deeper into the jungle, and that one day he would die and that would be the end. Still, Lyle could not help but fantasize a little. He very much enjoyed the image of the half-mad doctor-saint ranting out his own legend there in the jungle nights among the glowing ferns and ghostly mangoes. Perhaps he would live in some formal native epic until the last Indian died. But the Company proper did not concern itself one way or the other. Jaques was never as crucial to the case as, say, Robin Turner was.

Lyle suspected that a general feeling for Turner had already solidified. He knew that there were those, Ross among them, who probably wished that the boy were dead. But a formal hunt might stir up too much dust. So they would let him be for a time, as long as he lived quietly abroad in his own unknown heaven.

Officially, however, Robin Turner was a traitor, and probably fair game. Watson believed that there would come a day when they would bring the boy in, although the remaining old guard wanted no part of it.

Where then did Turner stand? One hardly dared to ask these days. Rather you were told that the whole matter was best forgotten, and for a while Lyle honestly tried to forget. As spring quickened the new stalks and the nights grew velvet and warm there were dinner parties. Lyle even delighted them once with claret and Cornish game hens in his drafty house. More often, though, he dined at the club while the chandeliers flared overhead. Occasionally old faces dropped by, and you rose to toast the years, smiling down a line of formal black lapels.

But even after the best of evenings, Lyle more and more found himself returning to the fragile ghosts that lingered behind in his empty home. Sometimes when he could not sleep he would walk for hours among the looming furniture. Nothing concrete was every fully revealed to him in those gray shapes of night, but in time he began to believe that he at last did understand.

267

Robin Turner was the stone that marked the real passing of his generation.

Possibly there was even a lesson here, Lyle eventually came to believe. Something that Turner learned early, while I have learned late. Either way, he knew this much for sure. This generation of his, these spies, these elegant gentlemen spies . . . they terrified him. Himself included. So that in the end he came honestly to hope that Robin and Kristian would keep on running forever.

THE WHITE MANDARIN

A brilliant novel of the Orient – a masterpiece of violent
action and complex intrigue against the mighty background of China in turmoil

THE DESTINY OF TWO MIGHTY NATIONS DE-
PENDED ON ONE LONELY SUPERSPY . . .

For two lonely, lethal decades John Polly had survived at
the deadly centre of a web of international espionage and
personal vengeance – a lone American who made his
home in the secretive heart of Red China.

By an ironic twist of fate his bitterest, most implacable
enemy was the CIA-backed opium magnate Fwng Chi.
Ironic because John Polly was a deep-penetration
agent – a CIA 'mole' at the highest level of Peking power.

THEY CALLED HIM THE 'WHITE MANDARIN'

'Dan Sherman is that very rare thing, a natural writer . . .
his work is exciting and rewarding reading'
Howard Fast

'A first-rate storyteller'
Morris West

THE WORLD'S GREATEST NOVELISTS NOW AVAILABLE IN GRANADA PAPERBACKS

Eric van Lustbader

The Ninja	£1.95	☐
Sirens	£1.95	☐
Beneath An Opal Moon	£1.95	☐

Nelson de Mille

By the Rivers of Babylon	£1.95	☐
Cathedral	£1.95	☐

Justin Scott

The Shipkiller	£1.95	☐
The Man Who Loved the Normandie	£1.95	☐

Martin Walker

A Mercenary Calling	£1.95	☐
The Eastern Question	£1.25	☐
The Infiltrator	95p	☐

GF781

All these books are available at your local bookshop or newsagent, and can be ordered direct from the publisher.

To order direct from the publisher just tick the titles you want and fill in the form below:

Name _____

Address _____

_____

Send to:
Granada Cash Sales
PO Box 11, Falmouth, Cornwall TR10 9EN

Please enclose remittance to the value of the cover price plus:

UK 45p for the first book, 20p for the second book plus 14p per copy for each additional book ordered to a maximum charge of £1.63.

BFPO and Eire 45p for the first book, 20p for the second book plus 14p per copy for the next 7 books, thereafter 8p per book.

Overseas 75p for the first book and 21p for each additional book.

Granada Publishing reserve the right to show new retail prices on covers, which may differ from those previously advertised in the text or elsewhere.